# SNOW IN GORKY PARK

# Snow In Gorky Park

Richard Pennell

authorHOUSE®

*AuthorHouse™ UK Ltd.*
*1663 Liberty Drive*
*Bloomington, IN 47403  USA*
*www.authorhouse.co.uk*
*Phone: 0800.197.4150*

*Published by AuthorHouse    01/28/2014*

*ISBN: 978-1-4918-9182-7 (sc)*
*ISBN: 978-1-4918-9183-4 (e)*

# ACKNOWLEDGMENTS

Many thanks to my daughter
Samantha Pennell who patiently read and original manuscript and
corrected the mistakes in grammar and text

**Publication by the same author:** *The Persuader by Richard Pennell*

# CHAPTER 1

Sam Tucker looked out of the window of the British Airways Boeing 737 as it landed at Domodedova, Moscow's international airport. Sam had flown many hundreds of times and many thousands of miles over the last twenty years but this was the first time that he had ever flown business class. Most of his flights had been in the back of military aircraft, flights taken during the twenty years that Sam had been in the British Army. Sam had never been to Russia before. He expected it to be a colourless, dismal place and as the plane taxied and he viewed the terminal he decided that his expectations were spot on. The terminal was a grey, shapeless, characterless concrete building. It was surrounded by a grey and white landscape, a grey sky and white snow. Even the snow looked a grey. Sam thought it was the most depressing place he had ever seen.

The inside of the terminal building was just as boring. The place was pristine clean but somehow had no colour or character either. The people too were grey. The immigration staff looked bored and just grunted at the people going through passport control. They only spoke Russian whatever the nationality of the incoming passenger. The same applied to the porters at the baggage carousel and the customs men who, just like customs men at all airports, stood around looking for a likely customer to pounce upon. Nobody smiled, nobody seemed to be pleasant, nobody seemed to be happy.

Sam was thirty-eight. He had been born in October 1970, in Canning Town in East London. He was born almost six weeks premature and had been a small baby and he was also small as a boy. As a result he was bullied by some of the bigger boys. The result of this was that Sam grew up fast. His defense was to attack. Sam had never backed down. His father, although drunk a lot of the time, had given him one piece of advice, 'get the bastards before they get you.' By the time he was ten he had grown to normal size and had a reputation that

1

ensured he was not picked on. It was as though Sam Tucker did not feel pain and he was fearless. He was in and out of fights all of the time although he was never part of a gang. He had a reputation as a hard case and a loner. Many of the adults who knew him thought that he would end up in trouble, probably in prison.

A turning point in his life occurred when Sam was fourteen years old. He was playing snooker at the local youth club when he stepped outside to have a cigarette. As he walked to the rear of the building to light up, he found Clare, his girlfriend at the time, leaning up against the wall having sex with one of the other boys. Sam went for both of them. He hit Clare across the head with his snooker cue and as the other boy stepped in to protect her, Sam head butted him. The boy was severely hampered by having his trousers around his ankles and as Sam's head connected the boy stumbled and fell over. Sam kicked him and stamped on him. By the time he was pulled off, the boy had a broken arm, three broken fingers, broken ribs, a fractured skull and severe concussion. He had also lost part of an ear, eight teeth and one of his testacles' was irreparably crushed where Sam had stamped on them

Sam was arrested, the juvenile court found him guilty of assault and he was given two years probation and a custodial sentence that was suspended. One of the conditions of his probation was that he had to meet with his probation officer once a week. On the third visit his case officer suggested that Sam would benefit from joining the local army cadet core. He explained to Sam that he thought that it would help get rid of some of Sam's pent up aggression. Sam reluctantly agreed as he felt that he needed to keep on the right side of the man. To everybody's surprise, most of all Sam's, he loved it.

They met every Tuesday evening and every other weekend there was an opportunity to go to an activity, often a weekend camp. He loved the routine, the friendship, he loved the activities especially the boxing and the weekend training camps, and to the surprise of his parents he spent ages shining his boots to a mirror finish and polishing his brass belt buckle and buttons. He learnt how to shoot a .22 rifle and he was the quickest cadet for stripping down and reassembling the rifle. He loved the cross-country yomps, the running and walking with full packs on their backs, and although he was not the quickest Sam had excellent stamina.

Sam left school when he was fifteen and all he wanted to do was to join the army but he was too young. He stayed in the cadets, being promoted to corporal, and took a job working on a building site. On his sixteenth birthday he enlisted.

He did his basic training at Aldershot and at the end of it he was offered the opportunity to go for additional training and assessment to judge his suitability to join the SAS. Sam was ideally suited to this unit and after six months in the army he became Private Sam Tucker SAS Battalion. During the next twenty years he would be trained to be an expert killer and he would see service in many areas of conflict throughout the world.

# CHAPTER 2

Although Sam was due to stay in Moscow for four days he only had hand luggage, a hangover from the army habit of travelling light. He walked through passport control and customs and out into the arrivals hall. In the arrivals hall the gloom and greyness disappeared for Sam. He saw Irina. She was standing just outside the arrivals gate, waiting to meet him. She was dressed in an ankle length fur coat, fur boots and a fur hat. She looked more beautiful to him than she did when he had first seen her just over a month before.

"Shammy" she cried out when she saw him. She rushed up to him and put her arms around his neck and kissed him on the lips. "Welcome to Moscow Shammy" she said. "You come with me now".

He held her and returned the kiss. "Hi Irina, How are you? Great to see you. I couldn't have asked for a nicer, more beautiful taxi driver". He put his arm around her waist and they walked towards the exit doors. Sam had known that Moscow in January would be cold but even though he had his ex army winter climate jacket and gloves on, he was unprepared for how cold it was, especially as it was early evening and dark. He was frozen by the time they reached the car in the car park and as he sat in it and Irena started the engine, he was greatful for the German efficiency of the Mercedes heater system.

Irina drove out of the car park and onto the new duel carriageway that leads to the city. She was a fast driver.

"How long have you been driving?" asked Sam as he gripped the seat tightly.

"Nearly a month" she replied.

"Is that how long you have had a license?"

"I don't have a license Shammy. Yuri say that you don't need one if you drive tourist, police never stop tourist".

Sam held on tighter, she was an appalling driver. In what seemed like an eternity but was in fact only about forty minutes, she screeched to a halt outside the Renaissance Hotel. A doorman rushed to hold the car door open for her. At last Sam could begin to breathe normally again.

"Whose teaching you to drive, Evil Kanivil?" Sam asked.

"Eh?" She obviously didn't know who he was talking about. "Yuri inside waiting" she said as she got out of the car and hurried to the hotel door. Sam followed. Yuri was standing beside the bar.

"Sam my friend, welcome to Moscow" he said as he moved forward and greeted Sam with a hug. "Irina will look after you while you are here, have dinner with you tonight and tomorrow morning bring you to the office and we talk about the business. OK?"

"That's fine with me" replied Sam. "Are you having dinner with us tonight?"

"No, just a drink now. I have business tonight to be ready for tomorrow. Irina, you go and check Sam in while we have a drink. Sam, scotch isn't it?" The barman produced a large scotch without having to be asked. "Cheers" said Sam.

"As you say. Cheers, here's to successful business."

Yuri left after about fifteen minutes and Sam followed Irena to his room. He had been surprised at how modern the hotel had been and as Irena led him into the bedroom he was again surprised at how large and well appointed it was. It was warm in the hotel and very comfortable in his room. Obviously this was one of the hotels where the central heating worked. He went to the window and looked out. Even though it was night the street lighting showed up a lovely vista of Ekaterina Park opposite. On the luggage rack were two bags. One was his, Irena picked up the other, opened it and started to take out her toiletries.

"Are you staying here the night with me?" said Sam, a bit surprised.

"Yes. You not want me to? she replied.

"No that's perfect for me but what about Yuri. You are his woman, what does he think?

"He said it alright. He has another woman anyway Shammy, I know this."

Sam didn't know what to say. "Are you hungry?" he asked.

"Very hungry" she said. "We can go out to a restaurant or we can eat here in the hotel. This is a good hotel for western people so the food is good". They chose the hotel restaurant and although the food was not brilliant it was certainly not bad. Sam had a steak and a bottle of red wine. The wine was from the Crimea and was not very good at all. However the food was not that important to Sam. He had had bad food, much worse than this, many times while serving for Queen and Country. More importantly he was with Irina. Sam thought again how very beautiful she was to look at and a lovely person to be with. She was bubbly, friendly, clever and he was in love with her.

Over dinner Irena told him again that she thought Yuri had another woman. She said that he had not come to her since they had returned from their holiday the month before. He had seen her but was using her more as a secretary or assistant than as a lover. During the year that they had been together he had bought her many clothes, some jewelry, a car and her apartment, which although small, was in a nice apartment block. Irina said that she had her suspicions when Yuri had arranged the holiday a couple of months ago. The frequency of their sex had become less and Irina felt that the holiday was a sort of a farewell present. She was not bitter in any way. They had been together for almost a year, which was a long time as far as she was concerned, and he had given her the flat so she thought that this meant that he did care something for her.

They finished their meal and went to their room. Sam felt slightly awkward about the situation but this vanished when, as soon as the bedroom door closed behind them, Irina kicked off her shoes and put her arms around Sam's neck and kissed him deeply. He responded and held her tightly. She pulled away from him, undid the zip on her trousers and let them fall to the ground. As she stepped out of them she pulled her jumper over her head and jumped on the bed.

"You can take my socks off" she said smiling broadly "and then you take all of your clothes off and I let you into my bed". She said everything with a smile on her face and a laugh in her voice.

Sam did what he was told, took off her socks, stripped himself and joined her under the blankets. They made love passionately. For a brief second he wondered if Irina was faking the enjoyment, if it was a job to her, if she had been told to do this by Yuri, but he dismissed it from his mind as soon as he thought of it.

# CHAPTER 3

After about an hour of exhausting love making they cuddled up together and Irina fell asleep. She lay in Sam's arms and breathed deeply.

Sam's mind went back to when he had first seen her, only a month ago in the dining room of the Crowne Plaza hotel in Sharm El Sheikh.

Sam had decided not to re-enlist at the end of his contract so he had been discharged from the army in October 2008 after twenty-two years of service. Because of his service record, despite the problems of the last year or so he received an honourable discharge and his army pension. Both of his parents were dead and he had one sister, Marion, who lived in Barking with her husband Mick and their two children. Although he had sent her Christmas cards, sometimes, and sort of kept in touch, they were not close. When Sam knew that he was leaving the army he wrote to her and told her and explained why he had reached that decision. She had written back suggesting that he should buy himself somewhere to live, also informing him that her house was too small for him to stay there. Sam had money saved up, he had lived frugally while in the army, and with the help of his sister Marion, had purchased a flat in a new complex in Beckton, just beside the Beckton flyover. He moved in during the last week of October and immediately decided that he wanted a holiday in the sun after his incarceration in Colchester. He went on line and found a good deal for a holiday in the first week of December at the Crowne Plaza hotel in Sharm El Sheikh, Egypt. It seemed both good value for money and a good hotel in a warm climate.

It was the first morning of his stay there. He was having breakfast in the large dining room. He had discovered that more than half the guests at the hotel were from Russia. He had finished his breakfast and was just drinking some coffee when she walked in. He couldn't help but notice her. Sam had always fancied Claudia Schiffer and to Sam, Irina looked like Claudia Schiffer, only more beautiful. She was fairly tall, about five feet eight. She looked taller because she was wearing gold sandals with four inch heels. She had shoulder length blonde hair and was wearing a short green skirt and gold t-shirt. Her skin was flawless and she wore very little makeup. Sam estimated that she was about twenty years old. He thought she was the most beautiful woman he had ever seen. He then noticed that she had a man with her. He was about the same height as her but twice her age. He had greying hair which was cut very short. He was stocky but not fat. He had bad skin, pot marked, and walked into the restaurant with a cigarette in his mouth. Sam felt disappointed. He knew instinctively that they were Russian and that he had a woman like this because he had bought her. Nobody who looked like her would otherwise be with a man like that.

Later that morning Sam was lying by one of the three pools that the hotel had, reading a book, when the couple came and lay on the sun loungers nearby. The woman still had on her gold sandals but was now wearing a gold bikini. The man was wearing a pair of Ralph Lauren bathing shorts. She was lightly bronzed while he was pale and pasty. They lay on the loungers until lunchtime and then went upstairs to the restaurant where a buffet lunch was served. Sam followed about ten minutes later, collected some cold chicken and salad from the counter and found a table about three away from the couple so that he had a good view of the woman.

In the afternoon Sam went to the hotel terrace by the sea, a man made strip of beach. He sat for a while looking at the people swimming in the sea for about an hour, to allow his lunch to digest. He then picked up his swimming mask and snorkel and walked towards the sea. As he went in he noticed the couple again. He looked at the woman and she saw him looking. She smiled as she saw him.

He made his way down to one of the rafts at the sea edge and dived off it into a wonderful world of coral and brightly coloured fish. Sam was an experienced diver, trained by the SAS, but here the coral was so near the surface that snorkelling was sufficient to see everything. He stayed in the sea for over an hour. When he came out the couple had gone.

He saw them again in the dining room at dinner. Again it was a buffet self service and Sam had a steak with some fries and a salad followed by fruit pie and ice cream. When he finished he left and went

to the bar. He was sitting on his own at a table when the man came up
to him.

"You are English?" he asked

"Yes."

"And you are here on your own?"

"That's right. It's a free country" said Sam wanting this man to go
away.

The man smiled. "I mean no offence but I have a favour to ask".

Bloody cheek thought Sam but he said "Ask away."

"I noticed today that you swim in the corals very well. I do not
swim I am afraid but I have with me a girlfriend that wants to go in
the sea and swim with the fish. You may have seen her, her name is
Irina. The favour that I ask is that you take her into the sea. We are
only here for another three days so I would ask that you take her
tomorrow."

Sam couldn't believe his luck. "Of course, I would be pleased
to." As he said it she walked to the table. She was wearing black high
heeled sandals and a short black dress.

"Hello my darling" the man said to her. "Mr . . . . . . . . . . . . . . . I am
sorry I did not ask your name . . . . ."

"Sam, Sam Tucker."

The man held out his hand. "My name is Yuri, Yuri Dolchenko".
Sam took Yuri's hand and shook it

"My darling, Sam said that he would be pleased to take you into
the sea tomorrow."

"Shank you Sham" she said "I am looking very forward to it". She
smiled at him as she spoke. He had to will himself not to stare at this
woman who had a voice to match her physical beauty.

The following morning after breakfast they met at the beach
terrace where they had been the previous afternoon. Yuri stayed on the
sun loungers as Sam went with Irina to the hotel shop to buy flippers,
mask and snorkel. As they walked back through the hotel complex they
talked.

"How well can you swim?" Sam asked her.

"In my home city when I was a girl we would go for swims in the
lake. We have very cold winters and the lakes and rivers freeze but the
summer was warm and we love to swim in the lake. It was polluted
and with no fish so I want to swim with fish here."

"Your English is very good. Did you learn that at your school?"

"I learn a bit, for three years at school, but mostly I learn from Europeans and also Yuri teach me. He say that English important and it good for my future."

They went onto a raft and Sam told her how to breathe through the snorkel tube. They slipped into the water, into the silent world of coral and fish. Sam could tell by her relaxed manner that she was enjoying being down with the fish. After about half an hour they got out and went back to the terrace where Yuri was waiting.

"Yuri, that was wonderful, you should see it down there, so clear, and the fish, all different colours and shapes and sizes. Can I go back this afternoon, please Yuri?" Sam thought she was like a child who had just been given a special present. She was so excited.

"If Mr Tucker says so it is fine with me" said Yuri "but you cannot go on your own. The Americans have a rule when diving, you have to have a dive buddy, that is so Mr Tucker is it not?"

"You should never go diving on your own, that is correct". Sam didn't want to point out that this rule was for diving not for using a snorkel. He didn't want to talk himself out of spending more time with Irina.

Sam continued. "I would be pleased to go with you this afternoon. I love it down there too". So they agreed to meet back at the beach terrace that afternoon at two thirty.

For lunch Sam had some cheese and biscuits, fruit and a cup of tea. He met with Irina and Yuri at two thirty and he spent almost an hour with Irina in the sea around the coral that was on the far side of the one they had swum along in the morning.

They came out and dried off with their towels. As Irina and Yuri were leaving, Yuri said "Would you join us for dinner this evening Sam? I know that meals are included in the tariff for us but I have found a good wine for us and I would like some male company".

"That would be nice, thank you" said Sam.

"We meet in the bar at eight o'clock? Drinks are on my bill I insist", said Yuri.

# CHAPTER 4

Sam walked into the bar at eight o'clock. Yuri and Irena were already there. "Exactly eight o'clock, very prompt," said Yuri.

"Habit of a lifetime," said Sam.

They had a drink in the bar where Irina spent most of the time talking about her swim with the fish. As they finished Yuri suggested that instead of eating in the buffet restaurant where most of the guests would eat, they should go to the Italian Restaurant that was on terraces near one of the pools. This restaurant was not included in the 'all inclusive package' that most of the guests had, so it was much quieter than the main restaurant. They went there and had a very nice meal, Sam had veal, Irina had some pasta and Yuri fish. They had a dry white wine that was produced from vines grown on the banks of the Nile near Cairo.

They were eating their main course when Yuri asked Sam what he did for a living.

"I'm retired," replied Sam.

"From the British Army?" asked Yuri.

"Yes. How do you know? said Sam.

"I was a KGB officer for more than twenty years. I was a major. I recognize a fellow professional when I see one. What rank?"

"I retired a Private" responded Sam.

Yuri looked at him for a few seconds when he said 'Private,' but did not pursue the matter.

The evening passed very pleasantly with the three of them talking about the hotel, food, swimming, in fact just making small talk. For Sam there was the added bonus of being able to spend three hours looking at the most beautiful woman in the world without appearing a pervert. Reluctantly Sam found himself warming to Yuri. He had wanted to dislike him because he had Irina, but in fact he found him to be very good company and he obviously cared for her.

The following morning Sam was dozing by the side of one of the pools when Yuri approached and sat down next to him.

"Hello Sam. How are you this morning? If I am rude to you please tell me but I have been thinking. What regiment were you in? You have the appearance of a specialist but I am surprised that you have just retired and that you are only a Private. Therefore I think that you have a problem and are busted as the Americans say".

Sam said nothing for a few seconds. "Yes, I was as you say, busted. I was in the SAS and yes, I was a specialist, I killed people. I don't want to appear rude to you either Yuri but I really don't want to talk about."

"I understand. Just one more question if you don't mind. Do you have a career when you go back to England?"

Sam wanted to conclude this conversation

"No", said Sam. "I'm going for a swim now". Sam got up and left Yuri sitting there while he went to the pool and jumped in. When Sam returned from his swim Yuri had gone. He didn't see either Yuri or Irina for the rest of the day or during the evening in the restaurant or the bar. Sam felt strangely disappointed. Maybe he had been a bit abrupt with Yuri when he asked him about his situation.

# CHAPTER 5

The next morning Sam was up early and had his breakfast. He selected a sun lounger by the quietest of the three pools, the one near the Italian Restaurant that they had eaten at two nights before.

It was about ten thirty, Sam was dozing in the sun when he heard, "Hello Sam". It was Yuri. "I apologise to you if I upset you yesterday. It was not that I was meaning to be rude to you."

"No, that's OK Yuri, its me that should apologise. You are right, I was busted, as you say, and it is still a bit raw. I came here to forget for a few days. I will have to think about it and sort my future when I get home."

"Maybe I can help" replied Yuri. "Let us go and have a coffee or maybe something stronger if you wish. I may have something of interest for you."

They left and walked down to the beach bar, the bar near the largest swimming pool which was just behind the beach. Sam sat at a table while Yuri fetched two coffees. Sam sat and sipped his coffee and waited for Yuri to speak.

"Sam, I run an organization. I have a vacancy for someone based in Europe. With your background and training you may be the ideal person for the job"

"What does your organisation do?" asked Sam.

"We kill people."

There was a long silence. "We are very selective, very discreet, and we charge a lot of money. You may call us an assassination agency but that sounds like a Hollywood movie. As I say we have a vacancy in Europe. Would you be interested?"

Sam didn't know what to say. He had not expected this. "If I was interested I would want to know a lot more about it," he said.

"Of course. I am not expecting a yes or a no today. But if you could be interested then we will talk again. I will investigate you and

13

you in turn will ask me the details of what you want to know. If you are not interested then we shake hands and when I go back to Russia tomorrow we will say goodbye forever."

Sam thought about it for several seconds. He had no real prospects when he returned to England. He had no money. He had been trained for only one thing and that was to kill people and here was a Russian ex-KGB officer offering the chance to earn a living doing something that he was an expert at. He decided that he had nothing to lose by finding out more.

"Let's say I am interested. What would be the next step?"

"We would talk in my office in Moscow. If we meet in one month you will have time to think about what you would need and also I would too. We would discuss it and maybe reach an agreement. If we cannot, we shake hands and say goodbye."

"OK, I'm interested," said Sam.

"Good, I am pleased" said Yuri. "In case we proceed and you are employed I would suggest that your cover is Irena. You will exchange e-mails when you return and that is how we will arrange for you to visit us in Moscow. If your security services are monitoring mail from Russia it will appear as if you are talking to a girl that you fell for while on holiday. That is your cover. Do you think that will work."

"It will work fine" said Sam.

"Good. I will tell Irina that she will be your cyber girlfriend. She will like that. She thinks that you are like James Bond, a sophisticated Englishman".

Sam smiled to himself at that description. One thing he was not was sophisticated.

"I have another favour to ask although now it may help our business. This is our last night here on holiday. Irina wants to go to a club in the town, It is called Back in the USSR, after the Beatles song. I have to work this evening. Would you mind if you took her to the club. It is mainly for the Russians who holiday here but Westerners go there too I am told."

"I had nothing planned for this evening. I would be pleased to take her." Sam wanted to cheer out loud. An evening on his own with Irina, paradise.

# CHAPTER 6

He had arranged to meet her in the hotel reception at ten o'clock. She arrived on time. When Sam saw her he caught his breath. She looked stunning. She was dressed in skin tight black satin trousers, black patent high heeled shoes and a white satin shirt. Her blonde hair was freshly washed and hung loose around her shoulders. She smiled when she saw him and the smile made her face light up. Sam felt himself blush, something he couldn't remember doing before.

She walked up to him and kissed in on the lips. He must have reacted to the kiss because she said "It's alright Shammy, we are going to be lovers on the internet so a kiss is a good start". She said it with a laugh in her voice.

They went to the club in town by taxi. As Yuri had said it was full of Russians with some other nationalities there too. It was a large club, the largest that Sam had ever been to. It was also very noisy, not really Sam's taste, but what was to his taste was the beautiful woman that he was with. Sam was very fit, but after about an hour and a half of continual dancing even he began to feel that he needed a short rest.

They left the floor and went to bar. He asked for some mineral water and to his surprise Irina had the same. "I thought all Russians drank vodka" he said to her.

"I prefer Champagne" she said, "but when I am hot and thirsty water is my favourite. You should not group all peoples together. Russians are different as English are, or Americans. Do all English drink gin and eat roast beef on Sundays?"

"Point taken. I won't jump to conclusions about you again," he said.

"You should not, because I am going to surprise you Mister Shammy, you see".

They danced on and off until the time reached half past one. Sam looked at his watch.

"You want to go Shammy? Irina said.

"Only when you want to" he replied.

"We go now. It's getting late, past my bedtime".

Sam suddenly felt that he didn't want to go. The evening would end when they got back to the hotel and he didn't want the evening to end. It was too late to change his mind now. Irina was holding his hand and leading him towards the exit. They took a taxi back to the hotel. They walked into the reception.

"I'll see you to your room" Sam said. "What's your room number?"

"Tonight I stay with you, only if you like of course. We are going to be lovers so I want to see what kind of lover you are so I can talk about it to you"

"But what about Yuri? What will . . . . . . . . . ."

"I tell Yuri that I find you very attractive man and think you sexy. He say I do what I want. I want to and he say it a good idea. Do you not want me?"

Sam thought that was the most stupid question that he had ever been asked. He took her hand and led her to his room. As soon as he closed the door behind them she reached out for him and kissed him on the lips. He responded. They took each others clothes off and fell on the bed. They made love, the first time passionately and frantically, an hour later, slowly and romantically. After they made love the second time, Sam took some water from the mini-bar. They both had a drink from it. Sam asked Irina how she was here with Yuri and did she mind that he allowed her to have sex and spend the night with someone else. He told her if she was his woman he would guard her jealously.

She lay there and told him about her life. She was twenty-three years old. She had been born in a city called Karabash in Russia. It was a large industrial city with many factories. Her father had worked in the large copper smelting and processing plant, one of the largest in Russia. The air inside was always very polluted, it was full of sulphur which spewed out into the air over the city. Her father was only fifty but could not work any more because of his lungs. They were full of poisoned air and he could not breathe. He spent all day sitting in a chair breathing heavily and coughing. He was getting slightly better and now at least he could walk to the shops and even go for short walks in the forest in the summer, which was better that he had been two years ago. She had two brothers, both of them older than her. They also worked in the copper factory. She thought they were mad. In Soviet times they would have no choice where they worked, the state would decide, but now they had a choice. The wages in the factory were very good, up to fifty percent higher than in other places, but rarely did a man who worked there live to be sixty. The plant had been closed in 1990 but had been reopened in 1998 because of its importance to jobs in the area. There were industrial waste mounds almost fifty feet high around the town and there is a high ratio of skin diseases, birth defects and organ failures.

In the winter the temperatures in the region dropped to as low as minus twenty-five, but the summer could be warm, as hot as twenty-six or twenty-seven in June and July. That is when Irina had gone to the countryside outside of the city and swum in the lakes. She told Sam that the countryside away from the city was beautiful in the summer. There were trees and bushes that had flowers on them of many different shapes and colours.

Irina had done well at school. She was the cleverest girl in her class. In Soviet times she would have gone to university, the state paid all of the costs. But now it was different and her parents could not afford for her to go. She was determined not to work in a factory and despite encouragement from her family, she was determined not to marry a factory worker and end like many of the girls that she knew, a housewife and mother of two or three children by the time she was in her early twenty's. When she left school she got a job in one of the hotels in the city. It was not very good wages and the hours were long and irregular but she met many interesting people and talked to them about the far away places that they came from. Most of the people that stayed at her hotel were from Moscow or St Petersburg and were visiting one or other of the plants in the city. Sometimes though a foreigner would stay. They would usually be someone who was looking to invest in the former Soviet industry. It seemed to her that all Europeans from whatever country spoke English. So if they were German, Dutch, Belgians, or the British, English was the language that they all used when they checked in and ordered food in the dinning room. She had learnt some at school so she could speak a small amount so she would speak to them in English when she could and learn some new words from them.

She had worked there for almost four years and had been promoted to an assistant manager. Part of her job was to fill in when somebody did not arrive at work. This is what had happened the first time Yuri had stayed there. He visited to sort out a problem with some workers in one of the factories. She was working on the reception desk when he arrived and then served at his table when he dined. The following evening she was on reception again when he came in for his room key but as the waitress had arrived for work, Irina did not serve at tables that night. Instead she was behind the bar. Yuri came for a drink and they chatted. Irina had told him that she hoped for something better than a life as a wife in Karabash.

Three weeks later Yuri was back to stay for three nights. On the third evening he told her that his business was concluded and that he would not be returning. He asked her if she wanted to leave and go with him to Moscow. She agreed. She had no illusions that he was offering for her to become his mistress and that people would think that she was whore, but he seemed nice, he seemed important, and she saw him as her passport away from her city.

She left home the next morning with her case packed. Her parents were both shocked and angry when she told them what she was planning and said that they would disown her. Yuri collected her from her apartment by taxi and they caught the train to Moscow, first class.

When they arrived in Moscow Yuri had taken her to a flat in the Presnensky area of the city and left her there to rest. The next day he returned and took her shopping. He brought her everything new, new underwear, trousers, skirts, dresses, shirts, jumpers, two coats, hats, gloves, handbags; she had never had so much.

That night he came to her in the bedroom. She was a virgin and when she told him this he was very gentle with her. They had sex three or four times a week, sometimes she even enjoyed it. He was always clean, sober and he never hurt her. He was not kinky and not into any weird practices. She got to meet with some of the other mistresses of powerful men and assured Sam that Yuri was one of the nicest. Some of the women were lent out as a treat or reward to other men for a night or a weekend. Yuri had never done this. Many of the men had power complexes and tied up the women or had anal sex with them. One man would watch while other men had sex with his mistress, sometimes four or five different men one after another. Yuri had never asked any of these things. He was her first and until tonight, he had been the only one.

It was about five o'clock when they eventually fell asleep in each others arms. The alarm went off at seven thirty and Irina got out of bed, got dressed, kissed Sam passionately and left. Sam had the terrible, empty feeling that he would never see her again.

# CHAPTER 7

Sam got showered and went down to breakfast. He hoped that Irena would be there. She wasn't. It crossed his mind that maybe Yuri knew nothing about her planning to stay the night with him in which case what would he do to her when she arrived back in their room this morning?

He spent the next three days thinking about her and then he returned home on 16ᵗʰ December.

He took a train from Gatwick Airport to Victoria and tube from Victoria to Barking. He caught a cab from Barking Station to his flat in Beckton. He walked in switched on the kettle, switched on his computer to boot up and went into the bedroom to unpack his case. He sorted his washing and went to the kitchen put it in the washing machine and turned it on. He poured some boiling water over a tea bag and returned to the living room to check his e-mails. The first one on the computer read:

*Hello Darling,*

*Got back to Moscow safely. Uncle Yuri sends his regards. We are both looking forward to seeing you early next month. Uncle Yuri is arranging the flights and will send you the details soon.*

*There is lots I want to say to you but it can wait until you are in my arms.*

*Lots of love from me*
*Irina*

Sam was over the moon. Everything was alright. He spent the rest of day walking around with a stupid grin on his face.

On 22nd December another e-mail arrived. It was from Irina. It gave details of the British Airways flight details that Yuri had booked for Sam. She said that she would meet him at the airport and to pack some warm clothes as it was cold in Moscow. He was to depart from Heathrow on 10th January, a Sunday. He felt that it would be difficult to wait that long.

He spent Christmas Day 2008 with his sister, the first time he had done so since he was fifteen. Her sons seemed to like him and he was happy passing the time playing with them. His sister pressed him about what he was going to do and she got slightly annoyed with him when he evaded answering her.

Sunday 10th January eventually arrived. He was at Heathrow Airport four hours before the plane was due to depart he was so anxious not to miss it. Yuri had booked Club Class seats so he could use the club lounge in the new Terminal 5. Sam was very impressed with the terminal and the lounge facilities.

# CHAPTER 8

Sam woke. It was still dark. He had to think for a second where he was. Irina was laying in his arms, breathing heavily. He looked at the clock; six forty-seven. It seemed surreal to him just then. He was in Moscow, in bed with the most beautiful woman that he had ever seen, about to go and meet a man about a job killing people. He lay there completely still, he did not want to disturb Irina, he did not want to break the spell. It occurred to him that he did not know what time they were supposed to meet Yuri or where.

After a few minutes Irina stirred. She opened her eyes and smiled at him."Hello Shammy my love. Is it nice to be here in Moscow with your cyber girlfriend?"

"Its nice being anywhere with my cyber girlfriend" he said. As soon as he said it he felt a bit of an idiot. What was happening? He was turning into a Mills and Boon novel.

He reached out and kissed her. He could feel himself getting a hard-on again. Irina must have felt it also. "Not now, we don't have time. We need to go and meet with Yuri. We will do it twice tonight instead".

She jumped out of bed and into the shower room. He heard her turn on the shower. She came back into the bedroom and pulled him out of bed.

"Come on Shammy, I must make sure you are clean and smell nice for your interview with Yuri".

She pulled him into the shower and started to rub the shower gel over him. He was immediately hard again. She looked at him, smiled and tutted. "I don't know what the word is but I cannot stop you doing this thing."

Sam laughed. "It's not me, it has its own mind you know. In England the woman have a saying. A man's brain is in his penis. It's my penis brain doing it, not me."

She laughed. She then went down on her knee's in front of him and took him in her mouth. He came within seconds. "That should make it sleep for a while" she said as she stood up and washed his genital area. When she has soaked him all over and rinsed him off he got out of the shower and left her to finish washing herself.

They dressed, went down to breakfast and at nine o'clock precisely the driver in a large Lexus arrived to take them to see Yuri.

# CHAPTER 9

The car took them to an apartment block at Str 9 Krasmaya Presnya. They took the lift to the third floor. They knocked on the front door of an apartment and very quickly it was opened by Yuri.

They went inside. The apartment had been turned into an office. The lounge was furnished as a boardroom. It had a large glass and chrome desk at one end with a cream leather executive chair behind it. There were two smaller chairs of a similar design in front on the desk. At the other end of the room were two settee's also in cream leather, placed opposite each other, with a glass and chrome coffee table in between them. In the corner was a large flat screen television. All of the fittings were very modern and looked expensive. The larger of the two bedrooms had been converted into an office. It had two desks in, both of which had computer terminals on them and two small filing cabinets. The second bedroom had in it a photocopier, fax machine, computer and scanner and a large printer. Only the kitchen looked as it was still an apartment. That had normal kitchen appliances in it, a fridge, kettle, coffee maker and microwave oven.

Yuri signaled for Sam to sit on one of the settees. As he did so another man walked into the room.

"This is Ivanov, a colleague of mine" said Yuri. Ivanov and Sam shook hands. "Ivanov will be with us for the beginning of our discussions so that he may get an idea of what we are thinking. Is that alright with you Sam?"

Sam nodded. As he did so Irina entered the room with a tray containing three mugs of coffee.

"Irina, please make sure that we are not disturbed, no phone calls, no interruptions" Yuri said as she was leaving the room.

The three men sat down; Yuri and Ivanov opposite Sam. Yuri started the conversation, "Well Sam, we have thought about it and investigated and I hope you too will have done so, so what do you think. What questions do you have?"

"Firstly a condition. I don't want to do any jobs in the UK. Anywhere else in Europe is fine in principle but not at home."

"We can agree to that" said Yuri. "Next condition?".

"There are no more conditions as such, more of a situation. One thing the army taught me is that preparation and planning are important for success. If I am not happy about the preparation or planning I walk away. I'm going into this not to get caught or to leave loose ends. I need to be satisfied that I can do that. That means the proper equipment and arrangements and information must be supplied."

"Sam, I told you in Egypt that I was in the KGB for many years. In the KGB I learnt to be a judge of men. I judged you to be the type of man who would require what you have said. We have an organisation that will give you all you need. I will talk about that later. Let us talk about you first".

Yuri looked at Ivanov. He pulled a file out of his briefcase and placed it on the coffee table. As he opened the plain manila cover Sam notice that the top page had an MOD stamp on it.

"Mr Tucker, I have your military record, very impressive".

Sam was annoyed and impressed at the same time. How had they managed to obtain his army dossier and done it in less than a month?

"It is a stupid situation that you are awarded The Military Medal for obtaining information in Iraq that saves many British and American lives in 1990 and are demoted and imprisoned for doing the same thing in 2007. I do not understand the western logic".

Yuri then took over from Ivanov to cover the main points of Sam's record. He had them memorised, which again impressed Sam.

Sam had been allocated to an SAS group based in Norfolk when he finished his training in early 1987. Once part of his battalion, Sam's training continued. He learnt quickly and impressed his officers. Within a year he was an expert marksman, everything from small pistols, to machine pistols and guns to high velocity sniper rifles. He was also expert at unarmed combat, winning the battalion competition for enlisted men. He was trained to fight with a knife and also trained to build and detonate explosive devices.

On August 2^nd 1990 Iraq invaded Kuwait. On August 7th all British forces personnel were put on amber alert. In November Sam's platoon were flown to a US airforce base in Saudi Arabia and set up a forward camp on the border between Saudi Arabia and Kuwait. On January 17^th 1991 the Americans started a bombing campaign of Baghdad. With the air supremacy of the US, the Iraqi airforce withdrew as many of their planes as they could to Iran, believing, correctly, that the US would not follow them into Iranian airspace and attempt to destroy them.

The air attacks ceased during February 1991 and on 23^rd February the American army entered Kuwait to liberate it. Unknown to most of the combatants a few small groups of selected men had already entered Iraq covertly. Their mission was to gain intelligence as to the size of Sadaam's forces and to try and find out where his crack regiments of guards were located and, if possible the readiness and strength of the Iraqi forces.

One such group was Sam's platoon. They were split into small units and Sam was in a group of five; four privates and a lieutenant. Their job was to go to a town called Ar Rutban, which was on the main road from Jordan to Baghdad. They were dressed as Arabs, with kaftans over army uniforms. They arrived on the outskirts of the town just after dark on 12th February. They came across a café on the outskirts of the town that had a large armoured vehicle park outside of it. The officer, Lieutenant Thompson, made the men lay up about one hundred yards from the building. They were then at the edge of the desert and in total darkness. He had already identified Sam as being the most capable of the group and was aware that although of the same rank, the others looked up to him, he was their unofficial leader. He signalled for Sam to join him to investigate the situation so, leaving the others, they crept to the café building. They found a window to the rear that had been left partially open. Looking inside they could not see anybody but could hear voices. They withdrew to wait.

They lay on the edge of the desert for over half an hour when a door opened and one of the soldiers came out. He walked around towards the rear of the building, opened his trousers and started to urinate on the ground. The Lieutenant and Sam crept forward. As they approached the man finished his toilet and turned around. Sam leapt at him, punching him in the face and then hitting him again as he went down. They then dragged him unconscious, the hundred yards to where the other men were. All of them then withdrew to a distance of about four hundred yards, dragging the Iraqi soldier with them.

They tied his hands behind his back as he came to. Lieutenant Thompson started to question their captive. He looked at the officer and said nothing.

"He isn't going to say anything asking him like that" said Sam. "Why not let me have a go?"

"No violence, he may not speak English" said the Lieutenant.

"He speaks English alright" said Sam as he moved forward.

The prisoner was wearing an army uniform, he was sitting up, hands tied behind his back and looked at Sam as he approached. He did not seem afraid. Sam took out a long bladed knife and swiftly cut open his shirt and then his trousers which fell away exposing him. Very quickly Sam moved forward, grabbed hold of the man's penis and cut off his scrotum. Everybody was very still, in shock, including the prisoner. Sam threw the testicles onto the ground and stamped on them. The man screamed. It seemed that he was more horrified at the thought of his testicles being destroyed than he was by the pain he felt having it removed.

"Now," said Sam quietly, "how many men are there in the café and where are Sadaam's guard units located?"

The man was still screaming. The Lieutenant was panicking. "He doesn't speak English" he was shouting.

Sam ignored him. He went towards the prisoner. He took his knife and just as quickly as before removed the mans penis. He held it up. "Who'd like this? he said. One of the young privates held his hand out. Sam was surprised that anybody had excepted his offer. The Private who had done so hero-worshipped Sam so was obviously trying to impress him, he threw it to the ground and started to stamp on it as Sam had done.

"What's next then, how about an ear, or maybe the nose"? said Sam.

"No, no, no. I will tell you" screamed the man.

Sam had been right, he spoke very good English. He told them that there were five others in the café. He told them that the crack Iraqi troops were still in Bagdad, some protecting Sadaam and others making plans to be behind the regular troops, most of them conscripts, many of them young, to make sure that they don't retreat and run back. This was known as the Stalingrad strategy. When the German army was at the gates of Stalingrad during the second world war, Stalin required all of the inhabitants as well as a conscripted army of mainly young recruits, to fight the Nazi's. He had his crack troops behind the lines to shoot anybody who tried to desert

This experience was a valuable lesson to Sam for the future. Inflicting pain itself on somebody is not as effective as showing the opponent that he lacked all emotion or scruples and that he would not stop inflicting more pain and doing irreparable physical damage to them as long as they withhold the information that he sought.

The Lieutenant decided that they should deal with the Iraqi's in the café. As they prepared to leave he asked Sam to gag the prisoner so that he could not shout a warning to his colleagues. Sam gagged his mouth and as the others moved off he went around the back of the man and slit both of his wrists. He bled to death in less than two minutes.

It took them almost half an hour to reach the café. They travelled most of the way crouched over in case they could be seen. The others had obviously heard their colleagues screams and were looking all around to try and locate where they had come from. Two of the soldiers were looking at the rear of the building. Sam and Lieutenant Thompson crept up behind them, Sam broke the neck of one and Thompson cut the throat of another. Both were killed silently.

The other three had moved towards the armoured vehicle. They all got inside as though they were going to leave. Sam jumped forward, opened one of the doors, threw two hand grenades inside and quickly closed the door again throwing himself to the ground as he did so. The Iraqi's were caught by surprise and had no time to react before the grenades went off inside an vehicles confined space. All of them were blown up.

They had the information they needed so returned to camp. Sam was awarded the Military Cross as it was thought that the information that he had gained saved many allied lives and shortened the war. With this knowledge the allies were able to move faster because they knew that they would meet little resistance until they reached the outskirts of Bagdad.

The award of the medal and the fact that he had removed the penis and testicle's, ensured Private Sam Tucker cult status among the enlisted men in his regiment. His actions did however concern some of the senior officers and this was posted on his record. Despite his successes over many years, on the occasions that he was reviewed for consideration for officer training, this episode and his actions were held against him and he never rose above NCO rank.

# CHAPTER 10

In 2007 Sam, now Sergeant Tucker was back in Iraq. Not much had changed as far as he was concerned except that this time the Americans had done the job they should have done all those years before and actually dealt with Sadaam Hussain.

After a number of successful missions Sam's unit was back in England on leave when the notification came through that they were to be sent to Afghanistan. Sam's SAS unit specialised in counter intelligence and assassinations. There were some Taliban tribal leaders who were giving the NATO forces some problems and they could not be located. In July 2007, Sam, with his battalion were flown into the American Air force base at Kabul.

In August he was with a small group of SAS and regular troops on a reconnaissance mission when they came across a group of Taliban. They spied on them and then moved in, killing three and arresting seven. They shackled the prisoners and returned with them to the barracks. Sam had already identified in his own mind who was the leader. He said so to the Lieutenant leading the squad who agreed with his opinion. When they arrived at their camp they split the prisoners up and put the leader in a room of his own. They needed to get information from this group about the Taliban activity and strength in the area, an area which had been targeted by the enemy over the past few months. The Lieutenant left to inform the Captain who he thought may like to question the man personally. Sam knew what that would mean in the new politically correct army. They would ask questions and the prisoner would not answer. The Lieutenant had left one of his privates with Sam to guard the prisoner. As soon as the Lieutenant had left, Sam told the private to wait outside of the room. He was reluctant to do so but Sam pointed to the three stripes on his shirt.

As soon as Sam was alone he said "I'm not pissing about. I know you speak English. I want information and either you give it to me quickly or I hurt you".

The man looked at him and grinned, "you are not allowed to mistreat prisoners, rule of war, Geneva convention".

It was Sam's turn to grin. "I don't even know where Geneva is" he said. With that he took a large hunting knife out of his trousers. The man was wearing sandals, his knife sliced through them and completely cut through two toes. The man screamed, the private rushed back into the room to see what was going on. Sam looked the man in the eye and without blinking he lifted the knife and repeated the action on the other foot, removing three toes from that foot. The Taliban soldier couldn't talk fast enough, giving all of the information that was asked of him, strengths, location and state of readiness of all of the fighting groups in the region.

"You had better take notes of this Private" said Sam as he turned and left the room.

Just over one hour later two military police detained him and he was charged with conduct unbecoming. He was court marshaled ten days later. He was found guilty of torturing a prisoner and was sentenced to loss of rank, reduced to Private, and a twelve month detention sentence in the military prison at Colchester.

# CHAPTER 11

Yuri finished summarizing the two incidents. "If you had done that when we were in Afghanistan you would have received the Soviet Order of Merit." he said. "In Britain you get put in prison. That is why the West will never win a war again. It is a new world, the world of Al Quaida, the world of the Taliban, the world of guerillas and terrorism. Battles will not be won by the rules of Eton or Harrow".

Ivanov then turned to other pages. "I see here that it was you who actually shot the Brigadier who was the personal bodyguard of Sheikh Khalifa Bin Hamad Al Thani in Qater in 1995, that enabled his pro-western son to take over as ruler. That was a sniper shot from over six hundred metres. We always thought that either the British or Americans were involved. But you must be an excellent marksman.

It also says that while under cover in Ireland you killed with bare hands a senior paramilitary from both the IRA and the UDA, quite an achievement. I have to say Mr Tucker you are very qualified for the job that we have in mind".

Yuri took over. "The job Sam is an assassin. My company gets paid to kill powerful, often corrupt people. We charge three hundred thousand US dollars per contract. You would get one hundred and fifty thousand, we get one hundred thousand and the rest, the other fifty thousand, covers the cost of provisions for the operation, weapons and paperwork mostly with some other small administrative costs. I have agents in Eastern Europe, I have two in the United States and one in Africa. I need one in Europe. That is the job I have for you. As you say it needs planning. You would be responsible for planning your own operations. I have a brother who is an attaché at the embassy in Paris. It is a good place. Most people do not like the French, they have no real friends so they want to be friends with whoever they can. They try with Russia. The Americans don't like us, the British don't trust us, the Germans hate us, so we let the French think that we like them. It is easy for an embassy of Russia to get guns, documents, anything we need into Paris. From there it can moved to anywhere in Europe. That is how we would supply you".

Yuri went on to detail the operation. And he and Sam went into great detail of how things would work in practice. Sam was impressed with Yuri's attention to detail and Yuri likewise was impressed with Sam's.

Before any of them realised, it was lunchtime and they stopped for some coffee and sandwiches which Irina brought in. She laid them on the coffee table with plates and knives. She was about to leave but Yuri asked her to join them. They made small talk over lunch and then Irina left them to continue their discussions. Ivanov left too.

Yuri picked up the conversation. "Sam, we need to arrange contact. As I said when we talked in Egypt, I would like that to be Irina. Would that be alright with you? You may need to meet from time to time to keep up appearances of being lovers".

Sam nodded, he felt if he answered it may betray how alright that was with him. This was business and he did not want Yuri to think anything else.

"Sam. I have a new woman. I have been with Irina for more than a year. That is more than I have been with any woman but I need to have a change now. I have an affection for Irina. She is a good girl and she is clever, not like most of my women who are sexy and attractive, good to fuck but not good for company. Irina is different. I will let her keep her flat, her clothes and her car but she needs to get an income. So I will give her a job as an assistant and she will be your link with me. She will be the girlfriend in Russia who you talk to on the internet every week. We will have a code. It will be 'snow in Gorky Park'. In the winter if she says 'there is snow in Gorky Park' or in the summer if she says that 'there is no snow in Gorky Park', then you will make contact. I will tell her this afternoon and I hope that she will understand and work in her new job. I would not want her to go as a whore in a Moscow club as many of the girls do when their masters are finished with them, or to go back to the shit hole of a town that I found her in."

Again Sam just nodded. He didn't really know what to say.

It was about four o'clock when they had concluded their arrangements. All weapons would be supplied to Sam's requirements through the Russian embassy in Paris. All documents would be arranged the same way or through a trade attaché in the London Embassy. Certain other code words were arranged for inclusion in e-mails from Irina. Yuri said that he would pay Sam a quarter of a million US dollars now, a sort of golden handshake to welcome him to the company. Banking arrangements were made and it was arranged that a company would be set up in Sam's name, a company who were security advisors. That legitimised some of the money Sam would be paid. The rest would be paid into a bank account in Sam's name in an Iranian bank. Yuri explained that the banks in places like The Cayman's would inform the Americans about money coming in, and the Swiss banks now didn't withhold information from the European authorities. Iran was a friend of Russia and told nothing to anybody.

They shook hands on the deal. Sam was now officially an assassin. Yuri called his car, the Lexus that had taken them to the flat, to take him to his hotel. He said that he would talk to Irina straight away and explain about his new woman and Irina's new role. Yuri asked Sam to be gentle with her when she returned to the hotel later as he felt that she would be very upset.

Irina returned three hours later. Far from being upset she was very happy.

"I told you he had another woman" she said as she entered the hotel room and held him tight. I am so pleased that I can keep everything and stay living in Moscow and have a job. And best of all my job is to talk to you". She kissed him hard. He was very aroused. He picked her up and carried her to the bedroom. He took off her coat and boots and then the rest of her clothes. As he did this she was taking off his. They fell into bed and made love. Sam knew instinctively that Irina was not doing this as part of her job.

The next day they spent sightseeing in Moscow. They visited all of the tourist sites, Saint Basils Cathedral, The Kremlin, Gorky Park and a huge department store that in Soviet times had only been for high ranking party officials.

When it was time to return to England , Sam was a bit disappointed that Yuri joined him and Irina. Sam checked in and was just about to go through passport control. He held and kissed Irina, a bit less passionately that he would have liked and shook hand with Yuri.

"By the way, get a new place to live. Beckton is a shit hole, your flat is a shit hole. Anyone that works for me has a standard to maintain and Beckton is not up to that standard. If you want to live in a shit place make it nice shit, maybe like Docklands. Move to Canary Wharf".

With that Sam walked through, past the passport inspector to wait for his flight home.

He was exited about his new life.

# CHAPTER 12

The day after Sam returned to his flat a package arrived, recorded delivery. It was a set of documents from a solicitor in London. It contained a company registration document confirming the details of Tuckers Security Consultants Ltd. This would enable Sam to not only have a vehicle to be paid money for his services but it was also a front in case anybody decided to investigate him. The package also contained details of a bank account opened in the company name. A covering letter explained that Sam would need to visit the branch of Barclays Bank in Barking, as soon as possible to sign some documents to activate the account. Half an hour after the package arrived, Sam was on the bus travelling into Barking to go to Barclays Bank.

When he got back home he e-mailed Irina. He told her that he had returned home safely and that his solicitors had sorted out his new company and that he now had a bank account so needed to start looking for some clients. He told her what a wonderful time he had had with her in Moscow and how much he missed her already. If the security forces did check his e-mails they would look like an innocent mail to a girlfriend or lover.

Sam searched the net to see what sort of flats were available in Docklands. He didn't really want to leave East London but he thought that he should pay attention to Yuri. Also the flat he was in now had rather thin walls. He could often hear the people in the flats on both sides of his and the flat immediately above his. There was also the constant noise from the traffic from the A13 flyover which was next to his block. He would like something a little bit quieter.

He saw some details of a new development called Baltimore Wharf. It was a complex of flats, cafes, restaurants and a health club. It was very close to Canada Wharf DLR station so access into London would be excellent. He decided to go and look at it and see what he could afford.

He was shown around a two bedroom apartment by the girl from the sales office. It was no larger than his present flat but much nicer. The fixtures were all of a very high quality and it had a balcony which overlooked the Thames, looking out over the river to what had been the old Millwall docks on the other side. It was very nice indeed and although it was in a large complex it somehow seemed private. Sam nearly fell over when she told him how much it was. It was more than three times the price of his present one for very similar accommodation, just a few miles nearer central London.

That evening he mailed Irina again. He told her about the flat hunt and how much it would cost, telling her that he would continue to look but not in such an expensive place.

Irina's reply, although outwardly just chit chat contained one of the pre-arranged key words, snow in Gorky Park. As they had arranged in Moscow, this meant that Sam had to buy a new pay-as-you-go mobile phone, the type that includes ten pounds worth of free phone calls. This means that the phone remains unregistered until the owner needs to top up the phone card. Sam would then make a phone call on this phone to a number he had memorised in the Moscow offices and have a phone call that lasted less than two minute. By doing this the phone call was completely untraceable. Sam was then to dispose of the phone safely and dispose of the SIM card separately.

He bought the phone from the large Asda supermarket near his flats and made the call. Ivanov took the call and just said "a quarter of a million pounds sterling has been paid into your Iranian bank account today, an advance on future earnings, so that you buy your new home", the phone went dead.

Sam returned into Asda and bought a disposable lighter. He took a bus to the Woolwich Ferry and went across the river as a foot passenger. Halfway across he dropped the phone, minus the sim card into the river. He returned on the ferry, took the bus home and once inside his flat he took the lighter and burnt the SIM card, the flame melted it.

The next day he returned to the sales office at Baltimore Wharf and put a deposit on the flat he had viewed.

# CHAPTER 13

Sam had no problem selling his flat in Beckton, This surprised him given that the market was so depressed and if you believe the newspapers, nothing was going to improve before the general election in May or June next year.

Sam moved into his new flat early in April 2009. But he was bored. He mailed Irina weekly, if anybody read them they would seem as though they were from innocent lovers, which is exactly what they were. There were no more code words and there was no sign of any work. Sam had set up a web site for his security company which said that his specialty was personal protection. He had had a number of hits, being ex SAS seemed to make people interested, but he had only had one job. A pop singer, a winner on X Factor, had been assaulted by a fan, so as a precaution the management wanted her protected. Sam was hired to protect her at a personal appearance at Tower Records in Leicester Square.

It was on 3rd May that he received an e-mail from Irina with a code word in it. She wrote that it was now spring in Moscow but there was still some snow in Gorky Park. Although it was a bank holiday Asda was open so once again he went and purchased a pay as you go mobile phone. He phoned the number. This time Yuri answered.

"There is a job in Cologne in June. Take a day trip to Calais next Saturday. Take the eight o'clock ferry, not the train. Opposite the town hall there is a coffee shop with tables outside and chairs with red plastic seats. Be there at eleven-thirty their time and be drinking coffee. A man will come up to you and ask what the coffee is like. You will say that it is very nice. He will say then it must be Italian. You will ask him to sit down. He will take over from there". Immediately Yuri hung up.

Sam went home. He burnt the SIM card and threw the phone in the river from his balcony when it was dark that evening. He e-mailed Irina telling her that he had decided to take a trip the following weekend to France and that he would send her a postcard. He thought that by doing this Yuri would know that he had understood.

He also booked his ferry ticket on-line, for eight o'clock as Yuri had said, returning at six in the evening. He thought he may as well make a day of it. He also arranged to hire a car as he had never owned one of his own. He felt very excited after all these months of inactivity.

He was in plenty of time for the ferry and once on board he went up to the decks, into a restaurant and had breakfast. It was a smooth crossing and took just over an hour. Sam finished his breakfast and then went up on deck to watch the ship berth. Once docked Sam drove off into the centre of Calais. He located the town hall and the café with the red chairs. He parked his car and went to sit in the café and ordered some coffee.

At eleven thirty precisely a man approached and gave the agreed greeting. He sat down and ordered a coffee. He looked just like a younger version of Yuri. "I have been watching you since you came from the ferry. I am sure you are not followed" he said in English spoken without almost any accent. He introduced himself as Yuri's brother from the Paris embassy.

"The person you have to deal with is a Korean industrialist. He will be in Cologne for an exhibition for three days next month. He must not leave Cologne. His movements and his photo will be delivered to you. A courier will call at your flat in three days time, on Tuesday at exactly eleven o'clock, he will ask 'are you Mr Franks with a S'? You will reply, 'no I am not Franks with or without an S'. He will say 'that is a pity I have a package for him'. You will say 'would you like a drink?' he will say 'a vodka would be nice'. He will be from the Russian Embassy. You must give him details of what you need provided, papers, weapons and such. I will arrange that and meet you when you have planned your trip".

He finished his coffee, shook hands with Sam and left. Sam paid the bill and then left. He found himself a restaurant in the town and had lunch, a rare steak and frites.

Sam arrived back home in the early evening and sat and thought about the job in hand.

The courier arrived as arranged, at exactly eleven o'clock. He gave the correct coded greeting. He entered Sam's apartment and gave him a buff coloured envelope. Sam examined the contents.

The envelope contained a photograph, details of the man's description, the hotel that he had booked for his stay in Cologne and his plans to visit the Messe where the exhibition was to be held. Having read all of the enclosures, Sam told his contact that he did not require a gun, only a small, sharp knife, but he would need a set of documents including a credit card and passport, in a false name. He gave the contact a photograph that he had had taken the day before with him aged to a man of about fifty five years old. That was what he wanted to reflect on his passport. He wanted it in a Danish or Dutch citizen's name, they spoke the best English and were in the EU so passport examination would be cursory.

Sam had been trained in disguise as part of his undercover activities with the army. One prime rule, never try to make yourself look younger, always age yourself. Trying to look younger never stands up against examination, while ageing is less easy to see. Sam could grey his hair, put some dental pads in his mouth to increase his jowls, apply some thin eyeliner to his face to look like shadows under his eyes, stoop so that he had rounded shoulders and put some padding under his shirt. The effect of these could age him up to twenty years.

# CHAPTER 14

Sam flew from Heathrow to Paris on British Airways. He took the airport bus to the Gare Du Nord and then a taxi to the hotel. Sam decided that he would be more anonymous in a large, modern hotel so he stayed at Le Mercure, one of the modern chains of hotels in La Defence. The evening he arrived he met with Yuri's brother in the public toilet on the ground floor just along from the bar and was given a small brown envelope. In his room later he took out the Dutch passport in the name of Jan Smitts with Sam's aged photograph in it, a credit card in the same name with a note that it had been set up with a two thousand euro limit. There was also a note that he was booked into the Crowne Plaza Hotel in Cologne for the three nights of the exhibition in the name of Jan Smitts with his new credit card used to confirm the booking. The final item was a small knife. It was the sort that was available in any kitchen hardware shop but Sam was taking no chances, he did not want to be tied to the purchase of a potential weapon. Anyway, he hoped that he would not need to use it.

The following day Sam spent wandering around Paris, acting as a tourist. He went to the Louvre, Notre Dame, Montmartre, Sacre Coeur and the Champs Elysees. All the time he was vigilant and was satisfied that he was not being followed. After his day of activity he returned to the hotel, had dinner in the restaurant and went to bed early.

In the morning he got up, packed a small bag and left the hotel with most of his clothes still in the room. He had arranged for Yuri's brother to disturb his bed and use the towels in the bathroom while he was away, so that it would look to the room service staff that he was still occupying the room. He walked to the Gare Du Nord station. He went into a cubicle in the public toilets and started his character change. When he emerged he was a grey haired older man with a slight stoop and a developing gut, he looked exactly like the passport picture of Jan Smitts. He booked a train to Strasbourg. He had planned a long journey by train but decided that he would not fly because surveillance cameras and security were much less stringent at stations than airports. Also nobody remembers people on trains, they are more anonymous than planes.

When he arrived at Strasbourg he booked another train to Dusseldorf and from there to Cologne. At Cologne he took a cab to his hotel. He arrived at almost midnight; it had taken him sixteen hours to get from Paris. He went straight to bed.

He had a leisurely breakfast and then went to the Messe, the large complex of exhibition halls next to the river in Cologne. He arrived just after ten o'clock. He registered as a visitor and paid for a four day pass. He went into one of the halls and walked slowly around. The exhibition was for industrial electronic companies and as he viewed the stands, Sam realised that he knew very little about the products or the industries that he was looking at.

The exhibition was a large one, it covered four of the halls. Sam found the stand of Kiamura Semiconductors in hall eight. His target was the president of Kiamura. Sam found a vantage point at a nearby coffee stall where he could keep his eye on the stand. At just after eleven o'clock the target arrived. He shook hands with some of the people working on the stand and after only about three minutes he left. Sam followed. The target went to the lavatory. He went into one of the cubicles. About three minutes later he came out, washed his hands and then returned to the stand.

Sam returned to his vantage point to keep watch. At one o'clock the target left. Sam followed. He went with four of his colleagues to the exhibitors' restaurant. They ordered lunch and the target left to visit the lavatory once again. An hour and a half later they had finished lunch and returned to the stand. On the way back to the stand the target visited the lavatory again. He finally left the stand just after five o'clock with two of his managers. He had visited the lavatory another two times during the afternoon. Sam watched him get into a taxi, one of the of white Mercedes cabs that are so common in Cologne. He then returned to his hotel. Sam had noted that the target had visited the lavatory at least five times in six hours during the day.

The following day was a repeat of the last. The target arrived on the stand shortly before eleven, went to lunch in the exhibitors' restaurant and left to go to his hotel at around five o'clock. He used the lavatory six times during the day. Sam followed him each time and noted that on every occasion he went into a cubicle. Sam had developed his plan.

The following day after breakfast Sam checked out of his hotel. He went to the Messe and checked his overnight bag into the cloakroom. As previous days, the target arrived shortly after eleven o'clock. He stayed on the stand until lunchtime, except for a toilet visit, and went to lunch at one o'clock. Sam was pleased to notice that, this being the last day of the exhibition, there were fewer visitors in attendance. The target returned to the stand after he had finished is lunch.

It was almost three thirty when the target left the stand and went to the lavatory again. Sam followed. The target went into one of the cubicles. Sam stood by one of the urinals. He put on a pair of latex gloves that he had carried in his pocket. There were two other people in the toilets. One left almost immediately the other left just as the target unlocked the door and began to exit the cubicle. Sam moved swiftly. He rushed at the target, catching him completely unawares. He spun him around, pushing him back into the cubicle. Sam placed one hand over the mouth and with the other, he reached around the victims head, turning it violently and breaking his neck. He then grabbed the head, pulled his backwards and forwards hard to ensure that the spinal chord was broken. The execution had taken only a few seconds. Sam heard somebody else enter the toilets. He sat the dead Korean on the toilet. He locked the door. He undid the victims belt and lifting him slightly, slipped his trousers and underpants down around his ankles. He stopped and listened. He still thought that there was at least one other person in the lavatory. Sam waited. After about five minutes Sam thought that the coast was clear. He climbed over the partition into the next cubicle and exited through the door. He took off the latex gloves, put them back in his pocket and washed his hands. He left the toilets, went to the cloakroom, reclaimed his bag and left the halls. He walked to the station and caught a train to Dussledorf and began the journey back to Paris. He hoped that when the body was discovered it would look to the unpracticed eye as though the man had had a heart attack. That would not only buy him time to get clear but until the truth was identified by a medical examiner, potential forensic evidence in the lavatories, hotel and anywhere else that the police may look, would have been compromised.

He had an uneventful albeit long journey back to Paris. At the station he again went into the toilets, washed the grey tints out of his hair, removed the dental pads from his mouth and removed the padded vest that he had worn for the past five days to make him look three stone heavier than he was. He walked to his hotel as Sam Tucker again.

He showered, changed clothes, and went to the dining room for an early dinner. After dinner he went for a drink in the bar. Sitting at one of the tables was Yuri's brother. They did not acknowledge each other. About ten minutes later Sam went to his room. Five minutes after he went in there was a knock at the door. He opened it and Yuri's brother entered.

"You were successful?" he asked.

"Yes" replied Sam.

"I ask because there has been no news in the press or the radio."

"Maybe they think it was still natural causes. There will be soon, don't worry, he's dead". Sam picked up his overnight bag and gave it to the Russian. He had placed the knife, latex gloves, padded vest, fake passport and driving licence, and the clothes that he had worn the previous afternoon in Cologne in it.

"I will dispose of these and inform Yuri of your success".

The following day Sam flew back to London.

# CHAPTER 15

It was the end of June in London. It was a beautiful summer day for a change; it had been a wet, cool summer so far. Sam sat on the balcony of his flat overlooking the Thames. He was bored. He had been back from his assignment for only a fortnight and he realised how much he needed action. His plans had worked well. His target had been missed after about an hour in Cologne. Some of his colleagues had been dispatched to find him. They had identified that he was in the cubicle by recognizing his shoes. They then found a member of the security staff who broke the lock on the door and discovered the body. As Sam had anticipated they assumed that the dead man had suffered a heart attack. They called an ambulance and the paramedics placed the body on a stretcher and took it to a mortuary. It was not until the following morning that it was medically examined and it was discovered that the dead man had a broken neck and had been murdered.

Sam had e-mailed Irena three times since he had returned from Paris but there had been no code words to signify another contract. They had professed their love for each other in the mails, Sam couldn't help wondering how much of what Irina said was what she felt and how much of it was because of the part she was playing. His doubts played on him. Why should the most the most beautiful and sexy woman that he had ever met want to be with him. He realised that when he was with her he felt secure, it was good; but when he was not the concerns crept in. Was it just a job to her?

Sam decided that he would go on holiday. He mailed Irina and told her. He decided that he would go to the South of France. He went on-line and found that there was a Holiday Inn Hotel just outside Nice. It had three swimming pools and its own beach. It was next to the marina that had a wide selection of restaurants. They also ran a courtesy bus to and from the airport.

The following day he received a reply from Irena. She asked what he was planning. He replied immediately telling her about his plans and adding that he wished that she could join him. He was amazed when less than an hour later she replied saying that she had told her Uncle Yuri about Sam's e-mail and he had suggested that she should go to France and spend some time with Sam. She added that it would take a couple of weeks to get a visa but if Sam wanted to wait until the end of July she would love to join him. He was over the moon, he couldn't believe how much he was looking forward to seeing her. For the time being all of his doubts evaporated.

He booked the hotel for the last week in July and booked his flights on Easyjet from Gatwick. He e-mailed Irina with all of his details so that she could book her flights from Moscow.

Two weeks before he was due to depart he got a mail from Irina. She told him that she had her visa arranged and her flights had been booked. She said how much she was looking forward to seeing him, how much she missed him and how much she was looking forward to visiting Europe. She said that she had seen on the internet that it was warm in France in July. She concluded that it was also warm in Moscow, so warm that there was no snow in Gorky Park. The words jumped out of the page at Sam.

He left his apartment almost immediately and walked across the road to the station. He took the Docklands Light Railway train to Beckton, walked across the road from the station into the large Asda store. He had decided to return there to purchase the mobile phone as he liked the anonymity. He paid for the phone and ten pounds worth of calls and went and had a coffee in Café Asda, the café that was just outside the main store, in the precinct. He took the phone out of the packaging and inserted the SIM card. He put the phone in his pocket and carried the charger, as he left the café and returned to the station and took the train back to Baltimore Wharf station.

Two hours later there was enough charge in the phone to make the call. Sam was reluctant to make it as he felt sure that it would effect his holiday arrangements. He made the call, Yuri answered immediately. Sam was relieved when Yuri told him that it was a project for August. It would be in Morocco.

"I know that Morocco is not Europe but I need you to do it as I have nobody else who could do it" Yuri explained. "My African man is in Cape Town but also this will need someone who is an accurate shot with a gun I think".

The target was a Lebanese. He was spending a few days on holiday in a villa belonging to a friend just outside Tangier. It was decided that he would be easier to hit in Morocco than at home in the Lebanon or where he sometimes lived, in Libya, Every morning, before breakfast the target would go for a run. He was always accompanied by two bodyguards, both of whom were former French Foreign Legion men. Both would probably be armed but Yuri had been unable to find out much about them.

Sam told Yuri that he would think about how to carry out the task, make a plan and let Yuri know what he needed.

Sam dismantled the phone and as before he burnt the SIM card. He left the flat, caught the train into London, and went for a walk along the Thames Embankment. He crossed the river, walking over Westminster Bridge and half way across he stopped. Making sure that there was not a boat passing underneath he dropped the phone into the river. He stood there for another minute or so and then disposed of the charger in the same way.

During the following week Sam researched on the internet in an internet café in Earls Court. He identified the location of the villa in Tangier. He assumed that the target would run along the beach, as behind the villa on the land side was a shanty town of cardboard houses. The town of Tangier was three miles away to the west and although there were some hotels along that part of the coast they were not as dense as those nearer the town. Sam worked out his plan. Using a public phone box in the entrance area of Earls Court Exhibition centre he phoned the direct line to Yuri's brother in Paris and said that he required a gun and silencer, preferably a Baretta 92F or if not a Glock 17. He wanted three clips of ammunition for the gun. He also needed a passport, if possible British, using the same photo as he had provided previously and a credit card in the same name. Finally he asked that Irina stay with him as part of his plan until after the job was done.

# CHAPTER 16

Sam's Easijet flight to Nice was on time. Irina was flying from Moscow on an Air Berlin flight to Frankfurt and then a Lufthansa flight from Frankfurt to Nice. Her flight into Nice was due an hour and a half after Sam's. He collected his luggage and settled down in a small coffee shop to wait for Irena. He could not believe how exited he was about seeing her again. It had been six months since he had spent time with her in Moscow. He kept on reminding himself that he was almost forty years old and not some lovelorn teenager.

Her flight was forty minutes late. It arrived at three o'clock. She walked out of the arrivals door and when he saw her he caught his breath, she was even more beautiful than he remembered. She saw him and her face lit up with a huge smile. She ran forward, dropped her case and hugged him. They kissed, a long lingering kiss. He didn't want to let her go and it seemed that she felt the same way. They walked arm in arm out of the terminal building and got a cab to the hotel rather than wait for the hotel bus. Irina told Nick that she knew of his request for her to stay until the middle of August and said how much she was looking forward to seeing London and where Sam lived. She seemed so happy.

They registered, went to their room, and as soon as they were inside they dropped the luggage on the floor and came together. They took each others clothes off and made love on the bed. It was quick and passionate.

They showered and unpacked their cases. "I have a letter for you from Yuri. You are to read it and then burn it and then you are to telephone his brother at the embassy in Paris at exactly four o'clock tomorrow afternoon with a reply".

The letter said that it was alright for Irina to stay with Sam provided she was not to be involved in the assassination and stayed in Nice while Sam was away. Yuri reminded Sam that her visa was for her trip to France and was only valid within the EU. Sam was very aware that the tone of his letter was very protective of Irina. Sam needed to show him that he would never risk putting her in danger. Yuri also queried the request for the three clips of ammunition.

The road that ran along the front of the marina started just outside the hotel door. That evening they walked along it and found a Chinese Restaurant to have dinner. They chatted all though dinner. Sam told her about his apartment and about London. She told him about her flat and how she had decorated it during the long Russian winter. She told him that Yuri had arranged for her to take lessons in English to improve her speech.

They returned to the hotel about ten o'clock and made love slowly and passionately. They then both fell into a deep satisfying sleep holding each other tightly.

The following day after breakfast they walked in the opposite direction to the marina, to a small shopping mall about half a mile from the hotel. They purchased some fruit and some mineral water and some chocolate for Irina and returned to the hotel. They spent the rest of the morning on the beach, had a club sandwich and a beer in the hotel bar for lunch and went back to the beach afterwards.

At a quarter to four Sam left Irina on the beach and walked back to the shopping mall. He had noticed a public phone box there and had decided that it would be better to call Paris from there rather than the hotel.

He phoned Yuri's brother. He explained that he needed the extra clips of ammunition for practice. He had been the best marksman in his battalion but had not fired a gun for almost two years. He assured him that he would not take Irina out of Europe and would never expose her to danger. He outlined his plan and why he needed Irina.

He returned to the hotel, hopefully having satisfied the questions raised by Yuri and his brother. As he walked through the reception area he went to the desk and booked another week in August for him and Irina.

The rest of the week passed too quickly for Sam and Irina. Apart from one morning when they took the local train along the coast to Monte Carlo, they spent the week on the beach or by the pool. They made love every night and usually during the day as well. It was time to check out and return to London. Irina reminded Sam that it was still like being on holiday as she was coming back to London with him.

They flew back to Gatwick and caught the Gatwick Express to Victoria. Irina seemed thrilled to be in London. "This is my first ever trip outside Russia except my holiday in Egypt and this is such a big city."

Instead of going on the underground they took the bus from Victoria to Stratford so that Irina could see London above ground. They took the DLR from Stratford to Canada Wharf.

They arrived back at Sam's flat just before dusk. They unpacked and Sam felt a warm feeling as she put away her clothes in his wardrobe and drawers. Sam sorted out the clothes from the holiday that needed washing and put a load in the washing machine.

They showered and changed and went to a small Italian restaurant in Canning Town. Sam told Irina that he had been born and bought up in Canning Town and how much it had changed while he was away in the army as the London Docklands had been developed. He showed her the block of flats that he had lived in before he went into the army and the building on the corner by the traffic lights that had been the London Electricity Board showrooms that had been the view from his bedroom window for sixteen years.

For the next week they were tourists. Sam took Irina to London most days. They had tea at the Ritz, visited Harrods, shopped in Oxford Street where Sam bought Irina some new clothes. They visited Buckingham Palace, the Tower of London, spent a day in Windsor and another in Oxford. They went to see some West End shows including Cats and Phantom of the Opera.

Irina seemed so happy. The day before they were due to leave to return to Nice, they were in bed one evening having made love when Sam told Irina that he was in love with her. He had thought hard about whether or not to tell her as he did not know exactly how she felt about him; how many of her actions were personal and how many were because of the job and Yuri.

She turned towards him. "Shammy, I think I love you too. But I do not know what we can do. Yuri has another new woman and I do not believe that he will want me again in that way but he is the sort of man that wants me to be near. Do you understand? I work for him. I live in his flat, I drive his car, I have a desk in his office, he needs me to work for him. I report to him everything you send to me. I do not think he will let me go just because I love you. He will not understand, he does not know love. We should make the most of what we have

50

at this moment I think." She held him tight. They fell asleep in each others arms.

The next day they got up and after breakfast packed their cases and headed for the airport. Sam noticed again how exited Irina was. This time she was so pleased that she had some new summer style clothes. When they had been shopping in London she had said that the selection was so much better than in Moscow and the fashions so much nicer.

Their flight departed on time and when they arrived in Nice, this time Sam had arranged to hire a car, a Citroen Saxo. Even after spending weeks together they still christened the bed as soon as they got into the room. After they had made love and lay on the bed in each other's arms Sam said "Irina, I need to talk to you about plans for this job". She sat up and looked at him.

"I need you to cover for me here. We will have all of our meals, breakfast and dinner on room service. I shall be away for three nights and four days. On the days that I am away you must order meals for two of us so that they think that I am still here. When they are due to come you will run the shower in the bathroom and answer the door in your towelling robe. That way they will think that I am in the shower. During the three days that I am away you must not spend them here. You can take the train to Monte Carlo, Nice and Cannes. You should not be seen around the hotel very much without me or it may be noticed. Even when I am here we will have our meals in the room so that it does not look strange, we will be consistent".

She took his face in her hands and kissed his lips. "I am pleased that I am able to help you" she said. "You will be safe won't you? You are very precious to me you know".

They made love again, slowly and tenderly and cuddled in the bed until just before seven o'clock. Sam got up and before he showered he ordered two steaks, salad, apple pies and a bottle of Merlot on room service.

The meals arrived while Irina was in the shower, just as he had planned. It helped that she was singing as she was showering. The waiter looked at the ruffled bed as he put the tray down on the table and smiled at Sam knowingly.

At exactly eight o'clock there was a knock on the door. Sam, now fully dressed, opened it and seeing Yuri's brother standing there slipped out of the room and followed him to the car park. He went to a car and took a holdall out of the boot. Sam looked inside and saw a gun, silencer and a bulky envelope. Sam thanked the man and told him to meet him back at the hotel in four nights' time, at the same time, in the car park.

"That won't be necessary. Yuri said for you to dispose of the gun but keep the documents as he has already another job lined up to do. He will make contact with you in the usual way when he has the arrangements made".

Sam took the holdall to his room and examined the contents. The passport, driving licence and credit card were British. They were in the name of Peter Smith. The gun was a Glock 17. Although Sam preferred a Beretta, the Glock was a very good weapon. It had a magazine of seventeen rounds, hence the name, each shot left the gun at around eight hundred miles per hour. The silencer would slow that down slightly and Sam was pleased to see that the silencer was a genuine Glock, produced in Switzerland, and not a Russian replica. Not for the first time Sam was impressed with Yuri's professionalism. He would know the importance of accuracy in a job like this and how sub-standard equipment could be inaccurate. The Glock is also very light, even with a length of seven and a half inches it still weighs less that two pounds Sam then checked the three magazines.

# CHAPTER 17

The next morning Sam left before breakfast while Irina spent her morning at the pool, He drove northwards up towards the mountains and the forests until he found an isolated spot. He took some cardboard targets out of his bag and pinned one of them to a tree. They were basic shooting club target cards, about nine inches square with a three quarter inch bulls-eye in the centre. He then measured out two hundred strides, approximately two hundred yards, turned and fired six shots at the target. He marked where he stood and then went to inspect the target. Two of the shots had hit the target card, none were in the bull's-eye. Sam was appalled. Two years ago he would have expected all six shots to be in the bull. He returned to his shooting position and fired another six shoots. He went back to the target. This time all six shoots had hit the target card but only one was in the bulls-eye. Once again he returned to his shooting position and fired the remaining five bullets. Five target hits, two bulls. He then repeated the process with the second magazine. His final five shoots gave him three bulls and two shots that were just outside of the bulls-eye circle. This was not good enough for Sam. He had been taught many years ago that when in an active situation you had to make every shot count. He had not planned on using it but he decided that he would continue to practice with the final magazine. Once again he returned to his starting position. He fired six shots. He went forward and inspected the target. Four shots were dead in the centre of the bull, a fifth was on the line between it and the circle outside it and the sixth was in the outside circle. Not good enough. Sam repeated the process yet again and this time he had five dead centre in the bull and one just on the line. Sam was now satisfied about his accuracy. He only had five shots left but he was intending to use only three of them, if his plan worked out. He retrieved the used targets and picked up the spent cartridge shells and left.

Sam returned to the hotel and spent some time by the pool with Irina. Just after two o'clock they went to their room and Sam packed a bag. Irina seemed tense.

"Please be careful Shammy. I am worried for you", she put her arms around his neck and pulled him to her.

"I'll be fine" he said. "I have a plan and there is no reason why it won't work". They held each other tight, kissed each other deeply, fell on to the bed and made love passionately; Sam felt that Irina was more passionate than usual. They phoned room service, had a late lunch in the room and just after four o'clock Sam left the hotel by a side door. He jogged to the station and caught the train to Marseilles. At the station he went into the toilets and put his wig and padding on and left the station as Peter Smith, fifty-six year old Englishman. He walked the mile or so into the town to the Hertz car hire offices. He had booked a Citroen C5, quite a large car, but he wanted the comfort. He passed over his driving licence and credit card in the name of Peter Smith, they were accepted and he was given the keys to his car.

He drove out of Marseilles, got onto the A7 to Orange and started his long drive to the South of Spain. He had planned the route before he left England and had a list of target cities and also the map that had been supplied with the car. He took the A9 passed Nimes, then Montpellier, on through to Perpignan. After Perpignan he picked up the motorway, the AP7, and into Spain.

"Good old European Union, no border checks" he thought to himself.

He took the Autopista del Mediterraneo and arrived in Sitges after nightfall. Sitges is a resort destination for many British tourists so Sam had no problem finding a restaurant and enjoyed a good quality steak with salad and fried potatoes. He returned to his car about ten o'clock and reclined the front passenger seat as far as he could and settled down to a nights' sleep.

He woke just after five o'clock. He was uncomfortable due to a full bladder. He used an empty water bottle to relieve the problem and started on his journey South.

He left Sitges and headed towards Murcia and then Malaga. He took the AP7 road to Marbella and stopped, again in the tourist area for a meal. Sam was dressed as a typical English tourist and as he intended, he blended well into the large number of British holiday makers. While in Marbella he went into one of the large holiday hotels and used the poolside showers and toilets.

He left Marbella and took the A7 towards Estepona and then on to Algeciras. He arrived in Algeciras just before five o'clock and booked himself a return ticket on the ferry to Tangier. The next one was due to depart at six-thirty. He parked the car in a car park near to the bus station, five minutes walk from the ferry terminal. He found a bar that had a number of British people in it, he assumed day trippers from Morocco, so he went in and had a drink and sandwich, again blending in.

He quickly returned to his car, collected his travel bag and went to catch the ferry. He joined a group of several Brits taking the ferry across the Mediterranean. The trip took an hour and a half. Sam disembarked just after eight o'clock. It was already dark. He walked into the centre of Tangier town and witnessed the large number of tourists, British, German, French and Scandinavian. He went to the central bus station and placed his overnight bag in a locker and set about both killing time and blending in for the next couple of hours. He visited a lively club where there was a large number of British holiday makers. He left the club just after midnight and collected his bag.

He strolled away from the clubs, hotels and bars, towards the residential areas. After only a few minutes he found what he was looking for, a rather battered, about ten year old, Toyota Corolla parked on a slight hill in a built up residential area. This was the part of his plan that carried the greatest risk, but Sam considered it a calculated risk. He needed to borrow a car for about eight hours. If he hired one not only would he leave a trail but it would be unusual for a European visitor to Tangier to hire a car. He figured that the sort of car that he had found would belong to a local worker, Toyota's were the most common cars in Tangier so the one he had identified should not look out of place anywhere in the city. He took a rubber hammer from his bag and hit the driver's door hard, in the area of the door lock. The pressure the impact caused released the central locking mechanism and Sam opened the door and got into the car. It took him about ten seconds to hot wire the car but instead of starting the engine he released the handbrake and let the car freewheel down the hill. Towards the bottom he slipped the clutch and put the car in gear. It jump started immediately. He headed for the beach and then took the coast road out of the city eastwards, in the direction of the Movenpick

Hotel. Three miles outside of the main tourist area he found the Movenpick. It was a large hotel right next to the beach. Sam pulled up on the road just past the hotel. He consulted the documents that Yuri had prepared for him and noted that the villa was situated about a further half mile along the road. Sam drove a bit further and found the villa that the Lebanese target should be staying in. It backed onto the beach and had large iron gates at the front entrance.

Sam turned the car around and parked on the road a quarter of a mile away, about halfway between the villa and the Movenpick Hotel. There were no buildings near and it was almost completely dark. There were no comfortable reclining seats in this car but Sam had slept in worse places. He spread out on the back seat and fell asleep.

# CHAPTER 18

Sam had trained himself many years before to wake up at a pre-desired time without an alarm clock, whatever the amount of time he had slept for. He awoke at ten minutes to six. He had been told by Yuri that the target was most likely to go for a run between six and seven o'clock. He moved to the front passenger seat and took the Glock out of his bag and fitted the silencer. He checked the bullets in the magazine and that there was one in the chamber. He wound down the rear window behind the passenger seat, the window that looked out across the beach. From this angle, at a distance of one hundred and fifty yards, three men running along the beach would be seen as three abreast, a clear shot at all three of them.

Sam's contract was only for the Lebanese but he had decided that he would need to deal with all three men. Sam needed to buy some time. If he shot the target and left the body guards they would raise the alarm. Sam planned to deal with the guards first. If he shot the target first, Sam concluded that by the time he had shot the second guard the third would have gone flat on the ground, making himself a difficult target. If the third shot was for the target it was likely that he would panic and would still be a good target after the first two shots.

It was six twenty five when the three men came into sight. As Sam had hoped they were jogging along the beach three abreast. Sam wound the seat back down as far as he could. He placed the barrel of the gun through the open rear window. The men were about one hundred and eighty yards away. Sam let them run a bit closer. He lined up the sights on the man furthest away. They approached, they were now only one hundred and fifty yards away. Sam eased the trigger backwards and fired. At almost eight hundred miles an hour it took only a fraction of a second for the bullet to reach its target. But before it had hit Sam was already lining up on the other bodyguard.

The first bodyguards head exploded in a mess of blood, brains and bone quickly followed by the second bodyguard going in exactly the same way. Sam hesitated for a second or two. He wanted to see the reaction of the target. As Sam expected he froze. Sam lined the sights up and fired. The targets head exploded less than a second later. Mission accomplished. Sam moved over to the driver seat, started the engine and drove back along the coast road and found the street from which he had taken the car. It was still only a quarter to seven and there was nobody about. Sam left the car about twenty yards from where it had been parked when he took it. He left ten, hundred US dollar bills on the shelf under the steering wheel. He hoped that this would maybe stop the owner reporting that his car had been stolen and returned. The car would not have been as much as a thousand dollars.

Sam took his overnight bag and walked away from the car, towards the ferry terminal. His ferry departed at five past ten. He had almost three hours to wait. He felt a bit conspicuous as there were no tourists around at this time of the day. He found a bar near the terminal and had breakfast. By nine thirty there were a lot of holidaymakers beginning to arrive, the ferries to Spain and Gibraltar would be leaving soon with the day trippers. Sam left on his ferry as planned without incident. He sat at the back of the ship. Half way across, forty-five minutes into the crossing, Sam checked that he was not being watched, slipped the gun out of his bag and dropped it overboard into the water.

The three bodies were discovered by a German tourist out jogging just before eight o'clock that morning. He ran back to the Movenpick where he was staying and the hotel receptionist phoned the police. Two policemen arrived at eight fifteen. They confirmed that they were bodies and had been shot and phoned their headquarters. Just before nine o'clock an inspector arrived. By now a crowd was gathering. He organised an ambulance and after another twenty minutes the ambulance arrived and took the corpses away. The main concern of the police was the tourists and so the police cleaned the blood from the beach and at the same time completely contaminated the crime scene. The corpses were taken to a mortuary, unloaded just after ten o'clock and a pathologist advised. The police chief arrived at the mortuary just before eleven. The police chief, inspector and the two policemen who first arrived on the scene then went to visit the beach. By now it was full of tourists enjoying the sunshine. The cleaning efforts of the policemen and the tide had obliterated any signs of evidence. The identity of the three men was not known as their faces had all been obliterated. The next step for the investigating team was to call at the hotels and villas along the beach to see if anybody was missing. Before they could do that however the local police reported a phone call had been received concerning a jogger who had not returned after his run. The informant, the targets host was interviewed but could give no clues as to why his guest had been murdered or by whom. The police team returned to headquarters at lunchtime with no clues other than a preliminary report from the pathologist that each had been shot by a single nine millimetre bullet, probably from a range of between one hundred and two hundred metres.

# CHAPTER 19

Sam disembarked on time at eleven thirty five. He walked to where he had parked the car near the bus station, and started the long drive back to France.

He returned using exactly the same route as he had used to drive to Spain. He stopped for a short break and something to eat twice, cat-napping in the car both times. He arrived in Marseilles the following morning before the car hire office was open. He put the keys into a box provided for out of hours returns and walked to the station. On the train he removed his wig, took the padding out of his mouth, removed the padding around his waist and alighted from the train as Sam Tucker.

He was back at the hotel, in his room with Irina, just in time for breakfast and while they waited for room service to deliver it, they made love, quickly and urgently.

They spent the next two days on the beach or at the pool. They held hands, kissed and cuddled, and made love three or four times a day. They both knew that soon this honeymoon would end and Irina would go back to Moscow but neither of them seemed to want to talk about it.

Two days after Sam returned from Tangier they checked out of the hotel and flew back to London. Irina was due to fly back to Moscow two days later.

The night before Irina was due to leave, they had made love and Irina was lying with her head on Sam's chest.

"Shammy, I want to stay here with you".

"I want you to stay here with me too Irina, but what would Yuri say? I don't think he is the type of person that would like surprises".

"I don't know Shammy" Irina said after a while. "Yuri does not want me as a woman any more but you are right, he rescued me from a life of drudgery and now I owe him. Maybe if I go back to Moscow

I can talk to him at the right time and see what he says. If he agrees, could I live with you Shammy?"

"You don't need to ask that Irina. Of course you could live with me. I could think of nothing that I want more".

She kissed him and he became aroused again. They made love once more and then fell asleep in each others arms.

While Irina was packing the next morning Sam turned on his computer and checked his e-mails. There was a mail from Yuri. He asked what time Irina's plane was due to arrive at Moscow as he was arranging for his limousine to collect her. The last line of his mail said 'tell her there is no snow in Gorky Park'. Sam replied to the mail with the flight number and estimated time of arrival.

He took Irina to Heathrow and helped her check in at the British Airways desk. He had booked her a seat in business class so there were no queues for her at the Club desk. Sam told her that there was a Club lounge once she was through security and to wait there until her flight was called. They held each other tightly before they kissed for the last time and Irina disappeared through the departure gate.

Sam waited until she was out of sight and then left the terminal for the underground station. He took the tube into London and changed on to the DLR. Instead of getting off at his station he continued through to the end of the line at Beckton and walked across the road to the Asda superstore. Although he could have purchased one nearer, he liked Asda as it was anonymous and he knew that he would not have a problem buying a phone. He then returned to the station, having first unpacked the phone and discarded the packaging in one of the rubbish bins at the supermarket, and caught a train home.

Once home, he put the phone on charge and during the afternoon he telephoned Yuri. He answered immediately.

"Congratulations. That was a very good job you did in Tangier. It was clever to remove the bodyguards as well, no witnesses. My sources tell me that the police are completely confused, they can find out nothing. Nobody saw anything or heard anything. It is a fact though that you will only get paid for one hit. That was the contract. But that is still a lot of money and we have a very satisfied client who may give us more work".

"Thanks" was all Sam could think to say.

"Did Irina get her plane on time?" Yuri asked.

Sam wondered if Yuri was just being polite or whether he was checking up on Sam. "Yes I took her to the airport and helped her check in. I left her as she went through the departures gate".

"Thank you for taking care of her Sam" said Yuri.

For some reason Sam felt uneasy about the way this conversation was developing but just as he started to think about how to respond, Yuri changed the subject.

"The next one is easy. A businessman from Georgia who has made too many enemies. He will be passing through Prague in three weeks time and will stop over for one night to visit some clubs and maybe a brothel. Our client is suggesting that he could be robbed and stabbed but as usual I will leave all of the details up to you".

"On the face of it robbery in Prague sounds like a reasonable plan. I'll have a think about it and let you know".

"That is good. It is important with this man that nobody suspect any Russian connection. When Georgia was part of the Soviet Union, this man was firstly a friend but was declared an enemy by Andropov when he was in power"

"There won't be anything to connect you Yuri, don't worry" Sam assured him.

# CHAPTER 20

Two and a half weeks later Sam was back in Paris. Once again he was at the Mercure Hotel and booked in for a week. He met with Yuri's brother as usual on the first night and arranged for his room to be 'used' for the two nights he would be away. Sam confirmed that the American hunting knife that he had requested together with a pair of scissors and some A4 plain paper, would be delivered to him in Prague.

The following morning Sam was a tourist in Paris. He genuinely liked the city and always enjoyed his visits there. He had an early lunch at a fish restaurant, Le Balloon Vert, he had eaten there before and they served excellent fish beautifully cooked. He washed it down with most of a bottle of Muscadet. Sam rarely drunk alcohol during the day but in Paris, with a meal, he made an exception.

He arrived at the airport at about one thirty, in plenty of time to change his physical appearance, again using the toilets, and boarding the fourteen fifty Easijet flight to Prague, booked in the name of Peter Smith. When travelling within the European Union a British passport usually only gets the most cursory of inspections and even then mostly by airport staff at a boarding gate. Today was no exception and Sam's passport was a good enough forgery that it didn't get a second look. Only entering the UK is the passport properly inspected. The forgery would be detected here but not elsewhere it seemed. The flight arrived on time at Ruzyni airport at half past four and Sam, with only hand luggage was on bus number 119 by five o'clock. The bus took him to the metro station at Dejvicka and from there it was a forty five minute journey to the city centre. Sam came out of the station and caught a cab to the Hotel Hilton Atrium where he was booked in for two nights. The Hilton Hotel had eight hundred rooms so once again Sam was working on his usual principal of large hotel equals anonymity. He had been in his room for less than a minute when there was a knock on the door.

"Who is it?"

"I am from the Russian Embassy and I have a package for you" a voice replied.

Sam opened the door quickly and pulled the man inside before he said anything else. "Who are you?" he asked.

"My name is Anotov, I am a driver at the Russian Embassy here in Prague and I was instructed to deliver this package to you. I waited for you to check in and then followed you to your room".

Sam took it, he opened the bag, had a quick look inside it and then reopened the door and virtually pushed the man out of room. "Thank you, goodbye, forget you were here" Sam said. The man was obviously not used to this type of delivery and Sam wanted him out of the way as soon as possible.

Sam checked the bags contents. All he had requested was there. He especially checked the hunting knife. It was perfect. It was the type of knife used by American hunters. It had an eight inch blade the leading edge of which was very sharp. The end of the blade was pointed, angled slightly upwards. The top of the blade was serrated. Hunters would use it when they had shot their prey. The tip would penetrate even a tough animal hide, the blade was sharp enough to cut skin and also to cut up raw meat and the serrated edge would cut through animal bone. Sam had used such a weapon before with great effectiveness.

Sam breakfasted early and went on a walk around the city. He had been told that the target was booked into the Intercontinental Hotel for two nights and was due to arrive today. Sam found Parizska 30 and located the hotel. He walked over to Letenske Park, where he had a good view of the hotel and then returned to the hotel. He entered the reception area and looked around for signs of CCTV cameras. The only ones that he could see covered the check in desk and the lift lobby. Other areas seemed not to be monitored. He sat at a table in the lobby and ordered a coffee.

He finished his coffee and sat and waited for another hour until, just after midday the target entered the hotel and checked in. Sam had a description and a photograph but was still surprised at the size of the man. He was about six feet five inches tall and Sam estimated his weight to be about eighteen stone. He was dressed in an expensive plain blue suit with a blue stripped formal shirt and no tie. He wore black Gucci loafers and had an expensive leather suitcase. He was allocated room 312.

Sam then returned to his hotel but he took his time; he was in no hurry. Before returning he walked around the city. It was a beautiful city with many medieval buildings, a lot of which were in urgent need of repair. He found the tourist area of the city for nightlife, bars, overpriced restaurants and hostess clubs serving the British and other European visitors staying for a few nights for a stag party.

Sam rested, showered and changed into a pair of dark trousers, casual slip on shoes, a light blue polo shirt. Over the polo shirt he wore what looked like a long sleeved, dark blue, lightweight jumper, but was in fact the type of jumper worm by golfers when they are playing in the rain. It has a cotton exterior layer with a waterproof membrane underneath it.

Sam had noticed a café almost opposite the Intercontinental Hotel when he had visited there earlier so decided that this would be a good place to dine. He arrived just before seven thirty. The food was average at best but he had a table in the window so could clearly see the hotel entrance. He stretched his dinner out to over an hour and a half with several cups of coffee, until he saw his target leave. Sam left the cafe and set off in pursuit. The target headed straight to the area that Sam had visited that afternoon. He had changed his clothes and was now wearing an expensive looking pair of black slacks, a beige cashmere jacket and plain blue shirt. Sam felt a bit shabby. He hoped that the target would not visit any expensive, upmarket places. He needn't have worried.

The Georgian was a big drinker. He visited several of the bars having a couple of drinks of whisky in each. As the evening drew on the bars that they visited became more seedy. They were now touring the strip clubs that catered for the stag nights and charged over the odds for watered down drinks.

It was almost midnight when the Georgian entered a club called the Black Cat Revue Bar. Sam followed him in. It was fairly full, the clientele exclusively men, most of them a bit the worse for drink. There was a small stage where three women wearing only thongs and garters, were gyrating around poles. Many of the customers were leaning across the stage and putting money in the garters of the girls. As they did so they were leaving their hands there for a few seconds, rubbing the crotches and buttocks of the girls as they removed them. The girls just smiled. Drunk tourists were easy money. The Georgian took a table at the front of the bar, close to the stage. Sam chose a seat in a booth towards the rear.

The waitresses were dressed as black cats. They had black stockings and basques with tails sewn onto the rear. They had hair bands with black cat-type ears affixed. To Sam the whole place looked very dated, as though it was trying to replicate a Playboy Club with cats instead of bunnies. There were also hostesses who approached the tables and sat with some of the clients. They were more tastefully dressed in black cocktail dresses. Every so often a hostess would leave the table with the client and exit the bar by a door just to the right of the stage.

The target had a bottle of champagne delivered to his table by one of the waitresses and as she left a hostess sat down. She was dressed in a black cocktail dress, short skirt and low cut top, black stockings and high heel shoes. Another glass was delivered to the table and the two of them set about drinking the Champagne. Sam ordered a Scotch and water, it was almost all water. The bill for it was about four times what it should have been.

The target and his new ladyfriend had finished the champagne and another was delivered to the table. With its arrival another hostess joined them dressed very similarly to the first. They were becoming more animated. The Georgian was being encouraged to push money into the garters of the dancers, which he seemed pleased to do. Each time he did so, he got a hug and a kiss from the two hostesses. Another bottle of champagne arrived. The three were getting very friendly. Less than an hour after they arrived the third bottle of champagne was finished and a fourth was delivered. The two hostesses got up from their seats and the target picked up his champagne and followed them across the bar and though the door at the side. A minute or so later Sam walked across the bar towards the door. He opened it a saw that it led to a flight of stairs. A bouncer approached. Sam thought quickly. "I was looking for the toilets" he said, "I thought they may be through here".

"Not here" he said in broken English. "Here you need much money to go upstairs here. Toilets there" he said pointing towards the door at the entrance. Then he said more softly, "Women here are expensive, you want better fuck for less money go round corner to

Sparta Club. Say my name, Sergio, and they find you a clean woman for half what you pay for fuck upstairs here". Sam thanked him and went to the toilets.

Sam had had enough of being cooped up in a cheap, sleazy club so decided to go outside and wait in the road. He figured that once the women had had sex with their client they would want to get rid of him and move on to the next punter. Sam was right. Half an hour later the target left the club. Sam followed. The target walked along the road and into another bar. Sam waited outside. He thought that it was unlikely that the Georgian would seek sex again so soon so Sam thought he would not stay inside for long.

Again Sam was right. Twenty minutes later the target came out. Sam followed. The streets were getting narrower, the night getting darker. The Georgian was now staggering slightly. He entered another bar. Sam waited in a doorway almost opposite. He felt that his opportunity may come soon so he put on a pair of his latex gloves. Fifteen minutes later the Georgian came out of the bar, staggering slightly more. He turned and walked towards where Sam was waiting. Sam moved forward. He pretended to stagger as though he too was the worse for wear for drink. He took the knife from his pocket bumped into the target and as he did so he plunged the hunting knife into the Georgian's ribs, using the serrated edge to carve upwards through the bone and into the heart. The Georgian stumbled forward almost knocking Sam over. Sam moved sideways letting the man fall forward and into the doorway that Sam had waited in. Sam removed the knife as the man fell. When he was on the ground, Sam felt his neck for a pulse, there wasn't one. He reached inside the man's jacket, took his wallet and hotel room key. He then slipped the watch from his wrist. Sam noticed it was a Rolex. Sam then walked calmly from the scene and started his walk to his hotel. On his way he emptied the targets wallet, putting the money and credit cards into his pocket and throwing the empty wallet away. After he had been walking for about fifteen minutes he dropped the knife down a drain having first wiped it carefully. He didn't think that it would be found this far from the scene of the crime but wiping it was still a wise precaution.

He arrived at his hotel and instead of taking the lift he climbed the service stairs to his room on the fifth floor. He entered his room confident that he had not been seen by anybody. He removed his waterproof golf top that had some blood on it. He was pleased to see that the waterproof membrane had done its job, no blood had seeped through to his shirt. He took the scissors that had been delivered to him by the Russian and cut and tore the waterproof into small pieces. He put some pieces of the A4 paper that had also been in the parcel and placed it flat into the toilet bowl. He placed the pieces of fabric onto the paper. He then took off his latex gloves and placed them on top of the pieces. He replaced them with another pair. He took the credit cards that he had taken from the corpse, cut them into pieces and put these too on the pile. The money he put in his wallet. He took a can of lighter fuel from his bag and sprayed a liberal amount over the pile in the toilet bowl and then set light to it. The latex gloves and credit cards melted and the material fabric started to burn. Once he was satisfied that it was beyond identification Sam flushed the toilet and saw all of the contents disappear. Sam then took the watch and using the foot of a chair leg, he broke the strap off and then twisting it, he broke the strap into smaller pieces.

He then put these pieces into the toilet bowl and maneuvered the pieces of metal around the u-bend. He flushed the toilet again so that the watch pieces would go into the sewer system and could not be found near his room. Finally he took off the latex gloves he was wearing, placed them in an ashtray and using more of the lighter fluid, set light to those too.

He then went to bed and fell asleep.

The following day he had a leisurely breakfast and checked out at about eleven o'clock. He walked around the city for a couple of hours before going out to the airport to catch the flight back to Paris. The journey was uneventful and he arrived back at CDG airport in Paris just before seven o'clock. As usual he caught the bus from the airport to the Gare Du Nord, where he went into the toilets, and came out as Sam Tucker. He treated himself to a taxi from the station to his hotel rather than take a bus. He went to his room, unpacked his bag, burnt the fake passport, driving licence and credit card and flushed the remains down the toilet.

He then went down to the restaurant for dinner. He enjoyed his meal and a glass of wine and then went to bed and slept soundly.

Two days later Sam returned to London.

# CHAPTER 21

Sam sat on his balcony and looked out over the River Thames. It was the last few days of September. The nights were drawing in and there was an autumnal nip in the air. He had never liked autumn that much anyway, to Sam it signaled the end of summer and warmth and sunshine. He was bored. He had only been back from Paris for two days and had nothing to do. He was sitting in an expensive chair, on the balcony of an expensive flat and was taking stock of his life. He had no friends. He had no family other than his sister and he was not close to her. He had no hobbies and no interests. In the army he had boxed, but he was almost forty now and didn't feel that he could start boxing again. He had been in the army shooting team but he did not feel that he could join a shooting club. Firstly with the restrictions on guns in the UK he could only shoot a .22 caliber, he was doing that when he was fifteen. Also he would stick out at any shooting club as being an excellent shot so he soon draw attention to himself, not good in his line of work. So he was bored with no hobbies and nothing to do. He was also missing Irena.

While he was on a job he thought about her only occasionally, but when he wasn't, she occupied his mind a lot of the time.

"This is how a man could be driven to drink" he thought as he sat there and pondered what to do between assignments.

On an impulse he got up, switched on his computer and sent an e-mail to Irina:

"Paris is the most beautiful city I know, you are the most beautiful person I know. Will you come and spend a week in Paris with me so that I can show the most beautiful person I know the most beautiful city I know?" He pressed 'send' and wondered how it would be received by Yuri when he read it.

The following morning the reply arrived:

"Sounds wonderful, you are wonderful. Would like to come soon. When can I come?"

Sam mailed back, "If Yuri can spare you how about two weeks time. If it is OK I will make the booking and see you in Paris". If she came then, they would be together for his birthday.

Four hours later the reply came, "Yuri says he can spare me, we are not busy. Tell me the plane to catch. I love you".

Sam was jubilant. He went on-line and booked her a return business class ticket on the Air France flight form Moscow to Paris and himself on a BA flight from Heathrow. He was scheduled to arrive in Paris three hours before her flight so even if he was delayed he would be there to meet her.

Instead of staying out at La Defence like he usually did, he decided to book a city centre hotel. He had heard somebody talking about a hotel called the Hotel Regent Garden so he looked it up and booked a room for five nights. Irina had said that this was how long she could stay away from the office. He e-mailed all of the details to Irina including the flight booking reference number so that she could print her own boarding pass.

The next two weeks passed too slowly but eventually Sam took the train to the airport to catch the plane to Paris and meet with Irina. He wondered if she had spoken to Yuri about her moving to London. He suspected not, as she hadn't mentioned it in an e-mail. He would find out when they met.

The flight was uneventful and arrived on time. Sam went through immigration and customs and waited for Irina. He had to wait for almost four hours for her to appear at the arrivals gate but when he saw her he forgot all about time. They ran to each other and hugged for what seemed like ages. He felt so good. They took a cab to the hotel which was just off of the Champs Elysees, very close to the Arc De Triumph.

They checked into their room and went to bed and made love. After laying and holding each other for a long time they got up, showered, unpacked their cases and talked about what sort of restaurant they wanted to go to for dinner. As they were so close to the Champs Elysees they decided that they would just walk to there and stroll along the famous street and find a restaurant that took their fancy. They got dressed, Sam put on a pair of Chinos and Yves St Laurent shirt and jumper and Irina wore a pair of black tailored trousers and a black silk shirt. She added a beige wool jacket. Arm in arm they walked from the hotel towards the Arc De Triumph. It was mid-October but the evening air in Paris was still warm. The trees had started to shed their leaves which somehow added to the romantic ambience of the city.

During Sam's time in the army he had been on many and various training courses. These were very varied in nature. There was the usual regular retraining on weapons, training on new weapons, unarmed combat and other methods of dealing with enemy combatants. There was undercover training, training in interrogation techniques both as an interrogator and being interrogated. Sam was considered to be an excellent student at all aspects but one thing that he could not be trained in was his instinct, it was thought that he had a sixth sense. He seemed to recognise danger signs that nobody else saw. It was a bit of a cliché but the hairs on the back of his neck did stand on end. He had developed a reputation for it, He thought that this was one of the reasons that he had survived in so many potentially dangerous situations.

As they left the hotel, those hairs were active again. It was the first time for many years and Sam did a quick mental check as to why. Sam walked without giving anything away to Irina but he had noticed a cars interior light turn off as he stepped out onto the pavement. In that split second he had seen that there were two men in the car. They had reached the end of the road and turned left. As they did so Sam looked covertly back down the road. The car had pulled away from the kerb and was coming slowly along the road. It was a Renault Sefrane, dark coloured.

They turned left onto the Champs Elysees, in the opposite direction to the Arc De Triumph. They were relaxed, hand in hand, lovers in the city of love. Sam surreptitiously glanced behind him and saw that Renault pull up at the corner that they had just turned. The man in the passenger seat got out of the car and started walking in their direction. Sam and Irina stopped to look in a shop window. The man stopped and looked in a shop window about thirty yards away. Sam and Irina started to walk again. So did the man, now about fifty yards back. They continued their stroll along the Champs Elysees, Irina completely unaware that anything was wrong. They reached a left hand turn and saw what looked like a typical French restaurant just a few yards down the side road. They strolled down and looked at the menu. They liked what they saw and went inside to dine. Sam forced himself to relax. He normally loved French food but he felt tense. Why was this man following them. Was he following Sam, was he somebody Yuri had arranged to follow them? Sam discounted that as soon as he thought of it. Was he following Irina? If so why? Was there something that he was not aware of about her?

They both started with moules mariniere with chunks of French bread and drank some Sauterne. They then both had venison with a selection of vegetables with a bottle of St Emillion Claret. Despite the problem outside Sam had to admit that the food was delicious. They chatted as lovers do, about what Irina had been doing since they had been in Nice, about Sam's flat and about what they would do for the next week in Paris. "I have not yet talked to Yuri about leaving Moscow." She told Sam "He has been away from the office most of the time. He has some new business that I do not know about that is keeping him away".

"Do you want me to contact him and discuss it?" offered Sam.

"No Shammy, I think it better that I speak. I can pick a moment when he is in the correct mind". She leaned across the table and kissed him. "Don't worry. I will do it soon, as quick as I can".

After the main course they decided that they did not want a dessert so Sam ordered coffee for them both. While waiting for the coffee Sam excused himself to go and visit the lavatory. While away from the table he went to the front of the restaurant to check the street. He could see nothing.

He returned to the table and they finished their coffees. As usual in France, food is to be enjoyed and taken at a leisurely pace. They had been in the restaurant for almost three hours.

They exited the restaurant intending to take a slow walk back to the hotel. Sam put his arm around Irina's shoulder and pulled her close to him. As they left the restaurant Sam noticed the Renault parked about fifty yards down the road. He decided that whoever they were they either wanted to be noticed or were not very good at surveillance.

Sam and Irina arrived back at the hotel. Sam was aware that one of the men had got out of the car at the restaurant and followed them along the Champs Elysees. He was sure that Irina was unaware of it. She was too relaxed and happy to know that anything was wrong. As they turned to go into the hotel entrance Sam noticed the car was parked about six cars further down the road. He could not see inside but assumed that the driver was waiting for his partner to get back, the partner who was about one hundred yards behind them.

While Irina took a shower, Sam put the security lock on the bedroom door and checked the window lock. He also put the fork that he had purloined from the restaurant under the bed, just below his pillow. A table knife is a useless weapon in a fight but a fork strategically placed can cause pain and damage to an assailant.

Sam showered and when he got into bed Irina reached out him. As he moved into, the tenseness of the situation evaporated and he forgot all about the tails and the Renault. As usual they fell asleep in each others arms.

The next morning over breakfast they studied the tourist guide book and decided on what they wanted to see. Today they would visit the Sacre Coeur and Montmartre. Paris is a very compact city and many of the tourist sights are within walking distance of each other. Both of them wore jeans and trainers, with casual shirts and light jumpers so they were dressed to walk but they decided to take the metro to Montmartre, it was just too far to walk to. They left the hotel and walked in the direction of the Champs Elysees as they had the previous evening. It was a nice day, Sam thought more like spring than autumn. The sun was shining and the sky was mostly blue with a few light clouds. It was not exactly warm, but it wasn't cold either. They both had jumpers on and this was quite sufficient for the conditions, they were comfortable.

Sam did a quick check. The Renault was not there. As they got to the corner he glanced back down the road. He could not see anybody following them. They arrived at the Metro station and purchased a book of tickets that would last them for a few days, Sam hoped. As they waited for the train to arrive the hairs on Sam's neck hairs were signalling to him again. He checked around him. He saw nothing that looked out of place, but his hairs had never lied to him before. He made a mental note of the people on the platform just as the train came into the station.

They entered the square at Montmartre. It was occupied by dozens of artists, all sorts of artists. Irina had not seen anything like it before and neither had Sam. Irina was so happy, to Sam she seemed like an exited schoolgirl. They found an artist who would draw a cartoon style portrait while they waited. Sam persuaded Irina to sit for him. While he was waiting and watching the artist he noticed the tail, a man who had been on the platform of the metro station and had got off of the train at the same station. He was studying a lunchtime menu at one of the restaurants that surround the square, a funny thing to do at half past ten in the morning. He was wearing a shirt and tie and a rather creased jacket, not what a typical tourist would wear. Sam decided to ignore him. If the tail, or whoever had organised the tail, wanted to harm him they could have acted by now.

They were both happy with the portrait and they looked at all the other stalls and the pictures on them. One of them was of the Arc De Triumph viewed from along the Champs Elysees which they both thought was great. Sam wanted to buy it for Irina but she would not let him. After failing to persuade her, Sam suddenly came out with "I'll buy it for you on our honeymoon then".

Irina screamed and grabbed hold of Sam. She put her arms round his neck and kissed him hard. "I accept Shammy" she said, "the picture and the honeymoon". Then she pulled away, put her arms around his waist, looked at his face and said "you do love me Shammy don't you, because I love you. You must know that".

"I do Irina, I do. We need to get this sorted out with Yuri". She didn't say anything, she just put her arms back around his neck and kissed him again. They strolled around the square with their arms around each others waists. They stopped at a café and had a coffee, not speaking but just looking and smiling at each other. All this time Sam had still kept an eye on the tail. He was still in the square, still watching them. Seeing coffee being served to Sam and Irina, the tail decided to sit at a table on the opposite side of the café and ordered something for himself. Sam and Irina had just finished theirs as the waitress brought a cappuccino and mineral water to the tail's table. Sam, feeling a bit spiteful, got up, gave the waitress a twenty euro note which more than covered the bill, and he and Irina left. The tail had only enough time to have one quick sip of his coffee and he too had to rush out and follow Sam.

Sam and Irina walked from Montmatre, up the steps and into the Sacre Coeur. They had been inside the cathedral only minutes when Sam noticed the tail slip in the door. They spent over an hour walking around looking at the art and architecture. Although Sam had been to

Paris a few times he had never been to this cathedral before and he thought that it was spectacular. Irina loved it too.

They left the square and walked down the hill on which Sacre Coeure was built. They found a small restaurant and decided to go in and have lunch. The restaurant only had ten tables so it was too small for the tail to enter and have anything to eat. Sam could see him in a doorway about thirty yards past on the other side of the road. Irina was very happy and relaxed so Sam knew that she had no idea that they were being followed. She decided that she would have frogs' legs for her lunch. She thought that was very French. Sam decided that he would start with fois gras. Irina decided to have canard, as her main course, Sam decided upon veal. The frogs legs tasted like chicken, rather tender but not much meat on the bone. The fois gras was excellent, apparently sent up from Le Patrons sisters' farm in the Dordogne. The canard and veal were also very good.

Towards the end of the main course Sam saw a car pull up next to where the tail was waiting. He got into the car, a Peugeot, and another man got out of the back seat and took his place in the doorway. The car pulled away.

"Not very good" Sam thought again, "unless they want us to know that they are watching. I wonder which one it is".

They finished their meal, paid the bill and left the restaurant hand in hand. They had walked about one hundred yards when a taxi pulled up at the kerb about thirty yards ahead, to allow two passengers to get out. Sam hurried to the taxi, pulling Irina with him, and quickly got in.

"Place De La Concorde s'il vous plait" Sam said as they settled back. Sam glanced behind at the tail and grinned as he saw him looking around for another taxi to follow Sam and Irina. He was not being successful.

They got out at Le Place De La Concorde and strolled through Les Jardins Des Tuileries and along the banks of the Seine stopping during the afternoon for a coffee. They arrived back at their hotel at about five o'clock and as they walked up to the entrance Sam noticed that the Renault was back on duty, parked fifty yards along the road.

During the next few days Sam and Irina visited the Louvre and the Notre Dame, they walked to the top of the Eiffel Tower, to the Arc de Triomphe and visited the Musee d'Orsay, as well as spending time walking around the Latin Quarter, sampling what the cafes there had to offer. At all times they were followed although it seemed that Irina was unaware of it. Sam began not to care. They were doing nothing that would cause any problems or look suspicious and it was obvious that it was a tailing operation rather than them being intercepted. It occurred to Sam that maybe they were working for Yuri. He could not think why this should be, he would deal with it when he returned to London.

# CHAPTER 22

All too soon their holiday was over and Sam and Irina parted at Paris Charles De Gaulle Airport, Irina on an Air France flight to Moscow and Sam on a British Airways flight to London.

As soon as Sam arrived home he switched on his computer. There was and e-mail from Yuri.

*"I hope you enjoyed your time in Paris and that Irina is safely on her way home. It is cold here in Moscow but it is too soon for there to be snow in Gorky Park".*

Sam immediately left his flat and took the train to Beckton. He had thought that maybe he should change this routine but Asda did give him the anonymity that he wanted. He purchased the usual pay-as-you-go mobile phone and returned to his flat to charge it up. Three hours later there was enough charge in it to make the call. He caught a train into Central London, changing trains at Tower Gateway, going to Embankment and walked alongside the Thames. Out in the open beside the river he phoned Yuri. As usual he answered almost immediately.

"Hello Sam, how was Paris?"

"Very nice, it would have been better if we hadn't been followed wherever we went".

There was a pause on the line. "What do you mean followed?" Yuri seemed genuinely surprised. Sam told him what had happened. He told Yuri that they were only watched, no attempt had been made to intercept them. He also told Yuri that Irina hadn't realised what was going on so he asked him not to tell her.

"I will make some investigations and tell you if I can find what is happening. In the meantime I have another job for you. It is a quick one in Ireland, in the South so it is not UK. An African is going to visit his old college, he went to Trinity in Dublin. He is giving a lecture there one evening, talking to current Business Studies students. The people that are paying want him to die in a traditional way, whatever that means, what is traditional in Botswana? That is something you will need to find out, you have two weeks, what do you need?"

Sam knew that security between Britain and Ireland was not very tight. The best part is there is nowhere where passports are checked electronically only visually, so a good forgery will have no problem being accepted.

Sam asked Yuri for a UK passport, drivers' licence and credit card. Yuri told him he would have them within a week and then he hung up. Sam returned home thinking on the way about his conversation with Yuri. He believed that Yuri was not responsible for the tails in Paris so the question was who was it and why? He was concerned. He decided that he must take extra care that he covered himself when he plans his visit to Dublin in a couple of weeks time.

# CHAPTER 23

The passport, licence and credit card, in the name of Jack O'Donnell, arrived by courier at Sam's flat six days later. In the package was a photograph of the target and a brief summary of his history. He had been a tribal leader, had a law degree from Trinity College Dublin, and he was believed to have skimmed millions of dollars from money given to his country in Foreign Aid. There were elections in less than two months time and it was thought that he would use violence and intimidation to ensure that his choice for Prime Minister, his puppet, was victorious. Sam had visited the library and found out that the traditional way of tribal killing was by contaminated spears. The tribes would go into battle with animal feces on their spears so that if they didn't actually kill the victim with the spear they would die later, in pain, from blood poisoning. One small point Sam realized was the tribes didn't have the benefit of penicillin. That would cure blood poisoning. He needed to deal with that.

Sam took a train from London to Liverpool. From Lime Street station he caught the bus to John Lennon Airport where he hired a car from the Avis desk. He left Liverpool and took the A55 from Liverpool to North Wales, into Holyhead where he caught the ferry to Dublin. The crossing took three and a quarter hours. Adopting his policy of wanting big, impersonal hotels, he had booked himself into the Bewley's Hotel at Leopardstown.

The following morning after breakfast in the restaurant, Sam took the Airbus which went from the hotel, across the city, to the airport. He waited at the arrival gate for almost two hours. Finally his target came through the doors having arrived on his flight from Paris. He was accompanied by two other men. Sam hadn't counted on this, he had assumed that the man would come on his own. The group left the airport, strode briskly, taking the walkway opposite the terminal doors, that go under the car park and out to the coach park. Here they boarded the courtesy bus to the Crowne Plaza Hotel at Santry. Sam had not been informed where they would be staying, he had assumed in the city centre. He had hoped that he would be able to bump into them when they left the hotel to dine in the city. Being outside of the centre, he realised that he may need to rethink his plans. He knew that he had four days to achieve his goal so he decided to return to his hotel for this evening and rethink his plan. He caught the airbus to his hotel, had an early dinner and retired to his room to consider his campaign.

The next morning he was up early and returned to the airport then catching the courtesy bus to the Crowne Plaza. He waited in the reception lounge area, enjoying a croissant and coffee. The target came into the lobby just before nine o'clock. He ordered a taxi with the concierge to take him to Trinity College. The taxi arrived within a few minutes and the target left with one of his friends. Sam then ordered a taxi and when it arrived asked the driver to take him to O'Connell Street. He left the cab opposite the Penny's store and walked across the river and found Trinity College. He made a few discrete enquiries and found out that the lecture at which his target was guest lecturer was that evening.

Sam had decided that he needed to be flexible with this assignment. He was uncomfortable that he could not plan the hit more precisely but given the brief and the lack of information he felt he had no option but to wing it to some degree. He found out that the lecture was not full so he managed to get himself a ticket. He left with the ticket in his pocket. He walked back across the River Liffe back towards O'Connell Street where he caught the Airbus back to the airport. He hired a car from the Avis desk for three days and headed out of the airport, taking the M1 towards Belfast. He had decided not to use the car he had hired in England, firstly because the English number plates might be remembered but secondly because the underground car park had CCTV and Sam thought it was a good idea for it not to have moved if anybody checked. He left the motorway at the Navan exit and headed towards the town. He found what he was looking for on the outskirts of Navan, a small agricultural supplies store. He purchased a small container of industrial strength rat poison. Sam then drove back to his hotel.

The rat poison was in crystal form so Sam ground it down to a powder. He put about a tablespoon full into a small plastic bag. He then lay on his bed and took a nap for about an hour. He got up at five o'clock, showered, dressed in casual clothes and took a cab to the college where he arrived over an hour before the lecture was due to start. He went into the college and walked around unchallenged. He found what he was looking for within a few minutes, the male student toilets. Normally anyone would look for a clean and flushed toilet but Sam was looking for the opposite. As he expected he found one. A student, obviously one whose diet contained too much fat, and whose consideration did not extend to his fellow students had left liberal traces of faeces on the toilet bowl. Sam took another small plastic bag out of his pocket and collected some of the substance. He went into a clean cubicle and mixed the rat poison with the human waste. He put the mixture into a third plastic bag, washed his hands and left the toilet area and the college. He crossed the road and went into a chemist and purchased a hairbrush, the sort with stiff wire bristles used for styling.

He went to the lecture and listened while the target told the audience about how he had helped save his country, the lessons that he had learnt while he lived in Ireland and how he had introduced western standards of honesty and democracy to his nation. He continued to say how he had almost stamped out corruption and was developing the system of law that was prevalent in Ireland. The lecture finished and there was polite applause. After the lecture there was some wine and finger snacks for the guests. Sam kept in the background keeping an eye on his target. The function broke up just after ten o'clock. The target and his two friends left and walked across the river to the restaurant and bar area of the city. Sam followed. The three men went into a bar, they were relaxed and enjoying themselves. Sam found a corner so that he could watch them and sat and drank tonic water. The trio had some food and consumed a bottle of wine and several pints of Guinness. It was two hours before the target left the bar and went, on his own, to the toilet. Sam followed. The target went into one of the cubicles. Sam waited by the basins. He took the plastic bag with the mixture in it and rubbed it on the bristles of the brush. As the target came out of the cubicle Sam staggered as though he was drunk. The target looked at him briefly and then looked towards the basins, walking towards them to wash his hands. Sam stumbled again, this time falling over and as he did so fell against the leg of the man. As he did so he lifted the trouser leg slightly and scratched the leg with coated hairbrush. The target jumped back. "What are you doin' man" he shouted.

"Very sorry" said Sam in a slurred Irish accent. "Trying to brush my hair and fell over, must have had a giddy spell".

"More like pissed" said the target, "piss off away from me you Irish slob". With that he turned and walked out. He hadn't seemed to notice the scratched leg.

Sam was immediately sober, he left the pub and caught a cab back to his hotel in Leopardstown.

# CHAPTER 24

Sam arrived back at his hotel shortly after midnight. He crossed the lobby and headed for the lift. He went up to the fourth floor, along the corridor, put the key card in the slot on the door and opened it. As soon as he did his senses kicked in, something was wrong. His room was mostly dark but there was a small amount of light coming in from the window. Silhouetted against the window Sam sensed rather than saw a shape of a man sitting on the bed. His training and instinct took over. He rushed over to the man as he began to rise off the bed. Sam headbutted him, breaking the man's nose. At the same time he grabbed his right arm, spun him around and pulled the arm upwards and outwards. He had gained the element of total surprise. While he was spinning the man he roughly frisked him, and found that there was a gun in a shoulder holster underneath his left arm. All of this happened in no more than a second. Sam then sensed that another man had been hiding in the bathroom, he had heard the door open and instinct told him that somebody was coming out of it.. He spun the man round so that he was between Sam and the bathroom door. At the same time he drew the gun from the man's shoulder holster and aimed at the bathroom as the other man exited through the door. The bathroom light was on and the man was silhouetted clearly against it.

"Very impressive Sam" said the man.

Sam let out a loud, deep breath. "You are a total pratt Yuri" he said. "Creeping around like that, breaking into my room, you could get yourself killed".

"I thought that I had my best man with me to protect me. Obviously he is not good enough".

Sam released the man. He fell back onto the bed. "Tell him not to bleed in my room. I'm careful not to leave traces. If he messes anything he can clean it up".

Yuri said something to him in Russian and the man just groaned. "I am asking him why he is, what do you say, acting like a big girl?"

"His nose is broken and his right shoulder is dislocated, so he is probably in a bit of pain. I could hurt him some more and put his shoulder back into its socket if you like, but it hurts like hell and I don't want him passing out".

Yuri spoke to the man again in Russian. "Yes please, put it back in. It will mean that we will not create any attention at a hospital or with a doctor having to explain what happened. I have told him that if he passes out or makes a noise I will personally throw him out of your fourth floor window".

Sam walked over to the man. "Hold down his left shoulder" he said to Yuri. He pulled up the edge of the bed quilt and told the man to bite down on it. Yuri translated it is Russian. The man did what he was told. Sam then grabbed the right shoulder with both hands, pulled the top of the shoulder outwards and then moved it forward. The man jumped forward, gave a muffled scream with the quilt in his mouth but the shoulder was back in place. "It'll be sore for a few days but it will be OK. Better get the nose seen to though. I can't fix that".

"We won't bother, he can be ugly all of his life as a punishment for not doing a better job, another second and I could have been dead."

Yuri then turned to the man, spoke to him again in Russian and signaled for him to leave the room. He made to get up and moved towards the bedside table to where Sam had placed the confiscated gun. Sam got there first. The gun was a Baretta, one of Sams favourite weapons. The man stopped and said something to Yuri.

"Vaslov would like his gun back".

"Tell him spoils of war, its mine now".

"It was got for you originally, for the Tangier job, but we could not get a silencer. I prefer the Glock anyway, but you can keep that with my compliments".

Yuri then said something again in Russian and the man left the room.

# CHAPTER 25

"What are you doing here in Ireland?" asked Sam. "You know that here in the West we knock at doors if we want to go into a hotel room of a guest. Doing what you just did can get you killed".

"I will explain in a minute. We have a lot to talk about. But first is the African dead?"

"Not yet, but he will be in about a week. You wanted a traditional death, in a couple of days time he will feel ill and by the time he does something about it he will have so much of his system poisoned that even antibiotics will not help".

"OK, I will leave that to you then".

Sam sat down on the bed and looked at Yuri waiting for him to start talking.

"Firstly, you were followed in Paris. It was only the Surete, and they are useless, that is why you were easily able to see them. But it is more serious now. Their bosses did not accept that you were just on holiday and have now passed it on to Interpol. Also your British special branch is involved. Both Interpol and the Branch are good, you need to beware".

"What are they investigating? I was always very careful".

"They are investigating the assassinations but it appears they have no evidence. I do not now how they have come up with your name but I have asked my contact to let me know anything that they have".

"Thanks, I appreciate that. It would be useful to know in case I am picked up sometime. Maybe I had better lay low for a while".

"That is something else I need to tell you. I am closing the agency. I have one job left, a job in France, in a town called Nancy. I would like you to do it because of a special skill you have but if you do not want to, then I will understand, it is up to you. I will tell you about it in a minute, but first, the agency. I am going to work for the Russian Government, in fact I already am. Our Prime Minister Mr Putin has set up a new secret agency to deal with internal terrorism. We have very good information that the problems we have with the Chechens is about to start and get worse again. Fucking murdering bastards, we should have killed them all when we were the Soviet Union and nobody would have been able to stop us. Now, we have to consider world opinion. They are terrorists who murder innocent people. Bloody Muslin fundamentalists. In 1999 they blasted an apartment building right in the centre of Moscow and killed many innocent people. You remember in 2004, in September, just as the schools go back from holidays, the bastard Chechen rebels invaded a school in Beslan and held young children hostage before killing some of them and their teachers when the Russian army tried to free them. Children and innocent civilians, that is who the murderers target. We have very good intelligence that they are planning another murderous atrocity. I am in Ireland because we have information that some of their people are being trained in Libya. The Libyans trained the IRA when they fought the English twenty years ago so I am here, in secret, on government business, meeting some old IRA soldiers who trained in Libya to try and get some information. So, I have to give up my private enterprise and become a policeman again. Instead of a major, I am now a full Colonel, what do you think of that?" Yuri smiled.

"That's great, as long as it means that I don't have to salute you". They both laughed. "So what about this job in France then, tell me about that".

"The man is a Chechen, he is a mass murderer. He is visiting some members of the European Parliament in Strasbourg. His grandmother was a Pole and it seems that some old King of Poland lived in this insignificant town called Nancy and built a great square. He wants to visit it so that he can tell his family that he has fulfilled his grandmother's dream. The reason that we need you is because it would require a shot of something between six hundred and eight hundred metres. I cannot get somebody from Russia quickly enough who can shot that well. We would obtain the gun, deliver it to you in a building in the square and take it away afterwards. All you would have to do is arrive, shoot the bastard and then we would arrange quick transport away from the scene before the police arrived. It is planned as a private visit so security would be not high. Two things you should know, I have to be honest with you. First, we will pay two million US dollars, second, it would be paid by the Russian government, so you would be working for us. The choice is yours, I will agree with whatever decision you choose to make."

"Let me think about it. If as you say it is only in and out, if it is planned properly, I can't see a problem, other than Interpol".

"We cannot talk openly, I am in Ireland on a diplomatic passport in another name, but we can e-mail each other when you are back in England. When are you going back?"

"I'm planning on leaving tomorrow, the jobs done and I don't want to hang around".

"That is good, I will leave here in three days so we can talk on a secure line again when I am back in Russia. You can purchase three dead phones and use one and then throw it away and still have two which we can use later".

"OK, I will buy them as soon as I get back to London".

Yuri looked at Sam for several seconds, it was almost an eerie silence. Sam didn't say anything, he sensed that Yuri had something else to say so waited for him to say it.

"Irina, she tells me that she wants to come and live with you in London, do you know about this?"

Sam was annoyed that it should be a matter for Yuri at all but he decided to keep his feelings in check. "Of course I know about it".

"Do you intend to marry her?"

"Possibly".

"Let me explain about Irina, Sam". Yuri hesitated for a while as though he was considering what he was about to say. "You need to know that I care for her and would not be happy if you let her down".

"Fucking hell Yuri, I'm . . . . . . . . ."

"No, please let me finish. In my world Sam almost all of the women that I have met are only good for one thing, that is fucking. I have fucked hundreds of women, maybe thousands. When you are a major in the KGB in Soviet Russia, nobody says no to you. I would go to a town in the Caucuses to deal with a problem. There would be a civic dinner in my honour, the mayor, the head of the local party, the state factory managers and their wifes and anybody else that they could include in a free meal would be there. The hotels in these shit towns were infested with rats and cockroaches so I would always be invited to spend the night at one of the senior party member's house. I would choose the one with the most attractive wife. I would always spend the night in the host's bed, with his wife, probably fucking her before I went to sleep and then again in the morning, while the husband slept somewhere else. Sometimes on the next night I would go to another house and fuck someone else's wife or maybe I would stay in the same house and fuck the daughter. Anything went, as I say nobody would say no. When the Soviet collapsed and I was no longer KGB I still had money and influence so I still had no problem with women. You know how I rescued Irina. Initially she was for sex, but soon she was different. She lasted almost a year. That is a long time for me. Since her, I am now on my third new woman, big tits, very athletic, no brain. Irina is special, I now see her as an uncle would see her, I care what happens to her. She is clever and lively and I would not want to see her hurt".

"I'm not going to hurt her Yuri. I have not had the same number of women as you and usually I have paid for it, but my view is the same, women were for sex, shag 'em and leave 'em. Irina is different for me too".

There was a silence between the two men. They both just sat and looked at each other. Finally it was Yuri that spoke. "I have a new office starting in my new position. I need it to be organised and I need staff. I am travelling a lot and I only trust Irina to do it. I would like her to stay until the end of March to start the office and pick the right people, then you would have my blessing and I would help in any way I could".

Sam got off the bed and walked across the room to Yuri and held out his hand. Yuri took it and the two men shook hands and smiled at each other. "I won't hurt her Yuri, I think that I love her, whatever that is".

Yuri laughed, "yes, whatever that is".

"I would like her to come to England for Christmas, if she wants to of course, and maybe come back to you early in the New Year".

"She will want to. That is good, we do not start back at work until 7th January for New Year so I will arrange plane tickets for her. She is getting decadent now because of you, she travels business class". Yuri was laughing as he said it. Any tension that was building up between the two men had disappeared.

Yuri got up to leave. "I haven't been here, not even Irina knows. It must stay that way".

"Fine by me, I don't think that Special Branch would be too impressed with me meeting an ex KGB officer and current Russian uncover officer, in Ireland, in secret".

They shook hands again and Yuri slipped out of the door. Sam went back to the bed and picked up the gun. It was an almost new one, in pristine condition. Sam wrapped it in a dirty shirt and placed it in the bottom of his case. The Barreta had been his weapon of choice for almost any occasion. He was pleased he had driven to Ireland, there was no way he would have got the gun back to England if he was flying. Going by ferry should prove no barrier to getting the small gun back to London with him. He liked the idea of having a weapon secreted away somewhere near to hand if he ever needed it.

# CHAPTER 26

Sam got up early the following morning, had breakfast as soon as the dining room opened and then checked out. He drove to the port and boarded the ferry to Holyhead. Passports were only used as photo ID when boarding the ferry, so there was no electronic checks. The crossing was a bit rough and Sam felt slightly sick but apart from that the trip was uneventful. Sam was relieved when the ship docked in Wales and he drove straight off and to the airport to return the car. From the airport he caught the bus into Liverpool City Centre and then walked to Lime Street Station and caught a train to London. On the train he had a meal so he would not need to cook for himself when he got home. He arrived back in his flat just before eight o'clock in the evening. He stripped off his clothes, put on his gym gear and went for a workout. All the residents of the apartment complex were automatically members of the Health and Leisure Complex. The fees were covered within the annual management fees for the flats. Sam regularly used the gym to keep himself in shape but others didn't. One resident who Sam had met soon after he moved in, lived in one of the other three apartments on Sams landing. The man was an Indonesian industrialist who visited London only very occasionally and used the apartment instead of a hotel. He never used the facilities. Almost a year before Sam had copied his locker key just in case he ever needed some unidentified storage. That time had come. Sam wrapped the Baretta in a tee shirt and making sure that the changing rooms were deserted, he placed the gun in the spare locker. After thirty minutes on the treadmill and some repetitive exercises on the weights machines, Sam finally returned to his apartment just after ten and e-mailed Irina about coming over to London for Christmas, just before going to bed.

The next morning after a breakfast of muesli, fresh fruit and coffee, Sam took the well trodden route to Asda at Beckton to purchase four pay-as –you –go phones. He initially purchased only two, being cautious, went to have a tea in café Asda and when he was sure that the assistant who served him the first time had been relieved, he returned to the counter and bought another two from her replacement. He thought that if he purchased four phones she would remember him if any investigation ever took place. He took the handsets home and charged all four batteries and late in the afternoon he took three of them down to the leisure club changing rooms and deposited three in the ghost locker, making sure, as he had done with the gun, that there were no fingerprints on them. Sam's training had made him always plan for eventualities and given the information that Yuri had gained, Sam was aware that he could get a visit from Special Branch. He did not want to have to explain why he had four unregistered, unused mobile phones.

Two days passed with no message from Irina. On the third day the e-mail arrived.

*Uncle Yuri has just come back from a trip. He has some wonderful good news that I will tell you when I see you. I am already looking forward to seeing you in England for Christmas my love. Uncle Yuri says that he will arrange the flights today. We are not busy in the office at the moment so I would like to come to England next week but I have to return on 5th January as we will be busy in our new offices here in Moscow. I hope the weather in England is good. Yesterday we had our first snow in Gorky Park.*
*See you soon my love*
*Irina x x x x*

Sam collected the phone and left the apartment immediately. He took the DLR train to Beckton and instead of going to Asda he caught a bus to the Woolwich Ferry. Sam was checking during his journey but he was confident that he was not being followed. He got on to the ferry and just as it cast off he phoned Yuri. The targets' visit to Nancy was in eight days time. Yuri had already put a plan in place. Sam would be collected from a hotel in Brussels by car, the car would take him to a town in France called Bar-le-Duc. From there he would be taken by motorcycle across country to Nancy where two men would have rooms in the hotel on the square, both overlooking the square. As soon as the shot had been fired, Sam would leave the hotel, be taken back to Bar–le–Duc by motorcycle and then by car to Brussels and then home by Eurostar. He would be home in London the day before Irina was due from Moscow at Heathrow. Sam would be miles away from the scene before the police would arrive and cordon off the area. All that Yuri wanted to know was if Sam was prepared to do the job and if so, what gun he wanted to carry out the hit. Sam confirmed that he would do it and gave the choice of weapon to Yuri; a Barrett Model 90. He had thought that there may be a problem in getting one but Yuri just said that it would be there on the day. Yuri said that getting such a large gun out of the hotel after the hit may prove a problem so suggested that it should be left in the room. The gun would be untraceable so all Sam had to do was to make sure that there were no fingerprints on the gun or bullets. Sam agreed that this was probably the best thing to do although he was always reluctant to leave a weapon behind, particularly a weapon of this quality.

The following day a courier arrived with a false passport, driving licence and credit card. As Sam had only agreed to the contract the day before, he realised that Yuri must have been confident that he would carry it out. The documents were in the name of Jason Williams with an address in Islington. Sam was thinking about another plan for the hit so he decided to check out the details of his persona. He took a train to The Angel station and walked to the square in a small road off of Upper Street where the address was. It was a large house which had been converted into three flats. Sam walked up to the front door and saw that there were three bells with an entry-phone speaker system. What he assumed to be the bell for the top floor flat, flat C, had the name of Jason Williams next to it. Sam rang the bell. There was no answer. Sam waited a minute or so and rang the bell for flat B. There was no answer from this flat either. Sam than rang flat A. After a few seconds a voice answered. "Yes?"

"Hello. I'm working on behalf of a London solicitor and I'm trying to locate a Mr Jason Williams. I have this address but there is no answer from his flat. Could you please confirm that he still lives here?"

"Depends what you call lives here" the voice said. "He's something to do with oil and spends most of his time in Kuwait. He lives here about three weeks every year. He should be back in the UK in about four months if things are usual. Otherwise I don't know how to contact him".

"Thank you" said Sam. "It is not urgent so it will wait until he returns. Thank you for your help".

Sam left and walked back to the underground station and returned home. By the time he returned to his flat he had formulated another plan. He decided that he would not tell anybody of the change, not even Yuri. Instead of travelling to Brussels by Eurostar, he decided that he would drive. The next day Sam hired a car in his own name. He drove around the streets of Redbridge until he found what he was looking for. In a road just off of the High Road in Chadwell Heath was parked a car with a 'For Sale' notice in its windscreen. It was a Y registered Ford Mondeo with six months MOT left and two months road tax. It was advertised at £950 ono. Sam had fifteen hundred pounds in cash in his pocket. He telephoned the mobile number on the windscreen and made arrangements to meet the seller in one hours time.

Sam left, went to a nearby Sainsbury's for a sandwich and returned to the car one hour later. It took less than five minutes for Sam to satisfy himself that the car was suitable and for the seller to agree a sum of nine hundred pounds. Sam signed the transfer documents in the name of Jason Williams at the address in Islington, took the keys in exchange for the cash and told the seller that he would collect the car the following day. He then returned the rental car and went home, enjoying a hard work out in the gym before his dinner. That evening he booked a ticket on the Euro Tunnel car transporter train from Dover to Calais, in the name of Jason Williams and using his new car's registration number.

The next morning he took the train to Holborn where he visited an insurance agency and insured his new car. He had chosen a branch in Holborn as the registered address was in Islington, close by, and also because an agent in Holborn is anonymous. He then travelled to Chadwell Heath, walked from the station to where his new car was parked and drove it away. He now had a new car, which was taxed and insured, fully legal, owned and registered to a man who should be in Kuwait for the next few weeks at least, which was enough time for him to do what he planned. He drove the car not to where he lived but to Beckton. The Asda store that was so familiar to him was located on a roundabout. Opposite the road into Asda was a road off the roundabout that led past the entrance of a Premier Inn hotel, where there were no parking restrictions. Sam parked the car there and took the train from Beckton station, which was only a matter of a couple of hundred yards away, back to his home.

# CHAPTER 27

The following week Sam picked up the Mondeo from where he had left it and drove to Dover. He had heard that passport control at the terminal was not strict, and this turned out to be the case. This was as he hoped as he was traveling on the false passport rather than leaving and entering the country on his own and switching when abroad. It was the first time that he had ever travelled on the train and Sam was very impressed with how efficient it was and how smooth the journey. They disembarked in Calais after what seemed like no time at all. The terminal exited straight onto the motorway and Sam headed in the direction of Brussels. He arrived at the hotel that Yuri had arranged without any problem. He checked in, paid for two nights in advance and went to his room, dropped his overnight bag on the bed and then left the room and went out of the hotel. He found a book store about half a mile from the hotel and purchased a road atlas of Western Europe. He found Rheims in the atlas and then Bar-le-Duc. Walking back to the hotel, he telephoned Yuri's number. Yuri answered almost immediately and seemed surprised to hear from Sam.

"Change of plan" Sam said. "I don't want to be collected in Brussels, I will meet the bike in the town as arranged. There is bound to be a town square in the centre. I will be there at two o'clock tomorrow afternoon. I will be sitting in a silver Ford Mondeo with English number plates".

"Noted", said Yuri. "I will instruct the men accordingly". The connection was severed. Once again Sam appreciated Yuri's professionalism, no questions, no explanations required. A telephone conversation that would be untraceable in such a short time and if anybody was monitoring it, it would mean very little.

Sam walked back to the hotel, had an early dinner and an early night.

The next morning he left the hotel, having paid for the two nights that it had been booked for, not intending to come back. He drove back into Northern France and found himself in Bar le Duc just after midday. He parked in the car park of a pizza restaurant and decided to have an early lunch. Something he had learnt when he had been on missions in the army, eat when you can, you never can be sure when you will eat again. If things went to plan he would not eat for many hours, not until he was back in England. Just before two o'clock he was parked in the town square. Less than four minutes after he arrived a large BMW motorcycle pulled up next to him and the rider knocked his fist on the passenger door window. Sam got out of the car.

"Monsieur Williams?" asked the man.

"Oui" replied Sam. The man held out a crash helmet. Sam put it on and sat astride the bike. The rider pulled away smoothly and they soon left the town behind. Sam was impressed with how quiet and comfortable the bike was. The roads were not busy and they arrived in Nancy just under an hour later. The bike came to a halt at the end of a road by an arch. The arch led on to the square.

"The 'otel is there" the man said in a French accent. "You are waited for in room twenty two and he will also have room twenty eight on the second floor. When you have finished I will be waiting for you right here in this place". Sam left the man and walked across the square to the hotel entrance. The square was indeed impressive. The hotel was a grand building that Sam assumed had been built originally for another use, maybe a grand home. There was a larger building on another side of the square. It had a French flag flying from it so Sam thought that it must be some kind of municipal building or maybe a court of justice now but had obviously been the palace when it was originally built. On the other sides of the square were restaurants and bars and some small boutique style shops, all very tasteful. Sam entered the hotel through the front doors, located the stairs and walked up to the second floor. He was now wearing a pair of thin cotton gloves which he would keep on until he was away from the town. He knocked at the door of room twenty two and it was opened almost immediately.

"You are Villiams?" said the man in a French accent, Sam had been expecting an Eastern European.

"Yes" was all Sam replied as he walked past the man and into the room. As the man closed the door Sam looked at the bed. Lying on it was the gun, the Barrett Model 90 that Sam had asked for. It was huge, over four feet in length and weighing twenty-two pounds, and it looked almost new. Not for the first time Sam was impressed with Yuri's contacts. Sam picked up the gun and checked the balance. He then checked the magazine that was on the bed beside it and saw that it was fully loaded with six bullets. He then went to the window to check the view.

"Lets look at the other room" Sam said. The man opened the door and walked along the passage. He took the keys out of his pocket and opened the door to room twenty-eight. Sam looked around, it was identical to the first room. Sam looked out of the window again. This room was slightly more central to the square so as he didn't know from which direction the target would arrive, he decided that this would offer a better vantage point for the shot. He returned to the first room, collected the gun and the bullets and, while instructing the man to keep watch by the staircase, he moved them along the landing to room twenty-eight.

He knew that he had some hours to wait before the target would arrive. He instructed the man to wait in the other room until he heard the shot then to move very fast to get away. The man left and Sam went back to the gun. He removed the shells from the magazine, checked them and then reloaded. The magazine holds six bullets, each are half an inch across and each weigh two ounces. They leave the gun at nineteen hundred miles per hour and can travel over eight hundred yards accurately. Sam had estimated that this shot would vary from between four hundred and six hundred yards, depending upon where the target was when Sam would get a clear shot. Sam then checked the gun. The Barrett 90 is a bolt action repeater. Sam was intending only to fire one shot but just in case, he checked the bolt mechanism. It was very smooth and well oiled. The gun had bipod legs attached to the barrel for stability. Sam tested these, they were fine. He pulled the chest of drawers in the room across the bottom of the window and rested the legs of its top. Making sure that the curtain obscured any view, in case somebody was looking, he looked through the viewfinder. All seemed to be in order. He loaded the gun by inserting the magazine and then lay on the bed to wait. He dozed for a while and woke refreshed. It was just after six o'clock. He pulled a bottle of water out of his bag and drank from it. He then positioned himself by the window to keep watch on the square below, He did not expect his quarry for another hour or so at least but it was better to be sure than to miss him. He had already wiped the gun of any fingerprints and was wearing the pair of thin cotton gloves.

The target arrived just over an hour later. As Yuri had predicted he had very little security, it looked like only one bodyguard. The target entered the square from Sam's right and started looking in the windows of the small shops that were there. He disappeared into one of them and came out about four minutes later, the bodyguard carrying a wrapped parcel of what seemed like some sort of ornament or statue. They continued to cross the square. They were heading for a bar almost opposite from where Sam had stationed himself. Although the bar had tables outside and it was a dry, bright evening, it was December and rather cold so Sam thought that the target would not sit out but go inside. Sam sighted the gun and followed him as he headed for the bar door. He was about five yards away from it when Sam lined up for the shot. Sam estimated that it was a distance of just over four hundred yards. Although this should not be a problem, Sam had fired one of these guns before and been successful over greater distances, you always need to allow for a slight drop in the trajectory of the bullet over such a distance when lining up the shot.

Sam took aim and squeezed the trigger gently. Firing a bullet of that size from a gun of that size is like firing a small rocket. The recoil is severe and so is the kick, but Sam was experienced enough to know this so was ready for it. He had known people break cheekbones and jaws when first firing a Barrett 90. Automatically Sam slid the bolt to put the next bullet in the breach as soon as the shot was fired. He needn't have bothered. As he looked at his target he saw that the targets back was disintegrating as the bullet hit home two yards from the bar door. Sam put the gun on the floor and left the room immediately. He ran swiftly down the stairs and out of the side door of the hotel. The noise from the shot being fired was very loud and the people in the square were looking around to see what had made the sound. Fortunately the smallish square surrounded by tall buildings on all sides, made the noise bounce off walls making it impossible for anybody to tell from which direction the noise had come. Few as yet realised exactly what had happened, only the one or two people near the target. Fortunately there was nobody sitting outside the bar and no women had yet seen what had happened and started screaming. Sam walked swiftly but calmly to the exit gateway of the square and found the motorcyclist waiting for him as arranged. He had barely sat astride the pillion when the bike pulled away. The ride back to Bar-Le-Duc and Sam's car was pleasantly uneventful. They didn't even hear police sirens as they left the environs of Nancy town.

The bike pulled up by the side of Sams' car. As he got off of the bike the rider took the crash helmet from Sam and rode away without saying a word. It had been a wordless journey but that suited Sam. He got into his car and started the journey back to Calais. He considered his change of plans to be good security. He doubted if it was the case, but if there was a leak inside Yuri's organisation they would be expecting him back in Brussels. It was a long drive. He headed for Paris, took the ring road around the city, The Parifarique, and then north to Calais. He stopped once just north of Paris in a motorway service area to use the toilet and have a coffee and a bar of chocolate to help him stay awake.

He arrived on the outskirts of Calais at 2 O'clock, parked his car and had a sleep. He caught the 6.10am Eurotunnel train which got him back to Dover just after 5.30. He got onto the M20 motorway and headed for home. At that time of the morning, the traffic was light and he didn't drop below seventy miles an hour until he slowed down for the traffic beginning to build up at the Dartford Tunnel. He drove to Beckton and left the car in the road opposite Asda. He then caught the train from Beckton, went back to his flat and cooked himself some bacon, made fresh coffee and sat by his balcony window and had breakfast. After about half an hour he went downstairs to the gym for a workout followed by a shower. He spent the rest of the day relaxing in his apartment. He tried to think about what he would do with himself, he was now unemployed. At least he had no money problems. With the fee from this last contract he would have a few million dollars in his overseas bank account. The trick would be getting it back to the UK. He then reflected how chance had played such an important role in his life since the army, how he had met Yuri while on holiday, and the odds of Yuri offering him a job at the only thing he was good at;

killing people. The chance that he met Irina, the only woman that he had ever loved.

On the spur of the moment he telephoned his sister. She was surprised to hear from him. Since he had been released from army prison he had phoned her and her children on their birthdays and had brought them presents; well actually he had sent his sister money to buy them presents. He used the excuse of asking what they wanted for Christmas as the reason for the call but actually he had the urge to tell somebody about Irina and sadly Sam realised that there was nobody else to tell. His sister said that she would ask the children and get back to him but also said that she would love to meet Irina sometime over the Christmas holiday.

# CHAPTER 28

The next day Sam was up early, fully refreshed. He took the train to Beckton and collected the car. He then drove to an area of Tottenham where there was a high incident of car theft. He wiped down the interior of the car with metholated spirits to remove any sign of DNA or fingerprints; he also wiped the door handles. When he was satisfied he put the keys in the glove box and walked away from the car. He then went by train to the airport. He was at Heathrow a good two hours before Irina's plane was due to land. Sam was surprised how much he was looking forward to seeing her again and spending the next few weeks with her. It crossed his mind that the next time that he would be waiting for her at the airport it would be for the last time, she would be coming to London to live here, with him, permanently.

It seemed an eternity but eventually she came through the arrivals door. They rushed up and held each other tightly. As they broke apart Irina said "Shammy, I have a message from Yuri that is urgent, well two messages really. The first one he said to tell you that the African from Ireland is dying and Yuri's contact is very happy because he thinks it is a witchdoctor curse. But the second is more important. Let us get away from where we may be heard".

Sam took Irina's case and she held his arm as they left the terminal building. Sam had decided to take a cab rather than the train so they walked towards the taxi queue. "Shammy, Yuri says that the police in England are going to question you. He has a contact in the French police who say that all of their information has been passed to the English. Yuri says that they have no real evidence but they have worked out that you were out of the country when some killings happened and that only somebody with your skills could have done some of the shootings. Yuri has given me a solicitor who is in London who will help you when they arrest you but Yuri says that they know nothing".

Sam smiled, "Good old Yuri, where does he get his information from?"

They got into the taxi and started their journey to Docklands and to Sam's flat. On the journey they talked briefly about their future together but mostly they just cuddled and kissed.

As soon as they walked into the flat Sam put Irina's case down and she turned round and kissed him hard. He responded and firstly took her coat off and then started to undress her. She was doing the same to him. By the time they reached the bedroom door they only had their underwear on and this was soon removed before they fell onto the bed and made love urgently. There was no foreplay and they both climaxed almost straight away. They got under the duvet and after a few minutes of holding each othe,r kissing, they made love again, this time much more slowly and tenderly. They spent the rest of the afternoon in bed, cuddling and talking about living in London once Irina had organised Yuri's new office and found the right staff. She seemed both relieved and pleased that her wanting to be with Sam had received Yuri's blessing. Sam was pleased too. Although he felt that it should not be anything to do with Yuri, he knew that in reality Yuri could make things very difficult for them or even stop it altogether. Sam liked Yuri and respected him but he certainly would not want to cross him.

They got out of bed at teatime, showered and dressed. Irina unpacked her case and gave Sam a note from Yuri which had a phone number and name on it. It was the contact details of the lawyer that Yuri had suggested. The note told Sam that although he didn't have to use this person, Yuri had used him in the past, he was very good, and Yuri had already briefed him about the problem. Sam committed the number to memory, wrote the name and number down in his writing and then burnt the note from Yuri. They went for an early dinner at a little Chinese restaurant in Poplar. Sam loved Chinese food and Irina was developing a taste for it. They held hands across the table, looked at each other and smiled. They talked some more about their future and what they would do when they were together, would they move from London to the country, would they move abroad, they felt that there were no barriers, they could do what they wanted. More than once it occurred to Sam that he was a forty year old man who had killed people for a living, not a sixteen year old kid with stars in his eyes. But right now he felt like the sixteen year old. Sam wanted to walk back to the apartment but it was a cold evening, too cold for Irina she said. They took a cab back to Sam's, made coffee and took it to bed with them. They made love again and fell asleep as usual, in each others arms.

# CHAPTER 29

The phone was ringing. It brought Sam out of his sleep; he was immediately wide awake. He realised that it wasn't the main phone but the internal phone that linked all of the apartments with the security desk at the reception area.

"Excuse me for disturbing you Mr Tucker, it's Chester from security here. Two men flashing warrant cards have just got in the lift. They asked how to get to your flat and told me not to tell you they were coming up, they wanted it to be a surprise. Thought you might like to know sir".

"Thank you Chester, much appreciated. You've just earned yourself a big Christmas box".

"Thank you sir, pleased to be of service".

Sam rushed into the bedroom. Irina was stirring. "What time is it, what is the matter?"

"Its not yet seven o'clock and the police are on their way up. Look, you stay in here, in the bedroom, stay quiet and when I have gone phone the lawyer that Yuri suggested, here is his name and number". Sam gave her the slip of paper with the details written on it. "Tell him that I have been arrested and as soon as I am able I will call him and let him know where they are holding me". Sam went over and kissed her. "Don't worry, they can't hold me for long, they have no evidence". Sam walked out of the bedroom just as there were three loud knocks on the door. Sam moved to the middle of the lounge and waited. They knocked again.

"Alright, alright I'm coming" he said in a sleepy voice. Sam opened the door wearing only his dressing gown. "What is this and how did you get past security?" The men both held up their warrant cards, they were special branch, an inspector and a sergeant.. "Bloody hell, what do you want" said Sam, seemingly surprised.

"Mr Tucker? Mr Sam Tucker? We would like you to come with us please" said the senior of the men.

"Am I under arrest?" said Sam.

"We can arrest you if you prefer it, but we would rather you would just come with us and help us with our enquiries".

"Can I get dressed first?"

"Of course sir" said the inspector. The two policemen started to enter the flat.

"Do you have a search warrant?" asked Sam.

"No sir" said the inspector, "we don't need one at least not at the moment".

"In that case you can wait outside at the door. I haven't invited you in."

The two policemen were unhappy about this but moved back outside the door. Sam walked away from them taking his dressing gown off as he walked to show that he was naked underneath. He walked into the bedroom putting his finger to his lips to signal to Irina to stay quiet. Less than two minutes later he came out of the bedroom dressed in a pair of his Ralph Lauren slacks and Polo short with a Hugo Boss jacket. He collected his coat which was hanging inside the front door in a small cupboard and closed the door behind him. He followed the sergeant to the lift, the inspector followed and they went down to the ground floor. They crossed the lobby and as they walked past security Sam said "Good morning Chester, cold one again today".

"Yes it is sir, another thick frost" was the reply.

Outside of the building was an anonymous black Ford Mondeo with a driver sitting in the front. The rear door was opened and Sam got in. The inspector got in the back with him and the sergeant sat in the front. Sam was completely relaxed and looked out of the window as they drove along the A13 into central London.

In many respects the British Army is considered to be the best in the world. It is underfunded, certainly over the last ten years or so, very often it has a problem with a lack of the right equipment, but to compensate the average British soldier is the best trained. This is even more the case when any special force member, be it the SAS or the SBS or even the Para's go into an unusual or clandestine operation. Only possibly Mossad can match the British for specialist training. As a result of some of his assignments in his twenty years service, Sam was very well trained in a wide range of disciplines and techniques. One of these was interrogation. Particularly before he went undercover in Ireland during the troubles there, he had a rigorous programme of interrogation procedures, not only if he was being the interrogated and to understand the best way to cope with being interrogated, but he was also taught the techniques of interrogation. Sam sat in the car recalling these courses. In almost all cases the interrogator does not have all the facts. They ask questions and hope that by answering them the person being interrogated will let something slip that helps the interrogator. The best advice when being interrogated is to say nothing. This has the added benefit of frustrating the questioner. Being interrogated by the British police, even Special Branch, Sam thought would be a piece of cake. They couldn't assault him or abuse him, within certain limits anyway, and they would have a time limit for which they could hold him without charge. He felt confident that he had not left a trail that could be proved without reasonable doubt and this had been confirmed by the information from Yuri.

The car pulled into a yard of a police station in the West End of London. The sergeant got out and opened the rear door for Sam. He got out of the car and the sergeant took his arm and propelled him in through a back door, the inspector followed. Sam was walked along a corridor and into a small room, no bigger than ten feet square, it had a table in the middle of the floor with four chairs around it. As he entered the sergeant went to the table.

"Empty your pockets" he said. Sam took out his wallet and put it on the table. "And the rest?"

"There is no rest, just my wallet". The sergeant patted Sam down just to make sure, he then picked up the wallet. "Watch too please". Sam took of his watch but said nothing.

"Sit down there and wait" said the sergeant as he pushed Sam inside, pointed to a chair on the opposite side of the table and closed the door behind him, leaving Sam in the room on his own. Sam sat down on a chair on the opposite side to he one that he had been told, with his back to the door. Sam looked around. The room had no windows. It had painted walls in a institution light green colour and along one side, to Sam's left, was a full length glass panel that was shaded black, obviously a viewing area. Sam sat back, made himself as comfortable as he could on the chair, crossed his arms and waited. He knew that this was part of the plan, keep the prisoner waiting a while and he will be more anxious to talk. They kept him waiting for over an hour.

"Would you sit on the other side of the table please" said the inspector as he walked in to the room followed by the sergeant. Sam looked at him and slowly got up and walked to the other side of the table and sat down on one of the chairs.

The inspector sat down, put a file on the table and said "Mr Tucker, my name is Inspector Jarvis and this is Sergeant Wilkins. We are assisting Interpol in the investigation of a number of murders which have occurred over the course of this year and we believe that you can assist us in these enquiries". The inspector then cautioned Sam. Sam said nothing, he just looked at the man. The inspector looked right back.

The sergeant opened the file that was on the table. "In early June you went to Europe. Where did you go?"

"If you are going to ask me questions shouldn't I have a lawyer here? I am entitled to a phone call".

"This is a matter of prevention of terrorism, the rules are different, no phone call". The sergeant had said this too quickly. Sam knew that he was lying and that he had an advantage with him but he had not yet been able to size up the inspector, he was more canny.

"So I'll ask you again, where did you go when you left the country in June?"

"I have nothing to say" said Sam.

The sergeant continued, "In August you left the country again, where did you go this time?"

"I have nothing to say" said Sam.

"What about September and again in October, you went abroad again then, where did you go?" the sergeant tried again.

"I have nothing to say" replied Sam again.

"Look Sam, may I call you Sam?" it was the inspector's turn to talk. "Obviously we know that you went abroad, you have left a passport trail. We also know that on each of these occasions while you were abroad, somebody, usually an influential person, was assassinated. Some of these killings would have required very specialist skill, skills that not many would possess, skills which you have thanks to your training in Her Majesty's armed forces. You see Sam we have details of your service record". Sam said nothing, he just looked at the man holding eye contact.

There was a silence broken by the sergeant. "Lets take your little trip to Nice. At the same time that you were there an influential man and his bodyguards were shot in Tangier. Not far from Nice to Tangier and it happens that there are direct flights". Sam knew that they had nothing to link him with the shooting. Just the fact that they had mentioned flights meant that they had no evidence. As Yuri had said it was all circumstantial.

"I have nothing to say" said Sam yet again.

"You can't keep on like this you know", the sergeant was getting irritated, just what Sam wanted. "You'll have to tell us eventually".

"Maybe I will when I have spoken to my solicitor. When can I make my call?"

"I told you, this is terrorism, no solicitor, you are . . . . . . . . ."

"What you told me is complete bollocks. Firstly what you have said is the issue here is not terrorism and secondly, even if it was, I would still be entitled to a phone call and a solicitor. What the prevention of terrorism act does is allow you extra time to question suspects, not to withhold a human right. Now, do I get my phone call because without it, I have nothing to say." Sam waited for a response. The sergeant got up from his chair and walked out, the inspector looked at Sam and followed him out of the room. A uniformed police constable entered the room and stood by the door.

A few minutes passed and Sam said "any chance of a cup of tea mate? They dragged me out of my home this morning before breakfast and I'm gasping".

"Sorry, I was told just to stand here. We do what we are told when the Branch are here".

Sam continued "That inspector seems a good guy but the sergeant, he seems a right pratt".

"Yeah, Inspector Jarvis is a goodun', a really nice bloke and a good copper. Some of the Branch guys look down their noses at us ordinary guys but he doesn't, he's been around a long time and is decent to all of us"

"What about his prick sidekick?"

"He's new to the job, only just come from CID to Special Branch, out to prove himself. Walks around like a bit of a big 'I AM' at the moment. We've been watching you through the glass, you're getting 'im rattled and your doing it on purpose". The constable was smiling slightly. Sam smiled back and said nothing. He had acquired a lot of useful information in this short interchange.

Sam was left sitting in the room for what he thought was at least another hour. At last the sergeant came in on his own. The constable was told to stay in position standing by the door. "There's a few questions being asked about you upstairs. The heavy mob will be down here soon, no more mister nice guy".

"At the risk of repeating myself what about my phone call?"

"There's no fuckin phone call" he had raised his voice, a good sign as far as Sam was concerned. Now he knew he was getting to him.

"What about a cup of tea then, and some toast, you dragged me out this morning before my breakfast and I'm famished".

"What do you think this is, the fuckin Ritz?"

"I need to go for a pee". The policeman was getting more uptight, Sam knew now that he had him.

"You are not leaving this room, you want a pee then as far as I'm concerned you can do it in your fuckin trousers".

Sam sat and looked at the man. Slowly he got up from the chair. The sergeant tensed and so did the constable at the door. Sam started to move away from the table and the sergeant stood up anticipating that Sam was approaching him. Instead of going towards him however Sam turned his back on him and went to the corner at the rear or the room. He quickly undid his fly zip and started to urinate on the floor in the corner.

"You filthy bastard" said Sergeant Wilkins as he rushed around the table and headed in Sam's direction. Sam turned, still peeing, and sprayed the front of the sergeants trousers with urine. Sergeant Wilkins stopped, stunned, and then, with his face full of fury, clenched his fists and made a move towards Sam.

Sam said softly, "that's right, hit me, make me happy".

"Sergeant" it was the police constable from the doorway, "maybe you had better go and clean up". His speaking had the desired effect, the sergeant stopped in mid track and with eyes full of hatred looked at Sam and then he turned round and left the room. Sam did up his flies and returned to the chair and sat down. Although he obviously didn't particularly like Sergeant Wilkins, Sam could tell that the constable thought that he had overstepped the mark, urinating on a colleague.

There was silence in the room for at least the next half an hour. Sam was now really getting thirsty, he had been trained to go for a much longer time than this without food or drink, he felt that he must be getting soft. He estimated that it had been less than five or six hours since he had been picked up from his flat.

The door opened and Inspector Jarvis entered the room. He was carrying a mug of tea and a bacon sandwich. He signalled to the constable to leave the room.

"Isn't that against protocol, you being on your own with me I mean" said Sam. The inspector put the mug and plate on the table and pushed them over to Sam. He sat down opposite him.

"I'm not questioning you any more, its been taken out of my hands. I think though that by the end of today you will wish you had been more co-operative with us. I have been told by a senior officer at the Yard that you are being collected by some heavy mob. I am now to cease questioning you".

"Then why are you?"

"Because I have read your service record, or what part of it they would let us have, and I respect you. It may be that if you had come clean we could have protected you from whoever is coming for you, or Interpol or whoever else might want your head on a block. At least the British police need to prove a case to punish the offender, there are organisations that don't."

"This bacon sandwich is very nice, please pass my compliments to the cook. Apart from that inspector, I have nothing to say".

Inspector Jarvis looked at Sam, he got up from his chair and held out his hand, offering it to Sam. Strangely Sam took the hand and shook it. "Goodbye Mr Tucker" said Inspector Jarvis, and he turned and left the room. The constable came in again as stood inside the door as before.

About an hour passed in silence and there was a knock on the door, the constable opened it and Sam heard a voice say "bring him out, his escorts are here". Sam got out of the chair and walked towards the door. He followed the owner of the voice, another constable, along the corridor and was followed in turn by the officer from the room. They reached the front lobby of the police station. Standing there were two men, both in their late thirties or early forties. Both were about six feet tall and upright in stature and both looked to have kept very fit.

Both were smart with very short haircuts, both were wearing pin stripe suits and white shirts. Both had highly polished shoes, their regimental ties confirmed to Sam that these guys were ex military.

"Mr Tucker, come with us please". Without waiting for an answer they turned and went to the door. The desk sergeant hurriedly passed Sam's wallet and watch to him before he followed them out of the police station. The black anonymous car this time was a BMW. Sam was shown into the rear seat. The two men sat in the front and the car drove away. Sam had not been prepared for this change of circumstance. His mind was now trying to work out what was happening. He was reluctant to engage these two in conversation, and even if he did, he didn't think that they would give anything away. They were a completely different proposition to the police that had picked him up this morning. He concluded that they must be from one of the security services, MI5 or MI6. As soon as he had concluded this the car turned northwards, towards Victoria, rather than heading to the Southbank where the MI5 headquarters are. Sam was not exactly worried by the turn of events but he was becoming a bit concerned. Before it reached Victoria the car turned off, towards Whitehall. It suddenly took a sharp right and pulled off the road through an arch, which led to a car park at the rear of a large, impressive building. The car came to a stop and the two men started to get out of the car. Without waiting to be told Sam opened the door and got out of the car too.

"Will you follow us please sir" said one of the men. They started to move forward towards a door at the rear of the building. Sam followed. As he was walking he noticed that some of the cars had military style number plates. He realised this must be the Ministry of Defence building. Now he was concerned. The military worked by different rules to the civilian police. What he could not figure out was why the military would be involved, unless one of his targets had been military and he had not known. As concerned as he was he decided that he would still employ the training he had received on interrogation, after all that was from the army. He would say nothing.

Sam followed the two men to a rather antiquated looking lift. It was the sort where the doors were manually pulled together. It shuddered and groaned its way to the third floor where the two men got out and marched down the corridor. Sam followed. They stopped at a door about half way down the corridor, waiting a few seconds for Sam to catch up and when he was with them they knocked sharply on the door.

"Come in".

The two men entered the room, again Sam followed. Both of the men stood to attention and saluted. "Mr Tucker Sir" said one of them. A man of about fifty came from behind a large mahogany desk and started to walk towards them. Sam had realised that these people were not ex military as he had first thought, but current military. He was trying to compute this in his mind. The man in the office was just over six feet tall, graying hair, and like his colleagues he wore a pin stripe suit, white shirt and regimental tie.

"Thank you gentlemen. Was there any trouble in getting him?" he said.

"None Sir" one of the men replied.

"Thank you very much, I'll call you if I need you".

The two men saluted, about turned smartly and left the room, closing the door quietly behind them. Sam took stock of the situation. The office was a large one. Apart from the large mahogany desk which backed on to the window, there was also another table to the side of the desk which had six chairs around. On the opposite side of the room to this meeting table were two settees facing each other with a large coffee table between them. This was a large, well furnished office so Sam knew that this guy was important. What he didn't know is why he was here and he felt decidedly uncomfortable about that.

"Good morning Mr Tucker, pleased to meet you at last" the man held out his hand and shook Sam's. "Won't you please take a seat" he said and indicated one of the settees. He then went back to his desk and picked up a buff coloured file. He brought it over, placing on the coffee table.

"My name is Brigadier Reece-Watkins . Can I offer you a drink, tea, coffee?"

"Coffee would be nice please" said Sam. The Brigadier went back to his desk, picked up his phone and asked for coffee for two. He then returned to where Sam was sitting and sat down opposite him.

"Well Mr Tucker, you've caused a bit of a ripple to some police forces in Europe we see".

Sam said nothing.

"Firstly lets get a few things clear, you are not under arrest here and you can leave at any time. Secondly I am not interested in anything that you have done or haven't done other than as a background for information. Thirdly we are going to get nowhere unless we have a two way conversation and yes, I know all about your army training and I know that you will have received training about interrogation, in fact I devised a good deal of it, but you may need to put some of your training and natural reaction aside for the purpose of this meeting".

Sam said nothing but he was trying to sum up the new situation. There was a knock at the door and the coffee arrived, on a tray, in a cafetiere together with two china cups, a matching jug of milk and a bowl of sugar lumps There was also a plate of biscuits. The Brigadier poured the coffee, passed a cup to Sam who helped himself to milk.

The Brigadier then sat back. "I don't know what you gleaned from our erstwhile police but here is a summary of the situation. During the course of the last two years a number of killings have taken place in various parts of the world. Many of the victims were involved in corruption and all were significant in their own fields. International agencies, civilian not military, became convinced that an organisation was behind a majority of these, what in effect were assassinations. All were carried out very professionally and all were well prepared and well executed. At the beginning of this year, targets were hit in Europe and as soon as it was suspected that the organisation was operating here, European police got involved. Initially it was a cooperation between the French and the German authorities but the Germans got a bit bored when their investigations got nowhere so left it to the French. The French involved Interpol who have excellent computer facilities for number crunching. They put a heap of information into their system and came out with a few dozen names, one of which was yours. They then found that on the dates when something occurred, not necessarily in France, but in Prague or Cologne, you happened to be in France. They became more convinced it was you when three men were shot at long distance, one bullet each, while running along a beach in Tangier. You were the only one of the suspects who could deal with that type of shot. Interpol, working through Special Branch, had requested your full service record, which of course we gave to them in the spirit of cooperation, having first removed a few sections.

This request flagged it up in my department so I had a look at your record and did a bit of digging into why you were under investigation. As I read your file I became more interested in you and dug deeper. It seemed that you may not have been treated exactly as you deserved while giving the army twenty years of your life. Normally I would have invited you for a chat before any police were involved but I only found out yesterday that Special Branch were about to act due to pressure from Interpol. That is why I had to pull you out from one of their stations rather than have a chat over lunch.

As far as the incidents under investigation are concerned it would appear that as usual the hits were very carefully planned and well executed and while they are convinced that you are involved they have no actual proof. For example they have scoured CCTV footage of days of activity at Nice Airport around the time of the Tangier incident. They have you coming in and going out but nothing in between. Its not my job to assist them but I don't believe that a skilled operator would go by plane, too much security. They would drive. They would hire a car, probably not from Nice where you were staying, but from somewhere nearby, maybe Cannes or Monaco but more likely Marseilles. I bet if they checked car rental offices near Marseilles station they would find that a car was hired to fit the dates in question, using a forged drivers licence and cloned credit card.".

Sam smiled inwardly, this guy was good, Sam respected that.

The Brigadier continued, "They think that you were involved a few days ago in Northern France, a shot of over five hundred yards. They are all jumping up and down because you made a mistake and left the gun behind, they now have evidence. Only problem is that there are no finger prints on the gun, the magazine or the bullets, no DNA traces that they can find so actually no evidence at all. Me, I don't think that leaving he gun was a mistake, it was just necessary. Its easy to slip away when all the focus is on the man who has been shot, much more difficult with a four foot long gun stuck under you arm".

For the first time Sam spoke. "As you say they have no evidence, so I have to ask sir, why am I here?"

"Indulge me by listening a bit longer, then maybe things will become more clear to you. When you came to my attention I read your file. I found it impressive to be honest with you. You were rather stupid in Iraq when you did what you did in front of a witness, the army had no option but to discipline you. I do however believe that it should have been handled differently and that your commanding officer should have taken charge rather than leave it to the regular station CO. I would think you were very annoyed at being imprisoned and demoted, maybe wanted to get our own back. You should have done it without witnesses and away from the camp like you did the first time.

Sam spoke up, "There is nothing about getting my own back. It wasn't the army, it was some chinless wonder, public school, never had shit on his hands, desk driving officer that did for me. He would have asked the rag head nice questions in a nice way and got nowhere. The army was my family for twenty years and they were probably the best years of my life, so don't run away with the idea that anything I may have done is a revenge trip". Sam was angry that it had been suggested.

The Brigadier smiled, "Just trying to get a reaction. Its nice to know that the army is held is high esteem and its we public school desk drivers that are the ones that are at fault. However, back to your records, it was the other skills of marksmanship, unarmed combat, the successful experience of going undercover in Ireland. For example did you know that your skill with the Barrett 90 put you in the top ten in the whole of the British army, and marksmanship with the Glock in the top thirty? It would tie in nicely with Tangier and Nancy if the police had that information. Don't worry, they don't, it was part of what we pulled from your file before we handed it over. Did you know that you had been considered for officer training on four occasions?"

"I knew of twice" said Sam, "didn't think I was up to it".

"The file says that you were not officer material due to not being a team player, you are a loner and have the propensity to take risks. It also says that you rely too much on your own initiative even if it means not following procedures. Your records however also state that you had the respect of all of those you served with and even generated some adulation in certain younger members of your platoons. You were an excellent marksman, excellent at unarmed combat, would have been decorated for the undercover work that you did in Ireland had it been possible to do so, could think strategically and act upon your judgment. It's all in here. More coffee?" The Brigadier poured himself another cup and as Sam had nodded he filled his cup too.

The Brigadier took a sip and then continued. "Once I had looked at your file I wanted to know more. Your visit to Russia in January this year, before the European killings started".

"I met a girl on holiday".

"Ah yes, the lovely Irina, who happens to be the ex mistress of one Yuri Dolchenko, ex KGB major and, if our sources are to be believed, suspected of running an agency offering to eliminate nasty people. I know, circumstantial, but very interesting you will agree. Quite a coincidence. Tell me Mr Tucker, do you believe in coincidences? I don't, not often anyway." Sam had to admit the Brigadier was very well informed.

"Don't worry Mr Tucker, the police don't have this information, its covered by national security issues. Now, again if our sources are correct, this little agency is closing down. Our ex KGB major is now back working for the Russian government as some sort of terrorist czar and has had to give up private enterprise. This could mean that you are unemployed. Is this the case?"

" I have my own company, we are security consultants, so I will earn a living". Sam felt that he had to put up some defence even if it was a bit weak.

"Ah yes, the security company, you did a bit of personal protection several months ago, a bouncer for a celebrity, and nothing since then. If there is more you had better not let the inland revenue know or they will be after you for back tax".

Sam was at a complete loss to know where this conversation was going. This man was very well informed, he had everything right, he had Sam's full service record and yet, what was he after, why was Sam here? "Well sir, you seem to have everything sorted and all the information but I still don't know why I am here".

"I want to offer you a job" said the Brigadier. Sam was stunned. He had never expected this. He couldn't think what to say. After a few seconds the Brigadier continued, "I run an operation from here inside the MOD. M15 and M16 are essentially civilian operations, we are military. Our objective is to target and deal with persons who are considered to be a danger to national security before they come to the UK and become a danger. We don't have a fancy name like MI5 or MI6, we are just department 3, we are on the third floor. We have no flashy identity cards, we are just soldiers, or from the Royal

Navy or Royal Air Force. Its not just killing people like you have been doing, sometimes the people stay alive. Its gathering information, usually working on your own, it often involves getting close to them, sometimes maybe even making them your friend. All information gathered comes to me and I decide, do they live or do they die. If they are to die you will have to dispatch them. We try and make it look like an accident but sometimes that is not possible. If we can't it must be done in a way that it does not come back to here, rather like you have been doing for this past year, allegedly".

Sam was sitting listening to his man in total silence, he was almost shocked. He was trying to think of something intelligent to say. "You said this is a military operation. Well I'm a civilian. As you know I have been for a year".

"Yes, you would have to rejoin the army".

"What rank, private or would you reinstate me as a sergeant?"

"Good god no man, nobody works for me who is under the rank of Major. You would have to be commissioned, although you have a chain and wouldn't have a desk, well you would have a desk here actually but you would hopefully not spend much time sitting at it. You would earn a Major's salary and that is all I'm afraid, somewhat less I would imagine than your recent income. All of the qualities, being a loner, working on your own, using your initiative, being able to judge a situation and change tack, all of the things that stopped you becoming an officer in the past are exactly what I need in this unit. That's apart from the fact that you are already a crack shot and can use a knife".

"How long to I have to think about it" asked Sam.

"Let's say a week" was the reply. "That takes us up to just before Christmas, there is a need for some training, that will mean up to three months in a camp somewhere, if I know in a week I can organize something for early January and have you operational by Easter". The Brigadier got up from the settee and walked to his desk. He reached in his drawer and brought out a business card. He gave it to Sam. "It has my direct phone number and e-mail address on. A yes or no in a week then?" He picked up the phone and told whoever was on the other end that Mr Tucker was just leaving. He walked him to the door and when he opened it one of the men who had brought Sam to the office was standing there.

Just as Sam was about to leave the Brigadier held out his hand, Sam took it and they shook hands. "One more thing of course, we are also offering you protection. As an officer in Her Majesty's Royal Army you will not be touched by the civilian police".

"And if I don't you will hand me back to them?" Sam asked the question.

"Good God no man. We don't hand anybody to anybody, but we would walk away from you as you will have walked away from us. Once we are no longer interested in you the police, or some other authority, would soon find out and they would just come back and arrest you".

Sam smiled and said "Thank you, I'll be in touch". Sam followed his escort along the corridor and into the lift. "What's the Brigadier like" he asked.

The escort looked at him, "He's a top man. He always looks out for his men". The lift arrived at the ground floor. Sam followed the man out of the lift and out of the door that they have entered through. A uniformed army sergeant stood outside. He saluted and stood to attention when the two men appeared.

"At ease sergeant. This is Mr Tucker. The Brigadier said for you to take him wherever he wants to go. Good bye Mr Tucker". The man turned towards Sam as he said it but did not extend his hand. He looked at Sam and then turned and walked back through the door into the building.

"This way sir" said the sergeant, as he led Sam towards an army plated Vauxhall Carlton. As Sam approached the sergeant held open the rear door.

"OK if I sit in the front?" said Sam.

"Fine by me if that's what you want. You're the boss". Sam went around to the passenger side and got in. As he put his seatbelt on the sergeant asked "Where to sir?"

"Head for Docklands and I'll tell you where when we get near".

# CHAPTER 30

Sam got out of the car in front of his apartment building. He walked through the main entrance door. "Good evening Mr Tucker. Is everything alright sir? said the security man. It was a different man to Chester but Sam was sure that he had been told the story of Sam being taken away by two policemen.

"Everything is fine thanks" said Sam as he headed for the lift. He turned the key in the door and walked into his flat. Irina came rushing into the hall and threw herself at him. "Shammy, Shammy I have been so worried. I have phoned Yuri and told him what happened and he has phoned me because you did not phone the lawyer and I have been so worried and I thought that they might come back and search the apartment and so I looked for something that should not be here but couldn't find anything and you have been gone all day and I didn't even know where you are and who those men were other than policemen and you did not even phone me and . . . . . . "

"Slow down, I'm here now. Get your coat, we are going out to dinner. I will tell you all that has happened while we eat, all I have had all day is a bacon sandwich and a couple of biscuits". Sam went to his desk and took out an unused mobile phone that was in the drawer, Irina went into the bedroom and was out in seconds with her coat. It had turned very cold in the last few days and although it was still early, not yet seven o'clock, it was below freezing. They walked to the station and took the train to Canning Town. As they travelled, Sam told Irina what had happened, how the police had wanted him for the work that he had done for Yuri and how the army had come along and taken him to the MOD and the offer that he had received..

"But that is good Shammy isn't it? Yuri is not working any more other than for the government to kill all terrorists. Working for your government must be good. Have you said yes?"

"Not yet. I've got a week to think about it". They walked from the train to the restaurant in silence. The owner welcomed Sam as a regular customer and at Sams request led them to a table tucked away in the corner. Without looking at the menu Sam ordered a bottle of Barolo and antipasti for both of them to start.

"You have gone quiet Sam, you are worried, tell me what about. Is it the job?"

"Its all sorts of things. Look Irina, this is not a conversation that I wanted to have now. I had planned to wait until you were here in living in England, but . . . . . . well look. I think that you must know that I love you".

"And I love you too Shammy".

"Look, please let me say what I want to say, it's hard enough without you saying anything. Well I love you and I want us to be married as soon as we can arrange it when you move to England next March or April". Irina beamed a huge smile and squeezed his hand. Tears started to form in her eyes, but she said nothing. Just then the waiter brought the wine. "Just pour it please" said Sam, "I'm sure its fine". The waiter poured the wine and left the table. "Bloody interruptions, anyway, I suppose what I am saying is will you marry me?"

"Of course I will Shammy, I love you more than you can ever know".

"What about me being in the army? I don't know the details of the job but it is possible, no it's certain, that I will have to go away on duty for maybe months at time."

"Shammy if that is job then that is what you have to do, I understand". The big smile came back on her face. "You will have to give me plenty of babies so that I don't miss you too much". The starter arrived.

They chatted over the rest of the meal and talked about maybe buying a house in the country, possibly in Essex, around the Chelmsford area Sam suggested. Irina said that she would Google Chelmsford on the computer. Sam had veal in a red wine sauce and Irina had pasta with a creamy sauce and crabmeat. The meal was delicious as usual.

They left the restaurant and started to walk to the main road to pick up a cab home. "Wait a bit" said Sam. "I need to tell Yuri what's happened".

"I had forgotten about Yuri with all of the things that are happening. You should phone him, he was worried for you."

Sam phoned Yuri's number on the new mobile phone. He answered immediately. Sam told him what had happened that day, how the police had detained him but obviously had no real evidence, just circumstantial, how he had not been allowed a phone call, how he had been taken to the Ministry of Defence and the offer that had been made.

"Are you going to accept?" asked Yuri when Sam had finished.

"I think so, yes"

"That is good. You and me Sam we are alike, we are old soldiers and will always be so. I am now a soldier again hunting bastard terrorists that threaten our country. You will be the same. You do have the same bastard terrorists but you have different ones, most of them Muslim brothers training in the same camps in Yemen and Libya and Pakistan. Who knows one day we may work jointly together, the British government and the Russian, hand in hand against the common foe. One thing I have to say to you Sam, I like you, you are my friend, so is Irina. You are always welcome in Russia but not if you are working against Russia. If you are working against Russia you are my enemy and Sam, no enemy that I have had is still alive. That is not a threat Sam, I respect you too much to threaten you, but it is a statement of fact".

"I will keep that in mind Yuri, but I hope that it won't come to that. As you say we have different enemies now, the cold war is long gone."

"Good luck my friend, and keep in touch. If I can help you let me know". Yuri hung up.

They found a cab and went back to the flat. Sam put his arm around Irina, "tomorrow we shall go to the West End and buy your Christmas present and an engagement ring". Irina moved tighter to him, squeezed his hand and kissed him on the cheek. They went up in the lift, entered the flat, held each other tightly as soon as the door closed behind them and kissed passionately. They found their way to the bedroom without letting go of each other, started to undress, fell into bed and made slow passionate love.

They lay exhausted holding each other. "Shammy, we are going to have a wonderful life. I love you so much and I am going to look after you and make you so happy".

"You make me so happy now Irina".

"But when we are married it will be even better. I will not have to think about going back to Russia and , you do want children don't you Shammy?"

"Of course, as long as they look like you and not me".

They chatted some more and Irina eventually fell asleep, laying on her side with her head in the crook of Sams arm. Sam lay on his back. Despite having been up for almost seventeen hours, Sams mind was racing. What a day. He had been arrested, interviewed by special branch, rescued by the army, offered a job, a commission in the army, and was getting married, all in less than twenty four hours. He thought back to his meeting with the Brigadier, he found that he not only respected him but he liked him as well, but most importantly, he trusted him. Sam considered himself a good judge of people, especially officers, he had come across some excellent ones and some who were useless. Sam had made his judgments soon after meeting them and felt that he had never been wrong in his initial opinions. He put the Brigadier into the excellent category. He tried to think of the disadvantages to accepting. Money was one, a major's salary was not brilliant, but he had money in the bank, albeit abroad, and anyway he had no income at the moment, he was unemployed. Then there was Irina, it would mean leaving her, possibly for long periods. She seemed OK with that, he would have to give her a load of kids as she had suggested. He smiled at the thought of it. If his sister could read his thoughts right now she wouldn't recognise him. He eventually fell asleep at about three o'clock.

Irina awoke just after seven, got out of bed and went to the kitchen and put on the coffee machine. Sam felt her get out of bed and followed a couple of minutes later. "There's a naked women standing in my kitchen" he said as he walked in..

"Would you like me to put some clothes on, maybe a big thick Russian dressing gown that we wear in the winter when we have no heat in the house, tight round our neck and all the way to the floor?"

"No the view is perfect the way it is thanks", they both smiled at each other. Sam thought again what a truly beautiful woman she was.

"I'm going to phone my sister" he said. "She will be up by now to get the kids to school. I want to shock her, tell her that I am getting married".

"You are close to your sister?" Irina asked.

"No, not close at all. I have been sort of invited there for Christmas though" Sam replied.

"Have we? I look forward to meeting your sister. What is her name?".

"Her name is Marion". Irina put some bread in the toaster, Sam went to the landline phone in his lounge.

"Hi it's Sam" he said as she answered her phone.

"What's the matter Sam? Its not yet seven thirty".

"Nothing's the matter. I just wanted to ask what you all wanted for Christmas. I'm going up West shopping today and if I see anything that you want, I could buy it".

"I don't know what we want Sam, I haven't asked anybody what they would like from you yet. It's a bit hectic here this time of the morning, getting the kids ready for school and everything. How about I ask them tonight and let you know. You don't need to go up West for what we want, you can get them in Romford market or anywhere else for that matter. Why are you going up West to shop anyway"?

Sam grinned, "I'm going with my fiancé to buy an engagement ring". There was a silence on the other end of the phone. Eventually Sam's sister spoke.

"Are you kidding me Sam Tucker? You, engaged? Has she met you? Does she actually know you? You must be the last person in the world I would think would get married; you are not husband material. How are you going to support a wife? Is she pregnant? Is she up the spout and that's why you are marrying her? When was it decided and has she agreed? Are you going to get a proper job?"

Sam was laughing now, Irina came in with coffee and toast for him just as his sister had finished the questions. "No she's not pregnant, yes she does know me, we have known each other for almost a year, I asked her to marry me last night and she agreed, and yes I do have a job, I'm going back into the army".

There was no response from Marion. "You still there? said Sam.

"Yes, I'm still here. I can't think of a time when I have been more shocked. Look Sam, I really would love to meet her. I'll have a chat

123

with the kids and the old man tonight and phone you tomorrow. I'll let you know what we would like for Christmas and we can talk and make arrangements for you to both come over for Christmas dinner. I assume that she can come, she doesn't have a husband and kids somewhere else or anything?"

"She would love to accept your invitation for Christmas dinner, we both would." Irina was smiling at him. "I have an idea for Christmas, get your old man to phone me this evening once you've told him about this phone call".

They said their good byes and hung up. Sam took a sip of coffee, it was still very hot. Irina came close to him; put her arms around his neck. Pulled him towards her and kissed him. They were both still naked and he could feel himself getting hard again.

"It wants to play" said Irina as she pulled away from him, " and my fanny wants him inside it". She pulled him down on to the settee and guided him into her.

Afterwards they showered, dressed and went to Regents Street, to Mappin and Webb to buy the engagement ring. It was a diamond solitaire set in platinum. It didn't have a price tag on it but Sam knew enough to know that it would be several thousand pounds. Irina was concerned about the price and wanted to know how much it was but neither Sam nor the jeweller would tell her. She loved the ring and it was exactly her size. Out of Irina's earshot the jeweller informed Sam that the cost was eight thousand five hundred pounds. This was a bit more than Sam had thought but if it was what Irina wanted that was fine by him. He had a Visa card with a credit limit of ten thousand pounds and nothing outstanding on it so passed it to the man. Once the transaction was cleared they left the shop with Irina clinging very tightly to Sam's arm. They caught a cab to Harrods and had coffee and a cake in the circle coffee shop. They then purchased a set of new clothes for Irina, from underwear, shoes, dress, coat, some accessories, for her Christmas present from Sam but also for her to wear at her wedding. "We haven't discussed dates" said Sam as they were walking round choosing the clothes.

"I don't want to wait, do you? said Irina. "I think we should not live together long before you make an honest woman of me".

"Fine by me" said Sam, "if you are coming over in April to stay, then how about we get married in May, it will just about be cold enough that you can still wear these clothes. If it gets to June you will need a different wardrobe."

"I accept" said Irina as she pulled him close and kissed him again.

They left Harrods and because they had so many bags they caught a cab to take them home to the apartment. While in the cab Sam phoned the Brigadier, he answered immediately, "Reece-Watkins".

"Sam Tucker here sir".

"Ah Mr Tucker. I didn't expect to hear from you so soon. Have you made a decision or do you have questions?"

"I have many questions sir but that doesn't alter my decision. There are a few things that I would like clarified but in principle I would like to accept your offer".

"That's grand Mr Tucker, I'm delighted. I would have been surprised if you hadn't had a few issues so lets discuss them. Lets say tomorrow, Ebury Wine Bar, Ebury Street, not far from Victoria Station, passable claret and excellent steaks, shall we say twelve thirty?"

Sam agreed and they hung up. They rode the rest of the way home in silence apart from stopping off at a service station in the Commercial Road at Aldgate which sold Marks and Spencer food where they brought a meal deal for two.

While Sam and Irina were heading back to the apartment, the Brigadier put some plans into action. He summoned his two main 'facilitators', the two men who had collected Sam from the police station. "Major Tucker is going to join our unit" he told them. "He has a Russian girlfriend who I don't think is a problem but I want to make sure. I want a tap on his phone line, I want his e-mails monitored and I want his mobile phone tracked too".

"Yes sir. Is there anything else that we should know about this woman?"

"I don't think so. She is living in Moscow, she had a relationship with an ex KGB officer and is working for him now. Tucker is intending to bring her to London and marry her. Our investigations show that its all above board and it's really a love match. But we have to be sure that it's not a plant; she is not a sleeper; just a precaution".

The two men left the room to carry out the Brigadier's instructions.

# CHAPTER 31

Sam got up and showered the next morning feeling almost exited about the prospect of lunch with the Brigadier. It was the same sort of feeling that he had had when he was about to go out on a mission. He cooked some breakfast for Irina and while they were eating Sam told Irina how to travel by DLR to Beckton and where the Asda supermarket was. He gave her some money, she was to buy some food to last them through the Christmas period but bearing in mind that they were spending Christmas day with Sam's sisters' family.. He told her to get a cab back to the flat as she would have a lot of bags and would have a problem carrying them on the train. He told her about a courtesy phone that was just inside the shop that was a direct line through to a local cab company. Irina had never traveled anywhere outside Russia on her own and Sam was a bit concerned for her. He was satisfied that she understood well enough but noticed that she kept on looking at her engagement ring while he was talking.

Sam showered and put on his best suit, in fact his only suit, but it was a Hugo Boss suit and he thought that it looked expensive. He added a plain blue shirt and one of his three ties, all of them fairly sober. He finished dressing by adding a pair of black-lace up shoes. He looked in the mirror and was satisfied that he at least looked something like an officer. At ten thirty it was time for Sam to leave. He would be very early at Victoria but he wanted to allow for any delays. He did not think that the Brigadier would like to be kept waiting.

He arrived at Victoria with an hour to spare, located the Ebury Wine Bar and then walked back towards the station and went into a Burger King for a coffee. While he had lain awake the night before, thinking, he had thought over a few things that he wanted to clear with the Brigadier before finally signing on the dotted line so to speak.

At twelve twenty eight Sam entered the restaurant. "Yes Sir?" he was greeted by a waitress.

"I am meeting someone here, Brigadier Reece-Watkins", before he could say anything else the waitress said "of course sir. The Brigadier hasn't arrived yet but I will show you to his table". She turned and led the way to a table for two tucked away in a corner. Sam followed.

Two minutes later at exactly twelve thirty the Brigadier entered and walked straight to the table. Sam stood as he approached and they shook hands. "Mr Tucker, I'm pleased to see you again so soon" he said as he sat down. The waitress appeared by his shoulder immediately with a menu which she put in front of Sam. "I'll have my usual please Julie and two glasses" said the Brigadier. "I can recommend the steak, sirloin, medium rare, with fresh vegetables".

"I'll go with that" said Sam to the waitress, "but the steak medium please". . She left the table.

"So, you have decided to join us. I'm very pleased. I am afraid with everything these days there is a form I will need you to sign but before I ask you to do so I would like to tell you a bit more about our little group. You should know exactly what you are signing up to. I head the operation and I have two Lieutenants, well actually they are Colonels but they share the job of being both my second in command and right hand men. Then we have the foot soldiers as I call them. Most of the these are Majors although there are three Lieutenant – Colonels. We presently have seventeen Majors in the squad, you will make eighteen. We are a secret organisation, I am subordinate to the Joint Chiefs of Staff but I report directly to the Secretary of State for the Armed Forces. It is important to say at this point that we still have to stay completely within the law. Nobody is executed without me authorising it first unless it is a case of self defence. Most of the time the operatives work on their own although sometimes it is necessary to team two or three up together. Sometimes too an operative may go on secondment to another unit, we have been known to work with the military police on occasions. It is not just a job of killing people either. We investigate, sometimes by going under cover, we analyse, and then we report. In some ways it is rather like the mission that you carried out in Ireland in the eighties, you were under cover for almost six months and fed back a lot of very useful information but in all of that time you only killed three people. The difference is that we do not usually investigate situations, we leave that to SIS and M16 and the like, we investigate people, people who may be security risks. Any questions so far?"

"No, it seems straightforward. I obey your orders and report back to you and you decide what I am going to do and I do it. Just like the regular army really" said Sam, said with a smile on his face to lessen the cynicism.

"Just so" replied the Brigadier. "Now let's talk about you. Despite your experience you will need to be completely retrained and assessed. We have a couple of places where this can be carried out. This morning I have booked you into one of our locations in Norfolk. You will be collected from Thetford Station on Wednesday 6th January from a train which arrives from London at ten eighteen. You will then be taken to the training camp where you will remain for probably about ten weeks. The actual time in training will depend upon the amount of training you need, obviously. If, at the end of that period you are considered to be up to scratch then you will be considered fit for operations. You will then be assigned to an operation if there is an appropriate one for you. The training consists of ensuring that you are at the peak of physical fitness, unarmed combat, weapons training; that includes knives, swords, chains and other such items as well as various guns and rockets. The training also includes other practical issues such as survival techniques, parachuting, speed driving, communications and even making a poison capable of killing a man from natural extracts. Any questions so far?"

"You say that I will be assigned an operation if one is available, what if there is no operation for me at the time?"

"Then you will be held in reserve. At such times you will be expected to report to the company gym at least twice a week to ensure physical fitness, from time to time there will be periods of retraining, this especially applies if a new weapon becomes available. Also you will be issued with a mobile phone which you must carry on your person at all times in case you are needed, but apart from that, your life is your own to do with what you wish. However if you are travelling more than two hour travelling time from HQ you must inform our admin people prior to travel. Any Questions?"

"No questions but I have three conditions".

"No conditions" the Brigadier quickly replied. "I cannot accept any officer making conditions at any time. You can make requests and I will deal with them as best I can if I feel that they are appropriate, but I cannot accept conditions. You should realise that after twenty years service".

Sam though for a second or two. Of course he was right, you couldn't have someone operating with individual pre-conditions. "Yes sir, of course you are correct. Requests then, first I wish to get married next year. She is Russian and she travels here on a tourist visa. I want to know that there will be no problems with me marrying her, her living here, and I want a UK passport for her". The Brigadier gave a short laugh. "What is that sir, don't you approve of your operatives being married?"

"Quite the contrary, I do approve. I find that the married ones are more grounded, less likely to take unnecessary risks, even more responsible. I appologise if I offended you by my reaction. I am assuming that the bride to be is the woman Irina?"

"Yes" replied Sam.

The Brigadier continued, "when we reviewed your file my two able lieutenants said that she was a cover for your clandestine activities. I said that it was more serious than that. I deduced that you would not have spent so much time with her, such as the Paris trip when you were first observed and did nothing that a tourist would not do, if you had not had more than a business relationship. I smiled because firstly I like being right and secondly because they both now owe me a gin and tonic. Anyway to the business end of your request, there is no problem. I can arrange for her visa to be upgraded to a resident's visa now and as soon as you are married I will speed through the application for dual citizenship. From the time I have the marriage licence in my hand to the passport being issued should be, let me think, let's say about four hours. Quick enough?" He was smiling again. He obviously enjoyed the power he had.

"That will be fine. Thank you" said Sam.

"Next request? You said there were three".

"I have quiet a lot of money in a bank account in a not so friendly Arab country. I need for it to be brought into the UK and deposited with a bank here no questions asked, no investigation of its origins by plod and no involvement of the tax man".

"Getting the money in is no problem. We have an arrangement with a central London branch of Lloyds Bank. We have an account there that we deposit money in case we need some quickly and don't want to explain why. They are totally secure. You would set up an account there and the source and origin of the funds would remain confidential. However I cannot control or influence customs and excise. They are a law unto themselves and very powerful. I am afraid that you would have to take your chances with them. My suggestion to you, with your Moscow connections, is to have the funds disguised as a Russian lottery win. As I understand it lottery winnings are tax free." Sam was once again impressed with this man's speed of thought. "And the third request?"

"No operations in Russia".

The Brigadier interrupted him before he could continue any further and explain why. "Out of the question. All of my operatives must be free to be in the theatre anywhere in the world. I cannot accept that if you are the best person to carry out an operation that I don't send you because your wife is Russian or because you know an ex KGB security officer. If that is something that your decision is dependant upon then lets us just shake hands now and go on our separate ways". He sat back and looked at Sam.

"Of course you are right again sir. I withdraw that request".

The Brigadier smiled. They had both now finished their steaks and the Brigadier had drunk most of the bottle of wine that had accompanied it. Despite that he appeared to Sam to absolutely sober and completely on the case. "Can I take it then that you wish to join us?"

"Yes please" said Sam

"Good. Then let's get on with the form filling". The Brigadier pushed his plate aside and pulled some pages from his pocket. "Sign here. You've already done the official bit twenty years ago so I'm not going all through it again but in essence to agree to serve the queen and her successors, obey the official secrets act, respect the chain of command etc etc". He pushed the forms towards Sam and offered him a pen. Sam took it and signed the form.

"Now, tedious I know but you need to complete this form with your clothes sizes. This is obviously for the issue of your uniform which will be ready for you in your quarters when you are registered in January. By the way as an officer you will be expected to be in smart civies when you report for duty in Norfolk, shirt and tie and all that, not jeans and trainers. What you are wearing today would be fine.

Need to maintain standards you know". Sam completed this form too and passed it to the Brigadier.

"That concludes our business for now. I will see you next probably late March" The Brigadier got up from the table. Sam did likewise. The two men walked towards the door. "Goodbye my dear" the Brigadier said to the waitress who was behind the counter.

"Goodbye Brigadier, see you again soon" she said and then looking at Sam she said "Goodbye sir, hope that we shall see you again too". Sam said goodbye and followed the Brigadier from the bar.

"Goodbye Major" the Brigadier said as he saluted. Sam returned the salute. "Good luck with the training. One thing, tell me if you don't mind now that you have the protection of her majesty, the shooting in Nancy, was that you?" Sam smiled and nodded. "And the three men on the beach in Tangier?"

"Yes sir that was me too, and you were right sir, it was a hired car from Marseilles with a forged driver's licence".

"I think that we are going to get along just fine you and me, great minds and all that. I'll say one thing, I don't think that you will need much sharpening up at marksmanship on your training session".

They parted company and Sam walked back towards the station. It struck him that he was now an officer in the army after years of them being the posh twits, well most of them. He vowed he would never be like that.

That evening his brother-in-law Mick phoned Sam. He said that the boys would like West Ham kits for Christmas although he added that the complete kit was a bit expensive. Sam agreed to take them to the Upton Park shop between Christmas and the New Year and kit them out. As his sister and her husband didn't know what they wanted and Sam knew that they were not that well off, Sam managed to get Mick to agree to him funding the whole of the Christmas expense. He did not want to embarrass Mick or his sister, and it took a bit of persuading, but eventually they settled of Sam giving them five hundred pounds. Sam knew that it was a small amount to him but a lot to them.

# CHAPTER 32

Sam had booked a cab for Christmas morning to take him and Irina to Dagenham to his sister's house. They arrived just before midday. Both his sister Marion and her husband were obviously very interested in who he was bringing, his new fiancé. Sam noticed Mick's look when he met Irina. It reminded him of how he felt when he first saw her over a year ago now. She was wearing a new dress that Sam had bought her for Christmas and Sam knew that she looked gorgeous. Mick took their coats and as he did so Sam discreetly slipped five hundred pounds in twenty pound notes into his pocket. He nodded his thanks and asked them both what they would like to drink. While he was preparing the drinks the boys started to talk to Irina asking her where she was from and when she was going to marry their uncle. Marion maneuvered Sam into the kitchen.

"Where did you find her? Is she one of these mail order brides or something? She's gorgeous, just like a model. You can't have just pulled her."

Sam smiled, "She's not a mail order bride, I met her on holiday last December in Egypt. We arranged to meet again and I went to Moscow in January and we have seen each other on and off since then. We have been able to keep in touch through e-mail and when she is able, which I hope will be end of March or early April she will come back to the UK and we will get married".

"Blimey, my big brother settling down at last. And what's all this about going back into the army?" Just then Mick came in with a beer for Sam.

"Yeah, how's that then? I thought they'd drummed you out".

"It's a bit of a long story but I was asked to go back into a special service unit, mostly admin and training I'm sure, but the offer was made and it was a very good so I accepted".

"Are they going to give you back your stripes?" asked his sister, "or have you got to start again at the bottom at your age?"

"Better than that, I've been commissioned, I'm going to be one of the poncy nose in the air gits". His sister looked at him opened mouthed.

Christmas dinner was traditional roast turkey, roast potatoes, roast parsnips, carrots and brussel sprouts. Sam really enjoyed it and it seemed Irina did too. He boys wanted to know if Sam was going back into the army to kill people and he told them that he would spend most of his time behind a desk in an office in London. Dessert was Christmas pudding, mince pies, brandy butter and ice cream.

After lunch Sam and Irina sat in the lounge talking to the boys while Mick and Marion cleared away the lunch table. They arranged to visit West Ham's shop the following day. Although it was boxing day the boys assured him that the shop would be open. When they had finished clearing the table, Mick and Marion joined them. The television was on but nobody was really watching it. They were talking about the army, what was Russia like, where were they going to live when they got married, did they want children, (Sam said no and Irina said six). It was very pleasant and very casual and Sam was surprised how relaxed he felt and how relaxed his sister and her family seemed bearing in mind that he had had very little to do with them for over twenty years. He sat and listened to them all chatting and decided that it may have something to do with the fact that they had nobody else, Mick's father had died when he was young and he was an only child brought up by his mother who was now dead. Marion and Sam's parents were dead and Irina had been disowned by her parents. They were in fact the only people that each of them had. Sam put his head back, closed his eyes and began to doze. He felt more content at this moment than he had felt for as long as he could remember, possibly for years.

# CHAPTER 33

Just at the time when Sam was closing his eyes, Yuri Dolchenko was lying flat on his stomach on a wet, muddy piece of ground, on the border of a copse on the outskirts of a small village in the Northern Caucuses of Russia. The village was fairly isolated, being about sixty kilometers from the nearest town and containing no more than twenty five houses. It was a rural, farming community. The village also had a small school with a mosque located next to it. The school and mosque were in the centre of the village, by a rudimentary village square, and the houses were built in blocks surrounding the square. The time difference between Russia and London meant that Yuri was already watching for his quarry in the darkness of early evening in temperatures of below zero. He was with thirty specially selected members of a Russian Army special service unit, ten of whom were with Yuri lying flat on the edge of the copse. The other twenty in two groups of ten, were concealed on the other side of the village watching the few houses that were there. Each of the other two groups were led by a sergeant and each of the three groups had a corporal as a radio communications officer so that the groups could talk to each other. At the moment though there was radio silence. Each group knew their function. The purpose of the other two groups was to encircle the village once they saw Yuri's group move forward into the village.

Yuri's new office was in the Lubyanka, the building that had housed the KGB in Soviet times and was now the home to the FSB, the Federal Security Service, the Russian equivalent of the American FBI. Yuri's unit had been allocated offices on the fourth floor. They were spacious, a large main area, freshly painted magnolia walls and white woodwork and doors. The desks were old army issue. There were two separate offices at one end, one was for Yuri and the other would be a meeting room in case privacy was needed.

The FSB and the FBI publicly state that they only work within their country's borders. Yuri's group was officially part of the FSB but in practice would operate anywhere in the world if it was necessary to fulfill their brief, which was to identify and then eradicate terrorists and terrorist activities that threatened Russia or Russians.

A little over a month before, in November, there had been a terrorist attack on a train travelling between Moscow and St. Petersburg. Many passengers on the train had died as it had left the rails and crashed. The full story and the investigation that followed had not been given to the media even within Russia. The government realised that with modern communications they couldn't keep the event a secret but they kept as much as possible within their own security system. They had strong evidence that the plans and the attack had been carried out by a dissident Chechen group, some of whom had died on the train in the crash. As fundamentalist Muslims they were prepared to sacrifice themselves for their cause.

During the investigation it had been discovered that the same group as had planned the train attack were planning a suicide bombing in the centre of Moscow on New Year's day, a main holiday for Russians. The FSB had identified some members of the group and had found out that one of the group had a father in a labour camp in Siberia. Yuri had arranged a visiting pass for the man's wife, sister and his two daughters. They had eagerly accepted as they hadn't seen the man for three years and visiting passes were difficult to get. Once they were in the hostel that was near the camp, word was passed to the group member that if he wanted to see his family again he would need to pass information to the contact. He reluctantly agreed and this information he gave was passed to Yuri.

The reason for the stakeout was due to this informant. He had said that a small group of no more than four men were making their way slowly to Moscow. In this village they would collect the explosives that would be waiting for them and receive instructions on how to place it safely into containers that could be concealed about their person and how to detonate the explosive at the correct time to cause maximum damage and casualties.

It was another three hours before Yuri saw the movement. Four men in dark clothing entered the village from the woods about four hundred meters to Yuri's right. Yuri's group had seen them too and all of them lay absolutely still and silent. The four men cautiously approached one of the houses, knocked on the doors and quickly entered as soon as the door was opened. The light inside the house had been extinguished before the door had been opened and soon after the men entered, there was light from inside again.

Yuri waited for another hour in the hope that when his group entered the house the men would be relaxed and there would be no resistance. When he felt that time was right he moved forward. He and five of his men burst in through the front door, the other five went to the back of the house and entered through a rear door. There was the sound of a gunshot from the rear of the house and shortly afterwards the group of Yuri's men entered the living area, pushing before them a man of about twenty years of age who had been shot in the shoulder. His gun, which was being held by the sergeant, was thrown on the floor. Yuri's group had covered six men including the four visitors, who were sitting at a table eating what looked like a vegetable stew.

Yuri nodded to the sergeant and without receiving any further instruction he and three of his men went and searched the house. It wasn't very large and they returned after only a few seconds pushing before them two women, one very elderly, and two teenage girls. In the background there was gunshot elsewhere in the village. The radio operator spoke to his colleagues with the other two groups. They confirmed that they had shot two men that had been trying to escape the village and that the village was now secure. Yuri instructed the six men and four females to follow him out of the house. He led them out and told them to stand in the school playground. One of the other groups of ten started to enter all of the houses one by one and instructed all of the residents to congregate in the school playground. The third group of ten was still on the outskirts of the village, unknown to the villagers.

All of the villagers were assembled in the centre within ten minutes of the group entering the houses. Yuri's men then started a search of the houses. While this was carried out, Yuri just stood and waited, he had ten machine guns pointing at the villagers. The search took almost and hour during which time the villagers started to become restless and complained about the cold. When the search was complete the soldiers had located several small arms, a number of machine pistols, some Kalasnikov rifles but more to the point, a quantity of semtex explosive with detonators, and a rocket firer with three rockets. They were all placed on the ground at the feet of Yuri. He spoke for the first time. "Who are the owners of these rockets and explosive?" Nobody spoke for several seconds. Then all of a sudden a village elder moved forward towards Yuri, swearing at him and his Russian bastard soldiers. As he approached Yuri, Yuri drew a pistol from his holder, pointed it at the man and fired from close range into his face. The elder fell to the ground and died instantly. This caused the crowd to become agitated. They were now surrounded by twenty of Yuri's men. Yuri shouted a command, "open fire". His soldiers aimed their machine guns at the crowd and pulled their triggers. When all of the villagers had fallen, Yuri's men then went from person to person to check that they were dead. Those that were only injured received some bullets to the head. Once they were satisfied that the entire population had been executed the soldiers then set about burning all of the houses, the school and the mosque. It would be some time before the situation was discovered and although the Russians would be suspected and even accused by the Chechnian's, there would be no witnesses and no proof. Job done, Yuri's men then started the six kilometer walk to their vehicles that had taken them there.

# CHAPTER 34

At midday on Boxing Day Mick and the two boys drove to pick Sam up from his flat. To his surprise and pleasure, Irina wanted to join the group on their trip to West Ham to buy the boys' Christmas presents. They all fitted into Mick's ageing Mondeo estate. He was a carpet fitter and used the car to carry carpets for his work. Sam sat in the front while Irina sat in he back with boys. They seemed to have really taken to her and her to them.

They were so exited when they entered the shop, a veritable Aladdin's cave to the supporter. Sam bought both of the boys a claret and blue shirt and had their names and a number nine printed on the back. He also bought them socks and shorts, some West Ham trainers and a track suit each. Sam had never understood the attraction of football and the fervor that it created among its fans. He was surprised then when Mick started to get enthusiastic about what the boys were getting. Sam discovered that he was a big fan too. Sam slipped a warm, winter, waterproof jacket off a hanger, in a size he thought would be Mick's. One of the boys told Sam that that was what Zola wore in the dugout. Sam feigned enthusiasm but he did not know what they were talking about or what a Zola was. Mick resisted Sam buying it for him but Sam insisted and eventually Mick gave in. To make sure that his sister didn't feel left out he decided he should buy something for her too. The only thing he could see was a tea towel, so he bought that. Shopping finished, they went back to his sister's house for a lunch of cold turkey, ham and mashed potatoes. Sam was surprised again at how well Irina seemed to fit in and how much everybody, not only the boys, but Marion too, liked her.

They left Dagenham in the early evening promising not to leave it too long before visiting again, and took a cab to London City Airport. Sam had arranged to hire a car for two days so they went to the Avis desk and collected the documentation and the keys for a Ford Focus.

The following day they went for a drive. They drove around Epping, Loughton, Chigwell, Theydon Bois and the villages in between. They looked at the various areas and chatted about the sort of house and area in which they wanted to live. The day after they went further away from London, to Chelmsford, Writtle, Witham and back via Shenfield and Brentwood. After dropping the car back at the airport they had dinner at a Chinese Restaurant in Limehouse and discussed their two day tour of Essex. Irina liked the Epping and Chigwell areas the most and this suited Sam as he would have to be within easy travel distance of the Whitehall office and both areas had a station on the Central Line into London.

The next few days seemed to fly by. It was soon New Year's Eve and they celebrated by having dinner at Sam's favourite Italian restaurant in Canning Town. They discussed their future and how much they both wished that Irina was not going to back to Russia for three months.

"It is not too much problem Shammy, after all you are going away to training so I would be on my own with my man in the army. Time will soon pass by and we will be together". Irina smiled when she finished talking and just looking at her made Sam smile too.

"Irina, I've been thinking about something for a while now and I feel I have to ask you. What about your parents?"

"My parents have disowned me, I have not heard from them since I left. They think I am whore, bring disgrace". Her face clouded up as she spoke.

"That's part of what I mean. You are not a whore, you are going to be married and we are going to be faithful to each other for ever. Do you not think that you should invite them to the wedding? Don't you think that your father may like to give you away, be part of the wedding? How about in years to come when we have children, won't you want to tell them about your roots? Don't you at least want to give them the chance to make things up to you?"

Irina sat silent for a while. Eventually she replied, "I always assumed that if I needed somebody Yuri would stand in as my father. You are right I would like them to come and I would like to make things better but I don't know, how do I do that and how would they afford to come to England?"

139

Richard Pennell

"Firstly money is not a problem, I buy the flight tickets and they just come, secondly just write them a letter. Tell them that you are getting married sometime in the middle of next year and would they like to come. Tell them that you are to marry an Englishman and will be getting married and will live in England. You could them tell them how wonderful I am, handsome, rich, funny, clever . . . ."

Irina started to laugh. "I will write as soon as I get back to Moscow, oh Shammy, you are so clever, so wonderful", she reached across the table, took his hand and kissed it.

They celebrated the New Year in the restaurant with everybody singing Auld Lang's Sine and toasting 2010. They left the restaurant just before one o'clock and as they could not find a cab they walked home. It was very cold and Sam complained how cold he was. Irina laughed at him. She reminded him that she was used to Russian winters and in her town it had sometimes dropped to minus thirty.

"You can warm me up when we get home them if you are not cold" was all that Sam could think to say.

"I will enjoy that" she said as she held on to his arm more tightly.

When they got back to the flat Irina did indeed warm them both up as they made love slowly and passionately. "That's the best start to any year I have ever had" said Sam as they lay together exhausted and sweaty. "Do you know my love, I have got a really good feeling about this year. Us being together forever, me being back in the army and an officer, us having a real home together with neighbours and enjoying doing things together. I just think that we are going to be so happy".

"Me too Shammy, I love you so very much. I just want us to be together for always". She cuddled up to him and soon her even, steady breathing let Sam know that she had fallen asleep.

# CHAPTER 35

On the last day of December, Yuri was at his desk in the Lubyanka Building. There was nobody else in the offices, tomorrow was a holiday in Russia so most of the people in Moscow had left early for the New Year celebrations. Yuri would be leaving soon to spend the evening with his new mistress. The only equipment that they had were the old desks, one for him and one for Irina and one spare, and a Dell laptop that Yuri was using as he sat there thinking about the future. He was thinking of Irina and how much he needed her to return. When he set the section up he persuaded his bosses that it should be staffed with civilians and not military personnel. He wanted trained secretaries, administrators and computer operators. He wanted the right equipment not some cast off from a military post that didn't need it anymore. It was a measure of how important Mr Putin himself considered the department that Yuri got everything he asked for. Irina had proved in a very short time how good she was at organising. She had ordered new furniture, five new Dell laptop computers complete with docking stations and compatible Hewlett Packard printers. She had anticipated that they would need a large storage base which could process information very quickly. She did some research and found that the biggest storage facility was Google's and that they used a system manufactured by an American company called Rackable. There were still some restrictions on American computer technology being exported to Russia but she had found a way around any problems and the new equipment was due to be delivered at the end of January and be operational by mid-March.

The recruitment of the staff needed would start as soon as Irina returned from England and then he could start doing his job properly. In the meantime he was coping. He was reading reports which had started to arrive about the incident on Christmas Day. As he expected the dissidents had blamed the Russian army but nobody in the West gave them any real exposure. The only thing he noted was the call from certain groups to exact revenge for the so called innocent women and children that had been murdered. He would be pleased when the new systems were in place and all of this information could be stored, accessed and analysed. There was a load of information coming into his department which needed to be stored, details of a car bombing a couple of months before which killed a number of civilians was an example. Some news of it had leaked out but not much detail so the story had soon died. Yuri sometimes wondered whether this old Soviet habit of secrecy, not letting people know what was going on, was counter productive. The Americans and the Europeans exchanged information. So did other countries, Australia and Japan, even Pakistan was cooperating with the West. If Russia gave them some information then maybe the Europeans or even maybe the Americans would share intelligence that might be useful. He would bring it up at the next joint staff meeting which Putin always chaired and try and gauge his reaction.

His mind again wandered to Irina. He wished that she were there to deal with these reports and get them into some sort of system now. Fleetingly he thought that maybe he should have married her to keep her in Moscow. The idea soon disappeared. Nobody like Irina would put up with his need for new and different sexual partners. His current mistress was an ex international gymnast who had had to give up the sport because of the development of her now oversized breasts. She had taken him to levels of sexual ecstasy that he had never experienced before but even with her, he knew that soon he would get bored with her and be on the lookout for something new. He was already thinking that she was too skinny. No, Irina would not have accepted that and anyway, he thought Sam was a good man and would look after her. He also liked Sam, which helped.

He finished reading the e-mailed reports, filed them for later and then turned his computer off and left the office to go home and prepare for the evening.

In a house in a small town in Chechnya, there were no plans to celebrate the New Year. Instead there was a meeting of a war council of a group with links to al-Qaeda and the Taleban that had fought the Russians for so long in Afghanistan. Usually such meetings only included men but attending this one were four widows, the wives of the four men who had entered the village and been shot by Yuri's men almost a week earlier. The group wanted revenge for the villagers, the wives for their husbands. Two of the wives offered themselves as suicide bombers to hit a major target. They suggested that the authorities do not usually consider women a terrorist risk so they should be able to place large quantities of explosives beneath their burkahs and travel completely undetected. The council promised to consider the idea seriously.

# CHAPTER 36

Sam and Irina held each other and kissed passionately. Irina had just checked in her luggage for her British Airways flight to Moscow. It was 4th January and she had to return as she was back at work on the fifth, tomorrow. Neither of them knew what to say. They seemed to have said it all in the taxi traveling to the airport. Parting seemed to get more painful each time but the compensation this time is that it would be the last. Next time they met it would be in London in March and it would be permanent. Eventually they parted and Sam waved as Irina went through the departure gate and he lost sight of her. Sam made his way to the underground station to take the train back to his apartment. He felt an emptiness now that Irina had gone, knowing that he wouldn't see her for three months. He boarded the train and tried to focus on the things he needed to do during the week. He had received an e-mail from the Brigadier confirming that he was to report for duty at a camp in Norfolk on Monday 11th March and that he would be collected from Thetford station from the train that would arrive at 10.18. The mail informed him that a travel warrant was in the mail to him and that had arrived the following morning. He was also given details of the Lloyds Bank branch at which the department had an account and the name of the manager, Mr Clore. He had contacted Mr Clore who had been expecting his call and had been briefed on what was required. He foresaw no problem but would need to see Sam with some proof of identity such as a passport and details of the bank and account where the money was currently being held. Sam made an appointment to see him on 7th January.

Irina sent a text to Sam to say that she had landed safely and arrived back in her apartment.

The week passed slowly for Sam even though he had a lot to do. On Wednesday the snow came. It was the heaviest snow that Britain had experienced in over thirty years. The most important thing was that Sam managed to transfer his money. He was impressed with the efficiency of Mr Clore and the fact that he didn't ask any questions. He told Sam that it would take about seven days to complete the transfer. Sam had well over two million pounds in his offshore account. He had told Irina that she could spend one million on their new house, that still left over one million in cash and whatever he would get when he sold the flat. He arranged for Mr Clore to invest the money once it had arrived although the return on capital was not very good in the present conditions. Sam didn't know what a Major's annual salary was but Sam's living expenses were not a lot, Sam lived cheap. Maybe it would cost him more when he had a wife.

Irina phoned Sam on 6th January, and e-mailed him on 7th or 8th. She told him that she was busy talking to recruitment companies looking for staff for Yuri's new office. She had seen Yuri only briefly when she had first gone back to work after the New Year, he had been in meetings all the time. She also told Sam that lots of information was being sent to the office about terrorist attacks in Russia and investigations that had been carried out by of the various agencies that had been dealing with terrorism before Yuri's department had been set up. All of this needed to be inputted onto a computer. She told Sam that she was waiting for the computers, at the moment they only had one and that one Yuri usually carried with him.

They spoke again on the Saturday night. This time there was no business talk, just how much they loved each other and plans for their future together. Sam told Irina that once he went into the training camp he may not be very contactable. When new cadets start initial training, for the first six weeks they are isolated, no phone calls, no visits. Sam thought that is was possible that he may be subjected to similar restrictions. They talked about the snow in London and Irina laughed at him and reminded him about how much snow there was in Moscow at this time of year.

On Sunday Sam packed. He knew that he would be kitted out with full army kit so he thought it would be sufficient to take three changes of civilian clothes. He also packed his passport and laptop. On Sunday evening he went to the gym on the apartment block and emptied the locker of his neighbour that he used for his clandestine items. He still had two false passports and driving licences and the Baretta that he took from Yuri's man in Ireland. He took them to his flat and hid them. It was difficult as his rooms had no floorboards or loft. He placed the documents behind a live double socket plug outlet. The gun he placed inside of a box of corn flakes. He opened the box very carefully and sealed it up just as carefully, so that unless there was a very detailed inspection by an expert the box would look unopened. In the evening he poured himself a glass of wine and sat and looked out of the window across the river. It was snowing again. Transport had been disrupted all over the country, Sam hoped that his journey tomorrow would not be too problematic.

# CHAPTER 37

Sam was up early on the Monday morning. He left the apartment and informed the security guy on reception that he was going away for anything from four weeks to three months. He caught the train to Liverpool Street station and from there he took the train that he had his travel pass issued for to Thetford. Because of the weather, it snowed all the way there, Sam arrived forty minutes late. He disembarked and as he walked out of the station he was met by a Corporal waiting by an army car. "Major Tucker?" the Corporal asked.

"That's me" replied Sam.

The corporal stood to attention and saluted. Sam returned the salute and said "at ease corporal". The corporal took Sam's case and placed it into the boot of the car. Sam opened the front passenger door to get in.

"Sorry sir, officers in the rear of the vehicle please". Sam closed the door and climbed in the back. He thought that he might like being an officer but would prefer not to sit in the back of cars. They left Thetford and drove out on the road towards Norwich. The weather was worsening. The snow was heavy and was being driven by a strong wind. The car was driving at less than twenty miles an hour. About five miles north of Thetford they turned left onto a minor road that ran into Thetford Forest. For half an hour they drove slowly along small, single track roads until they arrived at the gates of an army camp, Camp Armstrong. The driver wound down his window and spoke to the sentry. He gave him Sam's name, Major Sam Tucker. The sentry checked his clip board and waved them through. The car pulled up in front of the administration building. The corporal got out and rushed around the car to hold the door open for Sam.

"If you will follow me please sir" he said as he led the way into the main entrance of the building. He walked along a corridor and knocked on a door. A voice said "come in" and the Corporal opened the door and entered. Sam followed.

"Major Tucker Sir" said the Corporal.

"Thank you corporal" said the officer who was getting up from his seat behind a desk. The officer was a Colonel so Sam stood to attention and saluted. The colonel returned the salute. The Corporal left the room and closed the door.

"Good afternoon Major, my name is Colonel Yates, I am the CO here". He signalled for Sam to sit in a chair opposite his. "We are a small camp and we operate as a transport support unit as well as carrying out initial training for new recruits. We have a small compound at the rear where you secret guys go from time from time. There is separate accommodation for you, training ranges and even cooking facilities if you require them. The gym that was built for the new boys is also used as part of your training. If you wish as you are here on your own, you are welcome to use the officers' mess on the main camp and even billet here if you prefer".

"Thank you sir, I would prefer that if you don't mind"

"No problem, I will arrange it now". The colonel picked up a phone and instructed whoever was on the other end that Major Tucker would be billeted in room forty two and to place his case in there. "Dinner is served in the officers mess at nineteen hundred, we usually meet for a pre-dinner drink at around eighteen thirty. Dress is casual uniform. Today is for you to get yourself settled in. The Quartermaster will see you when you leave here and sort you out with underwear, boots etc and your uniforms will be in your room when you arrive. Tomorrow you will have a medical and there are a number of forms for you to complete. The Brigadier has arranged a programme for you. The rest of this week will be physical fitness training. You will be instructed by the Sergeant Major who trains the new recruits. Apart from him and the doc all other trainers are imported especially for you. You will be doing weapons training next week. The Brigadier has arranged for an officer from the Royal Artillery to come here that week to train you. That will be carried out on a specialist range in the compound at the rear of the camp. After that the Brigadier will programme your activities and let me know what needs to be done. He also arranges the experts to carry out the training. Do you have any questions?"

"No sir, I think that is quite clear".

"Good". The Colonel stood up, so did Sam. The Colonel walked to the door and called for the Corporal who was at a desk outside. "Please take Major Tucker to his billet. Goodbye Major, I'll see you at dinner time". Sam saluted.

"This way please sir" said the Corporal. He led Sam out of the building and across a parade ground to a building on the other side. It was still snowing hard. All of the ground was covered white. There were very few people around.

"No new recruits to march on the parade ground in the snow today then corporal?"

"No sir" he replied. "January is always a quiet month. It will pick up early in February. Apart from yourself sir, the only people here are the permanent staff".

He led Sam into a dormitory building and up a flight of stairs. He stopped by a door that had the numbers four and two painted on it and opened the door to let Sam in. "Your case is by your bed sir, your new uniforms are in the wardrobe. I will let the Quartermaster know you are here and he should be with you in about fifteen minutes". The Corporal saluted. "If that is all sir?"

Sam returned the salute, "Thank you Corporal, that is fine thank you". The Corporal turned and left.

The room was typical army issue. At least as an officer you got a room to yourself. It was ten foot by ten foot. There was a window on one side and a door on the opposite. The was a door in a side wall that led to a toilet that also contained a shower and hand basin. This was half the length of the room, five feet, the room next door would have a similar layout and have their toilet from the other half of the room. Inside the bedroom was a single bed, a bedside table, a four drawer chest and a wardrobe about four feet wide. There was also a desk with two drawers to one side.

Sam put his case on the bed, opened it and took out his mobile phone. No signal. He wasn't surprised. Most army camps in Britain and British camps abroad, have a low level magnetic charge running around their perimeter that acts as a barrier to the signals of mobile phones, wireless internet, blackberry's or iphones. It is a security measure and is very necessary in some of the overseas postings such as Afghanistan. It meant that he couldn't let Irina know that he was ok. He unpacked his case, putting the contents into the drawers and wardrobe. He noticed that already in the wardrobe were two standard uniforms, a dress uniform, four standard shirts with Majors tags on the epaulettes, two pairs of lace up shoes, one pair brown, one pair black and an overcoat. He was just about to try a uniform jacket on when there was a knock on the door, Sam opened it.

"Quartermaster Sergeant Major here sir. Sorry sir, can't salute, hands full". The Sergeant was carrying a large pile of clothes.

"No problem Sergeant Major, come in", Sam stood aside so that the man could enter the room. He placed the pile of clothes on the bed.

"I've taken your size sir from your uniform size sir. In case that is not correct I have also brought one lot of kit that is larger and one smaller, just in case sir".

"Thank you Sergeant Major" said Sam. The Quartermaster had guessed correctly and Sam was issued with five sets of socks, underwear, khaki tee shirts and handkerchiefs, three ties, two pair of blue PE shorts and two white PE tee shirts, PE shoes, two jumpers, one pair of boots, three sets of army fatigues and a set of army toiletries, toothbrush, soap, shampoo etc.

"You will also need some outside gear sir and a backpack and other items sir. These will be available to you at the end of the week sir. You will need to come to the stores for those, may I suggest you leave it until Friday afternoon sir. I shall be on duty then and I am sure that they will have arrived sir". The Sergeant Major stood to attention as he was talking to Sam. "Is there anything else sir?"

"Yes there is actually sergeant major. The Colonel said that officer mess dress code was casual uniform. What precisely is that?" The sergeant major pointed out the appropriate clothing. Sam thanked him.

"If you don't mind my asking sir, are you not very familiar with officers' mess protocol?"

"Not very, no Sergeant Major"

"Come up through the ranks have you sir?"

"Yes, went in at sixteen as a private. It shows does it?"

"I'm sure not to everybody sir, but I can spot a real soldier when I see one. I would bet that you had seen lots of action too sir. If you don't mind sir, where you in the first Gulf War? SAS?"

"Yes, why?"

"You won't remember me sir, I was a Lance Corporal then, you was a rooky private, but you was the one who chopped the rag 'eds bollocks off and got the information that saved a lot of our lives. Bloody hell sir, the bastard yanks were more of a threat to us than the Arabs after that, friendly fire, bollocks, there is nothing friendly about being shot at by one of their idiot fighter pilots".

Sam smiled, "Yeah, don't I remember. Sorry limeys, we just shot up a couple of your tanks by mistake". Oh that's alright Yank, just pay a bit more attention next time. Fucking idiot commanders". Sam felt his frustration of all of those years ago start to return. He remembered the men cowering whenever an American plane was near. The Sergeant Major jogged him out of his trance.

"Sir, there was a rumour at the time that a couple of the American pilots that had shot and killed some of our lads had been taken out, off camp, and tortured and killed. It was rumoured sir that one of them had been scalped, both had had their pricks surgically removed, and they were found, one with his hair over where his prick had been so it was like a fanny, and the other with his mates prick in his mouth. It was rumored sir that it was some of your SAS lot that had done it. I wonder sir if you may have heard the same rumour?"

Sam looked at the man and smiled. "I heard the same rumour but know nothing about it. The day after they were found I was shipped very quickly back to the UK".

"I had a funny feeling that you would have no idea sir" The Sergeant Major stood to attention and saluted.

Sam returned the salute. "Can we keep my background between ourselves please Sergeant Major. I would appreciate staying as anonymous as possible".

"Absolutely sir, my lips are sealed. Anyway if I was to tell anybody about some of the things you are alleged to have been involved in, they wouldn't believe me". He smiled, turned and left the room.

Sam checked his new uniform. The Brigadier had done a good job they fitted well. He unpacked his case and put the clothes from it and his new army allocation, away in the drawers and wardrobe. He lay on the bed, it was comfortable enough. For an army billet it was about the best Sam had stayed in. It was the first time he had ever been allocated his own room; privilege of rank. Sam was surprised how at ease he felt. He had been away from real army life for more than two years, although one had been in detention. Despite this Sam felt relaxed and almost at home. He showered and dressed in army clothes, a pair of khaki trousers and shirt and highly polished brown lace up shoes.

Just after six thirty Sam left his room and made his way to the officers mess which he had noticed was in the main building that he had been received in earlier. It was still snowing very heavily and the snow had settled and was fairly deep.

Sam was greeted as he entered the mess and was introduced to the other officers already there. It seemed that they all knew why he was there in the camp and although they were polite they all seemed somewhat guarded. The meal passed with small chat and shortly after nine o'clock Sam was back in his room. The mess opened for breakfast at six thirty in the morning and his medical was scheduled for eight.

# CHAPTER 38

Sam arrived for his medical. The doctor was a Major as he was. It occurred to him briefly that it was somewhat peculiar that these senior, qualified people were the same rank as he. To start with Sam was given a form to complete. It required answers to questions such as did he smoke, how many units of alcohol per week did he drink, did he or had he ever taken recreational drugs and various questions about his diet and exercise. He then had a very full physical inspection which included the doctor taking blood and urine samples and x-raying his lungs and scanning his kidneys and liver. It took so long that the doctor had ordered sandwiches and orange juice which they both had during a short break. At the end of several hours the doctor declared Sam fit for duty pending the results of the blood tests which would take about three days to analyse.

Sam was not surprised that he was fit for duty. When he considered this period of training, he knew in advance that he would have no problem with any aspect of it. He knew that he was healthy, he had kept himself at peak fitness since he had left the army, he was an expert shot, he could still deal with anybody in unarmed combat, so it was only some communication techniques and maybe some survival tactics that he would actually benefit from.

He returned to his room. He still had a few hours to kill before dinner time. He would have liked to have gone out for a walk but the weather was awful, the snow was very heavy. Sam could not remember when the weather had been as bad as it had been over the past couple of weeks.

At dinner his fellow officers were again polite but still Sam felt that they kept their distance. As the previous evening, Sam was back in his room at about nine o'clock. He had found out that there was an officer's lounge with a television and a selection of books and magazines in it for when he had a few hours spare as he had today.

The following morning after breakfast Sam reported to the gym for his fitness training. It took Sam about ten minutes to realise that the sergeant instructor was a sadist. He introduced himself to Sam and told him that his objective was to get Sam fitter than he had ever been by the time he left the camp. They would spend the next three days assessing Sam's needs and then drawing up a programme for him to follow over the coming weeks. Having had a very pleasant, informal chat the instructor told Sam to drop and do twenty press-ups. Sam dropped onto his hands and completed them fairly easily. As he went to get up after completing them, the sergeant said "another twenty". Sam found the second twenty more difficult. As he finished those the sergeant repeated, "another twenty" only this time he placed a heavy backpack on Sam's back so he was pushing that too as well as his body weight. He felt exhausted by the end of the third set of twenty. There followed an hour of torture for Sam. He had pull-ups on a bar, having to get his chin to rest on it, sit-ups, running holding a medicine ball and various other exercises. It seemed an age but was in fact just over an hour when the sergeant said "OK Major, take a break now. There's a water tap in the corner, take on some liquid". Sam staggered to the water and gulped down three full plastics cups. After fifteen minutes the torture started again, more sit-ups and stretches. Then Sam was led to a multigym and he had a session on weights. Another hour, another break.

By the end of the day he was exhausted. He had considered himself to be fit but not this fit. He had dinner in the officer's mess and as soon as the meal was over he excused himself and headed to his room for an early night. He was missing not being able to contact Irina. He wondered how she was getting on in the new job.

The following morning when he got out of bed Sam ached. He had a hot shower and then turned the tap to cold for 30 seconds before getting out, drying and dressing> The aches had almost all disappeared by the time he got to the mess for breakfast.

That day and the next were much the same, circuit training followed by weights followed by more circuit training. By the afternoon of the third day, although he was tired, Sam felt that he was dealing with the regime a bit better, he found the exercises slightly easier. On the Thursday evening, when the course had been completed the instructor came up to Sam. "I have to admit major that you are far fitter than I had expected, in fact you are in pretty good shape".

"I feel bloody knackered" said Sam.

"I have pushed you hard to see what you can do and you did everything that I could have expected. You're very fit. While you are here on camp we will schedule a half day to keep you in trim. You won't find that as difficult. The Brigadier usually has his men back here once or twice a year for a refresher. Once we know what your timetable is for next week I will let you know when I will see you again". The instructor saluted and turned and left. Sam shuffled back to his room feeling very weary but pleased with what the instructor had said.

# CHAPTER 39

The weekend arrived and passed. On Monday morning Sam had been instructed to report to the shooting range where he was to meet Captain Levy of The Royal Artillery. The Captain was waiting when Sam arrived. He stood to attention and saluted. Sam returned the salute.

"Good morning Major" he said. "My name is Charles Levy and as you know I am here to teach you how to shoot with a number of different types of guns. We will start with a .22 and work up the scale. I don't know what experience you have had sir, but you are in good hands with me, I am the battalion champion marksman".

Captain Levy was everything in an officer that Sam hated, public school, Sandhurst, over-confident, cocky and so sure of himself that he automatically thought that he was better than anybody else. Sam decided that he would stay quiet and just lets his shooting skills speak for themselves.

They started with static targets at 100 yards and then 200 yards with a .22 rifle. Captain Levy scored six bulls eyes on each target and so did Sam.

"That's very good Major. Now lets try with pistols. Ever fired a Glock 17?"

Sam grinned inwardly. What did this clown think he had been doing for over twenty years in the army. He responded, "Once or twice".

"Well we'll start with this, it's a few years old but is still in good nick. It's mine actually. There is a new one, same model with just a slightly different grip, back in my room. We'll save that for later in the week".

Once again static targets were placed one hundred yards away. Captain Levy told Sam that the Glock kicked when fired so he would need to get used to it. He then shot at the target and fired seventeen rounds into the target. He put fourteen of the bullets into the centre circle and three just outside. Sam noticed that his sequence of firing was not completely regular. Sam took the gun from him. Again the Captain told Sam to take it easy with his shooting. Sam checked the gun. He started to breathe. Sam measured his shooting by his breathes. He would breathe regularly and then fire as he breathed out. Sam aimed and fired. He emptied the seventeen shot magazine into the target, seventeen in the bulls-eye.

Captain Levy's attitude changed. "You are a very good shot Sir".

"Other people have said so" was all that Sam would say.

"Shall we put the targets out to two hundred yards?" said Levy.

"Three hundred if you like" said Sam. The target was set at three hundred yards and again Sam scored seventeen hits in the centre.

"Excuse me sir but I realise now that you are an excellent marksman. I have to go through the programme for my report but I may not be able to teach you much, if anything indeed".

"That's fine, what is next in the programme then? Better lead on".

After lunch in the officer's mess they went into a mock village at the rear of the camp and shot at moving targets, firstly with a Glock pistol, then with a Kalashnikov rifle and finally with a Thompson sub machine gun. Captain Levy scored a hit rate of ninety one percent, Sam scored ninety eight.

Captain Levy was billeted at the camp so the two men dined together in the officer's mess that evening. Sam was somewhat apprehensive but he had become aware that the Captain was not as cocky as he had been earlier, so agreed when the Captain suggested it. Also, although the resident officers were polite to Sam they did not include him so he had started to eat alone, not that that troubled him.

After a few minutes of awkwardness Sam relaxed and the two men started to talk about guns and the point of the planned week. "Normally when I am asked to educate and evaluate, I don't discuss the programme with the people involved beforehand. However you are different Major, so far, and I know its only one day, but you are the best shot that I have seen. What we did today was two day's schedule, static was for today, moving targets tomorrow. Wednesday was supposed to be more pistol work and Thursday long distance firing. Given your obvious experience I would like to ask you how you would like to proceed. I don't want to make myself look like a prat again and instruct you about something at which you are better than me".

"Good plan son" said Sam smiling. He felt that to admit what he just heard, was an effort for the young Captain and Sam respected that. "What pistol's then? We've done the Glock 17. What was for tomorrow then, a Baretta?"

"No, I've got one of the new SIG Sauer P220's".

"Now you have got one up on me, I've never even heard of that".

The Captains eyes shone as he started to talk. "It's a new automatic pistol, 45 calibre, it will stop an elephant. The Americans are looking at it, both for their army and the FBI, in fact the FBI are trialing it at the moment. Although its made in Germany by Schweizerische Industries it is likely to be too expensive for the British army to have issued, or even NATO unless the Gerry factory want to discount it to them. But I've been given one to trial so it may be that you special ops types will get them. Hence, training with one tomorrow". The Captain was obviously into his guns. "For the next day they have loaned me a Barrett. Have you even shot with one of those beasts, they are awesome".

"What model, a 90?" asked Sam.

"Yes, used one?"

"Once or twice".

Captain Levy looked at Sam. "I won't make the mistake of telling you how to fire it then, in fact sir, maybe you would give me some advice. I also have a couple of the newer Glocks, the new 17 I told you about and a model 26. Both of them are being used by our security police, you know the guys who look after the royals and the politicians"

"What's the difference between the two models?" asked Sam. "I've used the 17 but am unfamiliar with the 26".

"The 26 is smaller, it only fires ten rounds whereas the 17 fires seventeen. The 17 also has a three and a half inch barrel and is almost five and a half inches high while the 26 is only just over four inches high and only three and a half inches in the barrel. Some say the 26 is a woman's gun, but after today, I wouldn't think that would be the case with one in your hands sir".

Once again Sam felt increased respect for the man. It must have taken a lot to admit that he had been wrong earlier in the day.

They were up, breakfasted together and on the range shortly after nine o'clock. The captain produced the SIG P220. He handed it to

Sam who was surprised how heavy it was. "How many times have you fired this weapon" asked Sam.

"I had it issued last week and fired a couple of rounds on the range before I came down here. It's got quite a kick. Would you like to fire it first?" Sam took the gun, loaded it and fired a shot at a target two hundred yards away. He hit the top edge of the target, outside of the centre area.

"I see what you mean about the kick" he said as he took aim again. The second shot was a little closer but still well above the centre of the target. Four shots later Sam was still not hitting the centre of the target. He reloaded and fired again. It took four more shots for Sam to hit the centre of the target. He reloaded again and this time he fired six shots into the centre of the target.

Sam then handed the gun to the Captain. "Your turn" he said. Captain Levy then loaded the gun and fired at the target. He too missed on the first round. It took another three rounds before he got the hang of the kick and the weight of the gun. They then spent another hour taking it in turns to fire the SIG. Sam reflected afterwards that it was just two men enjoying what they were doing.

They broke for lunch and went into the officer's mess. "Do you mind me asking you sir, how long have you been in special ops?"

"I'm not really sure what you would consider special ops. I joined up over twenty years ago, as soon as I was sixteen. During initial training they decided that I would be a good candidate for the SAS and sent me for training with them. I had a natural talent for shooting and other armed combat so was placed in the SAS doing various jobs in various theatres".

"If you joined when you were sixteen you must have been a squady, you must be very good to have made Major from Private" said the Captain. Sam just smiled.

After lunch they went back to the range. Captain Levy brought the Barrett. "When did you last fire one of these? he asked.

"Not long ago, a few months I suppose".

"What range?"

"About eight hundred yards".

Captain Levy looked at Sam. "Wow" he said, he smiled. "I'm glad that I asked you first. I was going to suggest that we started at four hundred, I have not shot beyond six".

"Let's put the targets at six then and see how we go".

They both hit the six hundred targets and then put them out to eight. Sam took careful aim and fired. He hit the target. He repeated it three more times and then passed the gun to Levy. He fired and missed. "Will you take some advice son" said Sam.

"From you, anytime" he replied.

Sam told him to relax and breathe regularly. "Get your breathing right, it is in time with your natural body rhythms, use the breathing as a metronome for pulling the trigger. Relax, breathe, and squeeze the trigger as you breathe out".

He still missed with the next shot but was closer. Four shots later he hit the target. He was obviously very exited about having hit it at eight hundred yards. Sam was pleased for him.

They then finished off the day firing AK47's at moving targets. Both of them were experts at this so no tuition was required. It was like two boys in a playground. When they finished they arranged to meet in the mess at nineteen thirty. The initial cocky attitude that Captain Levy had displayed was now completely gone, he only showed respect and admiration for Sam.

# CHAPTER 40

The two men had a drink in the bar and then went together into the officers mess for dinner. The camp was beginning to get busy with new recruits arriving for their induction training so the mess was becoming busier with more officers arriving to supervise.

"I was due to be here with you for a week but there is nothing that I can teach you, rather the other way round. I have to report to my c/o every day and I have reported as much this evening. He has asked for a written report to be faxed to him tomorrow. I have already typed it up. I have told him that I have never seen somebody who is as natural a marksman as you. Tell me sir, why have you never competed in service shooting competitions. I am assuming that you haven't or I am sure that I would have heard of you".

Sam thought for a minute. "It's something that has never come up. Over the years I have been in covert situations and in front line positions and sometimes even beyond the front line. Possibly best that I am not known".

They continued their meal making small talk. Sam said that he had to report to the gym for a session on Thursday afternoon, Captain Levy said that he thought he may be gone by then. They decided that they would meet on the range the following day and spend some time on target practice.

The next morning Captain Levy told Sam that he had been told to leave later that day and report back to his regiment. The two men shook hands warmly as they parted.

On Thursday Sam got up late and found that he had missed breakfast time in the mess. They made him some toast and he had some coffee. He wandered around the camp for the rest of the morning just killing time. The snow had stopped for a while but there was still plenty lying around on the ground, and it was still very cold.

Snow and cold, his mind went again to what Irina was doing and how she was.

He went to the gym in the afternoon and was given a hard workout and told that he should report back again at the same time the following week.

He returned to his room. He had only been there for about ten minutes when there was a knock on his door. "Excuse me Major", said a Corporal as Sam opened the door, "the c/o has told me to come and get you. You have a visitor sir, waiting in the Colonel's office". Sam followed him out and closed the door behind him.

He knocked on the Colonels door and when instructed he went in. The Brigadier was seated opposite the Colonel. Sam saluted to them both. "I'll leave you two in private" said the Colonel as he got out of his chair and left the room.

"Well my boy, its seems that you are very healthy, very fit and a better marksman than the best that the Royal Artillery have to offer us. Very well done."

"Thank you sir, does that mean that I can get out of this place?" asked Sam.

"Absolutely. You can have a long weekend off, report back on Monday morning. There is a train that arrives at Thetford Station at 07.52, where you will be met by car and taken to an RAF station for two days parachuting and abseiling training. You will then come back here on Tuesday evening for two days unarmed combat training. That takes us up to Thursday evening when you can go again, all being well, and then back here the following week for survival training and communications. You will need to arrange your own transport to and from the station after next week. Today I was on my way down from a lunch in Norwich, thought I would pop in and say hello as I was in the area. About to leave now and drive back to London, give you a lift if you can be ready in fifteen minutes".

"I'll be ready in ten sir", Sam saluted, left the room and hurried across the parade ground to put a few things in a bag. He was back with the Brigadier eight minutes later.

On the drive to London the Brigadier told Sam that he was genuinely pleased with his progress. He always knew that he was a good shot but the report he had received was excellent. He was pleased too with the level of Sam's fitness and his general health. He told Sam that he had arranged for a civilian to be with him for the communications training, an ex executive from Sperry Rand, who had been major suppliers to the military. The unarmed combat instructor was an NCO who also would show Sam the latest techniques with knives. The last instructor was a major who had a degree in applied biology and was an expert in living on natural products when on a mission and also making poisons from natural plants and substances which were readily available in the community. This training would involve two days of theory and then they would be flown to RAF Lossimouth in Scotland where they would depart for four days in the highlands, in the winter, with only emergency supplies. The intention would be to find food and shelter in the natural environment.

"Once you have finished here you will be back in London for a spell. I think that I already have your first assignment, we have an investigation that needs to be done in Nigeria, should be easy but you never know. But first you will need to familiarize yourself with our procedures etc back at base in London. Anyway that's for the future".

The Brigadier had instructed his driver to take Sam home, which he appreciated. He decided that it wasn't the done thing to invite the Brigadier in, he just thanked him and as he closed the door the car pulled away.

The first thing he did when he got into his flat was to turn his laptop on so that he could e-mail Irina. He hoped that she may still be up and would phone him. While waiting for his computer to power up he realised how much he had missed talking to her and hearing her news.

# CHAPTER 41

January had been a very busy month for Irina. The computer equipment had been delivered and so had the new office furniture that had been ordered from Germany. This was very unusual but as the unit had the personal backing of Prime Minister Putin, it seemed that she could request whatever was needed from any source. She had assisted Yuri in recruiting three new secretarial staff to deal with the inputting and collating of information. She was now training them. She and Yuri were both working very long hours and on a few occasions had left the office late and had dinner together. They had discussed various situations of the new operation, not least of all was how surprised both of them were about the amount of information that was coming in from various agencies within Russia about terrorist activities that had occurred over the last few years. Yuri was of the view that not all the reports were actually terrorist incidents but the police were reporting them as such as an excuse for not being successful in apprehending criminals. He was also somewhat surprised at some of the actions of the security forces. Some of the reports that he had read suggested reprisals were being used for personal vendettas.

In what little time she had to herself Irina often thought of Sam and wondered how he was getting on in his new position. She felt happy for him as she thought that he had deserved better from his army. Yuri had once aid to her that in the Russian army Sam would probably be at least a Colonel and would be very decorated. She was very proud of Sam and couldn't wait to go to England and live there with him. She recalled one of their last conversations about inviting her parents to the wedding. She had told Sam that she would write as soon as she got back to Moscow, that was a month ago and she still hadn't written.

On a dismal, wet, cold, winter afternoon in Moscow, at the beginning of February, Irina wrote a letter to her mother. She told her how much she had missed her and her brothers since she had left. She told her about the job she was doing for Yuri Dolchenko and about her life in Moscow. Finally she told her about Sam, the English officer who she had met and fallen in love with. She told her that she was going to move to England in March and marry her Englishman. She asked her mother if she thought that she and her father would come to England for the wedding. She posted the letter on her way to the office the following morning.

When she arrived she found a note from Yuri saying that he had had to leave to go and investigate a reported problem in the South. He would be away a few days. At this time of the year Irina thought that the weather would mean he would be away for longer than that. When the women arrived for work Irina stressed to them how important it was to hurry with the inputing of the data that was coming in about terrorism, but although urgent, accuracy was more important than speed.

Yuri meanwhile was travelling by train, not his favourite mode of transport, to his destination. He was accompanied by two recently recruited field operatives, both with a rank of Captain. February in Russia meant that many of the roads were closed due to snow and although it was a milder than usual winter, he did not want to risk getting stuck so all three men were travelling by rail. He arrived at his destination, a city called Omsk, near the border with Kazakstan, in the early evening. He was met at the station by the mayor and the chief of police. It was like being in a time warp, back to when he was in the KGB. One difference now though was that everybody involved knew that his team had the personal backing of Prime Minister Putin, probably the most powerful man in Russia.

The three travellers went straight to police headquarters and were quickly briefed on an incident that had occurred only thirty six hours before. The basic facts were that a group of armed men, allegedly about twenty in number, had crossed the border and blown up a police station in the south of the city, killing the six policemen that were inside at the time. Normally this would be too small an incident for Yuri to become personally involved with but on this occasion he had acted because the analysis showed that the explosive used was a cocktail that up until then had not been known before. It appeared from the report that it could be compact but very potent.

Yuri listened to the report of the police chief and after he heard it asked him to arrange for his team to be shown the police station the following morning. The arrangements were made and the mayor invited Yuri to dine with him which he accepted. Then Yuri and the two Captains were taken under police escort to the best hotel in the city. The police chiefs deputy took them into the hotel where the check in formalities were waived. Yuri had been allocated a large suite. It had a bedroom with a king size bed complete with a flat screen television, an oversize bathroom with a separate shower and a spacious lounge with two settee's and arm chair and another flat screen television larger than the one in the bedroom, There was also a well stocked bar in the lounge. Apart from the televisions it was all a bit old fashioned but it appeared clean and comfortable. Their cases were taken to their rooms while the police officer took the two Captains into the hotel bar, ordered their drinks and introduced them to two young ladies that were drinking in the bar, female company for the evening if they wished it the deputy police chief said. Both the young Captains said they did wish it so the policeman left and the two men settled down for and evening and they hoped a night, with two attractive young women.

Meanwhile the Mayor took Yuri to a restaurant. It was in the main street about one hundred yards from his hotel. The chief of police joined them there. When they arrived they were shown to a private room that already had a number of people in it joining their party. Yuri was introduced to the mayor's wife, the police chief's wife, the mayor's daughter and son and to the husband of the daughter, the daughter of the police chief and her husband, and to a woman of about twenty five who was introduced to Yuri as a niece of the mayor but who very obviously was not. It really was just like the old days Yuri thought. Tonight he would accept the woman on offer, the so called niece. He was in the mood for some stress relieving, uncomplicated sex with an attractive woman, even if she was a prostitute, but tomorrow . . . . . . . . .maybe he would try the mayor's wife, or maybe one of his daughter's, possibly the married one just to be spiteful, or maybe the daughter of the police chief.

The food was unexpectedly good and the wine reasonable. Yuri tried to shut out the mayor droning on about how frightened the local populous were about terrorist activities so close to their town, while in his other ear he was told by the police chief that he was starved of funds to employ enough police to cover all of the region for which he was responsible.

After dinner, Yuri told his audience that he was tired, he would see them tomorrow morning and arranged to be collected from his hotel at eight o'clock. He walked back to the hotel with the 'niece' on his arm. She was obviously experienced and good at her job. After about one hour of sexual activity Yuri was exhausted. As Yuri lay on his back on the bed, covered in sweat, the niece, who name was Tanya, asked him if he wanted her to stay the night. He told her that he would like that and instructed her to follow him to the shower and wash him before he went to sleep.

The next morning he woke early, Tanya was still asleep next to him. He woke her, rolled on top of her and then took her quickly before going to the shower. He had decided to take a cab to the police headquarters and arrive early, just to see what sort of operation they were running.

He was not surprised that it was lax. He entered the building, said who he was, told the officer in charge that he would wait in the police chief's office and was shown into it without being asked to show any identification. Given that a police station had been attacked and policemen killed less that two days before in a neighbouring town, he would have hoped that security would have been better.

Thirty minutes after Yuri had entered his office the chief of police arrived, slightly flustered. Yuri spared nothing in telling him that his security was disgraceful, his officers lax to the point of incompetence, he added that the atmosphere when he entered had been so offhand that it was unreasonable to expect the co-operation of the local community in any matter, in short, he stripped bear the persona of the policeman, leaving him in little doubt that his whole future in his current position was in severe jeopardy.

# CHAPTER 42

Yuri's two men arrived on time and a subdued police chief drove the three men South, to the village where the attack had taken place. A police car with four armed police in it followed. Yuri set up an office in the village hall and instructed the police chief to arrange for anybody who saw anything or heard anything to attend at the hall that day. The police who had been on duty were already there, they had obviously been told to be on duty when the team from Moscow arrived.

Detailed interrogation of both the police officers and some local people who had seen the terrorists enter the town, identified that there was not twenty or so as had been originally reported but only between ten and twelve. They had been well organised and only concentrated on their target. This had not been a random attack, it was aimed at the authority in the town. What was of great concern to Yuri was the appearance that some of the attackers, probably three, had been women. This supported intelligence reports that he had received from elsewhere that women were again becoming more involved in terrorist activities. He knew from fighting in Afghanistan against the Taliban that women were important behind the scenes in supporting their men. Indeed in Afghanistan the Russian soldiers were more afraid of being dealt with by the Taliban's women than by the men. The men would just kill them, the women would kill them slowly. A favourite trick of theirs was to wait until nightfall, then carefully skin the men. The pain was excruciating and their cries and moans could be heard for miles over the plains of the country. It was very unnerving for the young Russian conscripts manning sentry positions to hear this. In the morning worse was to come. As the sun came up and its rays hit the raw flesh the pain was even worse. The captured soldiers died a very slow, agonising death. Yuri knew from experience that these ethnic women were to be feared.

According to information that Yuri's group had compiled, women had become more involved in the front line activities since the early part of the twenty first century. Many men and even boys were killed by the Russians fighting in the Chechen wars of the nineteen nineties. Women witnessed their husbands and sons and other relatives being killed. The bond of "blood revenge" is very strong in the ethnic Muslim groups in the Northern Caucuses and although it has traditionally always been the men who would take on the duty of avenging murdered relatives, evidence showed that the women were assuming the role too. Some are not willing according to information gathered. They are blackmailed by the authorities, widows may have run up debts that they cannot pay, or in some cases they are raped by the community leaders which would lead to being unacceptable in the very conservative society that prevails in Chechnya. These women have been given the name of The Black Widows. Nineteen of the forty one terrorists who took a theatre audience hostage in Moscow in two thousand and two, were Black Widows. They were also present at the assault on the school in Beslan in two thousand and four when over three hundred people died including one hundred and eighty six children. The Russian media has not made much of this public, as they feared that it would strike fear into much of the population, especially in the cities. But all of the information has been made available to Yuri and his team.

At the end of many hours of interviews, Yuri's team had gathered enough information to finish and return to Omsk. On the way he travelled in the front of the car with the police chief. Yuri decided that he did not like the man very much so he thought that he would have some fun. "We have collated the information from all sources provided, it seems that your initial reports to me were inaccurate" Yuri said in an accusing tone.

"I am sorry sir, in what way?" the police chief replied in a whiney, defensive voice.

"Numbers, you said in your report that there were at least twenty, we believe the figure is nearer to ten. The most important omission however is that three of the attackers were women. You did not report that to me. It is of paramount interest as it may be involved with something that we are dealing with in another area".

"I am very sorry sir, I will reprimand the person responsible first thing tomorrow".

"I would have thought as police chief for the region, it is you who are responsible", said Yuri, enjoying the man squirming in his seat. It really was like the old KGB days when Yuri had virtually absolute power when he was out in the provinces. They drove the rest of the way in silence until the pulled up in front of the hotel.

"It has been a long day sir, maybe you would prefer to have a quiet evening in, and eat in the restaurant of the hotel". It was obvious that the police chief did not want to spend the evening with Yuri.

"Not at all" said Yuri, smiling both inwardly and outwardly. "This is our last evening in your town so we should all meet again, all of the people from last night, the mayor, his family, your family, and maybe we could have some music tonight. We shall have a farewell party".

"I am not sure that they will all be able to come sir, it's very short . . . . "

Yuri interrupted him. With no sign of humour at all he said "I am sure that you can arrange it. Let's say that everybody is a suspect in any conspiracy against the state in this region. I would hate to think that any of the wonderful people that I met last night may feel awkward about spending time with me in case they gave themselves away".

"I will make sure that they are all invited sir".

"Good. I will see you in two hours when you collect me and my two officers to take us to the party you will arrange". Yuri got out of the car and walked into the hotel without looking back. He smiled at himself visualising the panic that the police chief was now experiencing having to organise the dinner and guests at such short notice. In the past some had told Yuri that he had sadistic tendencies. He didn't agree, he considered that he was just having fun because the people involved were weak.

# CHAPTER 43

Irina arrived home tired from another long day. She turned on her laptop as she always did. She didn't expect to hear from Sam, she knew that while he was in the special camp he would not be able to contact her, but sometimes Yuri would e-mail her something that he had forgotten when they had last met.

Today though was a surprise. She had an e-mail from Sam saying that he had the weekend off and was at home. She was so exited that she phoned him immediately. He was so happy to hear from her and she from him. He told her all about his time at the camp, she told him about how busy her office in the Lubyanka was and how much time Yuri was spending out of Moscow. He told her about what he was doing next week and that he would have a weekend off then too. She told him that she had written to her mother and told her all about Sam and that she was getting married and going to live in England. Sam asked her what her mother had said and she told him that she had not yet had a reply. He told her about how cold it had been in England and how much it had snowed. She laughed at him and told him that Moscow had more snow but actually it had not been as cold as usual. She told him that their offices, in the old KGB building, had obviously been for senior people in Soviet days as it was a part of the building that had working central heating. Yuri had told her that he had managed to get them because the computers needed to stay warm and dry. Sam told her that he may have to go on a mission soon after he finished his induction and said that they needed to firm up on the dates that Irina would come to England so that Sam could try and arrange to be there when she arrived. They chatted on for about thirty minutes.

"We had better hang up" said Sam. "This phone call will cost a fortune. I will e-mail you over the weekend before I go back to camp on Monday. I miss you and I can't wait until you are here".

"I love you too Shammy and miss you terribly. I hope that I will be finished here by the end of March and then we can be together". They hung up. Sam felt much better having spoken to Irina. She seemed fine and happy and was looking forward to coming to live with him in England.

Sam spent the weekend relaxing. He went to the gym on Saturday morning, went shopping for some food afterwards and in the evening went to his favourite Italian restaurant in Canning Town. He telephoned his sister Marion and they arranged that he would visit her and her family on Sunday for lunch.

At lunch the boys wanted to know all about what he was doing, had he shot anybody, had he driven a tank, and when he explained the pain that he had experienced when he started the fitness training they wanted to know why he hadn't killed the instructor. After lunch they sat and watched football on the television. Sam's sister had Sky which Sam had never thought about getting but she explained that the cost was worth it as they all watched either the sport or the films that were on about six channels at the same time.

While he was there his sister went online and found him the train times from Liverpool Street Station to get him to Thetford in time to meet his car. During the afternoon they were alone in the kitchen, Marion was making a pot of tea while Mick and the boys watched the football. "You've changed Sam" Marion said suddenly. "I don't know whether its Irina or the fact that you've gone back to the army, but you have changed".

"For better or worse?" said Sam, a bit surprised.

"Oh for the better, much better. Its taken forty years but I actually like you now, you seem settled and the unnecessary aggression has gone".

"Its probably a bit of both, the army and Irina. I suppose that at last I have a home and roots now. When you're a kid you don't realise it and in the army, at least the units that I was in, you never knew where you would be a month ahead. I still don't know where the army will send me but it is unlikely to be for months on end like Ireland was, or Iraq or Afghanistan, and anyway, when I come home I shall come home to Irina and a home that is ours, not a barrack residence somewhere. Maybe its just peace of mind". Sam went quiet after that.

He left them after tea at about six o'clock and went back to his flat. He took a cab and arranged with the driver to collect him the following morning to take him to Liverpool Street Station. During the drive home he mused about what Marion had said about him being changed. He decided that he had changed and for the better. Not for the first time he thought how lucky he had been to meet and fall in love with Irina and she to fall in love with him. That was the big change. What he had said to Marion about having a home to return to after an operation was the key.

# CHAPTER 44

Yuri and his two colleagues were collected promptly from the hotel reception by the police chief. He had expected no less after the conversation he had had that afternoon. They drove about one hundred yards to the same restaurant as the previous evening. As the food and wine had been reasonable, Yuri was not disappointed. They went to the same private room and were greeted by the mayor and his wife. There was a man setting up a disco rig in the corner. Yuri smiled to himself. This must have taken a bit or organising in such a short time.

He turned to the police chief. "Surely it is not just the seven of us that are dining here tonight. I thought that you were arranging for all of last night's guests to attend"

"Yes Colonel I have done so. But it is rather short notice and they have had to make arrangements but they will all be here, all except my niece, I have not been able to contact her but I do have two other nieces coming instead which I hope will meet with your approval. The mayor's family and mine will be here shortly. I will order some wine while we wait".

"No wine yet" said Yuri, "We will toast in vodka while we wait". The mayor scuttled away to organise Vodka and glasses.

Within thirty minutes the other people had all arrived, including the two 'nieces' who were a lot more obvious than Tanya had been the night before. They both gravitated towards the two younger men in Yuri's team which Yuri didn't mind at all. In fact he stopped the mayor from intervening when it was obvious that he was going to speak to the girls and redirect them. Yuri was aware that they were the same two girls that his men had met in the bar the evening before and presumably spent the night with. Yuri, buoyed partly with the four large vodka's that he had consumed, had other plans tonight. The previous evening he had taken a dislike to the mayor. He considered him the type of person who must have achieved his position by creeping to everybody all his life, as he had to Yuri since he had first met him. Yuri had planned to spend the night with his wife, or maybe his daughter, just to spite him. But over the course of the day he had decided that he disliked the police chief more, so maybe he would take his wife to his bedroom instead and maybe he would let the police chief wait in the lounge of his suite while he fucked his wife so that he could hear what was going on. Yuri smiled inwardly to himself. What a lot of choices he had.

They sat down and the food arrived. As the previous evening it was more than reasonable and the wine was from the same vintage, two years old from the Crimea region. The D J played music throughout the meal and when the meal was finished and the table cleared, Yuri suggested they start dancing. His two major's were up on the floor immediately with their two partners. Yuri asked the mayor's wife and they took to the floor. As soon as they started to dance, Yuri, pretending to be more affected by the drink than he was, started to fondle the woman. She didn't resist but it was obvious that she was uncomfortable. Yuri was keeping an eye on her husband who was trying very hard to look anywhere but at what was happening on the dance floor. When the music finished he returned to the table and asked the police chief's wife to join him. She was obviously reluctant but went anyway not feeling she was able to refuse a man in Yuri's position. He repeated the performance with her, groping her bum and fondling her boobs when she moved apart from him. Following his lead, his two men did the same but with very different results. These were two experienced prostitutes so they just laughed and encouraged the men more.

Yuri realised he had a problem. With the vodka and the wine, although not by any means drunk, some of Yuri's senses were dulled and he was aware that he had not been aroused at all by either of these women. They were both overweight, plain peasant stock. He would probably be unable to get it up enough to shag them even with their husbands being tortured outside. The only attractive woman was the police chief's daughter. When he returned to the table, the mayor got up immediately and took his wife onto the dance floor, in an attempt to keep her safe from Yuri. Yuri then invited the police chief's daughter. She was even more reluctant than the two older women but she was encouraged by her father. Yuri started dancing close to her and feeling her bum too. He could see her husband becoming irritated. The tempo of the music changed and they pulled slightly apart. So did his two men. The breast groping started again and this time one of the hookers took the man's hands and put them inside her blouse onto her breasts, The other one, laughing did the same. Yuri, pretending to be slightly drunk also put his hands inside the jumper that the woman was wearing and onto her boobs. She tried to pull away but he just laughed and gripped her breasts tightly, hurting her. He saw her husband start to get up to protect her but he was restrained by her father who urgently whispered something in his son-in-law's ear. He sat down again. The music slowed down again and they moved closer together. She whispered in his ear, "you hurt me".

"I'm very sorry but you tried to pull away and you have such lovely tits".

She said nothing.

"I will make it up to you tonight. I will be very gentle when we make love in the huge bed I have in my hotel room".

She jumped back. "What?" she exclaimed.

Yuri pulled her closer to him again and whispered in her ear. "I have decided that I want you, you are my partner for tonight. We will enjoy each other for one night only, but it will be memorable".

She was obviously shocked and didn't know quite what to do. "I am a married woman and cannot be unfaithful to my husband".

"Of course you can. It happens all the time. Anyway I have made my decision, it is you that I want".

"Do you always get what you want?"

"On the very rare occasions that I haven't the parties that refused me have spent many summers in labour camps in Siberia. We still have them you know only now they are referred to as correction centres". Her body seemed to droop slightly as the meaning of what Yuri had said began to sink in.

They returned to the table and sat down just as another bottle of vodka arrived. The police chief's son-in-law took his wife's arm and began to leave saying his goodbyes as he got up. His wife looked at Yuri, followed her husband towards the door and started to talk to him quietly. He suddenly looked at Yuri with a face full of hate, looked again towards his wife and stormed out. She returned to the table.

"Well I think the evening is over for me" Yuri said, and then turning towards the police chief he said, "Eight a.m tomorrow you can pick me up. We have unfinished business as to what to do about the problem on the border. Come my dear let us find heaven" he said to his new bed mate.

Having been abandoned by her husband she gave in to her fate. Once in bed she seemed to accept the inevitable and as such she may as well enjoy it, thus she proved a willing partner, Yuri thought that she must be bored with her husband. She had a very attractive body, nice hips and boobs and looked good naked. Despite his alcohol consumption, Yuri had no problem getting it up both at night and again in the morning.

He was met at eight by the police chief and taken to his office. No mention was made of Yuri's conquest. Yuri offered to supply a small detachment of troops on the border to repel any future excursions by terrorists and also told the police chief that he would investigate increased funding so that a more permanent solution could be found to provide more men. He told the police chief that he would return in six months to review the situation. When the police chief said that he would look forward to it, Yuri did not believe that he was telling the truth, unless he didn't like his son-in-law and liked Yuri showing him up.

On the way back to Moscow by train Yuri mulled over the notes that he had made during the investigation. He sensed that the female component was becoming more serious and it was something that needed to be given a higher priority.

He briefed his two men accordingly. They would be the ones out in the field more than he, they needed to know what to look out for.

# CHAPTER 45

The car was waiting as Sam arrived at Thetford Station. There was still remnants of the severe winter snow on the ground on the fields on the outskirts of the town. They were heading south, down the A11. They turned left about ten miles outside Thetford and soon arrived at an RAF camp. Sam, dressed in his Major's uniform, returned the salute of the sentry once the identification pass had been examined and the barrier raised. Sam was met by a Group Captain who led him to an office. He was just over six feet tall, well built but no fat, had blonde hair that was worn longer than is usual in the army, and had a big smile with perfect teeth. He looked like the sort of RAF officer that would be featured in a film rather than real life. He also had a rich baritone but soft voice. "Well Major, what experience do you have jumping out of planes?"

"I have some but I am a bit rusty. The last time I was in a drop was behind some lines in Helmund province but it was about five years ago".

"Helmund? Rather you than me. Still if you have done that what we shall do here will be a piece of cake, even if you haven't done anything for a few years. Bit like riding a bike really, you never forget. What about abseiling?"

"Never done it".

"Good. That gives us a starting point. We are going to deal with that part today so let's get your kit to the billet and you can change into fatigues and then we will start. Sergeant" he called out. A Sergeant appeared at the door. "Pleases take Major Tucker over to the guest officers block and show him his room. Back here in say, twenty minutes?" he said to Sam.

The room was much like his room at the army camp, just a different colour of emulsion paint, grey/blue rather than khaki.

They went to the top of a concrete and wood tower and the Group Captain showed Sam the harness and how to put it on. "This is for beginners, I would hope that by the end of today you will be going down without the harness. It's a drop of one hundred and fifty feet which is a fairly typical drop in an operational situation."

"Can we just back up a bit please Group Captain. You say that by the end of today I am going to jump off of this tower without a harness?"

The Group Captain laughed. "Firstly, I'm not sure what the protocol is in the army but how about you call me Steve when we are together, and I call you Sam. And yes, I have absolute confidence that you will be going down without a harness before we break for dinner tonight".

Sam put on the harness as he was shown and clipped a thick rope to a bracket on his belt. He followed Steve to a platform on the edge. "Turn round so that your back is facing away from the platform. The rope that you have just linked to you will take a weight of twenty tons, it is twelve inches shorter that the distance from the top of the tower to the floor so if you fall, you will land twelve inches above the ground so to speak. See, it's completely safe." Sam was still sceptical.

"This other rope here", said Steve, picking up a rope that was dangling over the edge, "this is thirty inches longer than the height of the drop and it is this one that you abseil down on. You go hand over hand like this". Steve showed Sam the procedure for holding the rope. "We will go down together very slowly so I will guide you every step of the way. Hold tight and just step off the edge".

Sam held very tight and followed Steve over the edge. Sam was dangling on the rope and seemed frozen. He couldn't remember when he had been more scared.

"OK, just relax a bit and kick out from the wall like this. As you do it release your right hand and grip the rope lower down with it, like this". Steve showed Sam what to do. Sam followed. They then repeated it with the left hand being released and gripping further down. Progress was slow at first but about half way down Sam seemed to get the hang of it and found a routine. Steve kept pace with him and when they reached the ground he said "There, nothing to it. You did really well once you relaxed a bit. Come on then, back to the top".

They unlocked Sam's harness and walked up the stairs to the top of the tower. "There are two hundred and thirty steps to the top of the tower. A few more climbs and you will feel happier going down than you are going up", Steve joked. At the top, after only climbing it twice, Sam felt that the Group Captain may be right.

The next descent was easier and the following one more so. After five Steve suggested removing the harness and showed Sam how in normal use, the drop rope would be buckled to a smaller harness. Steve had been using this since the beginning of the lessons. Sam said he would give it a go, changed the harness for the belt and followed Steve over the edge. He got a rush of adrenalin as he abseiled down the side.

"See, you've got the harness off before lunchtime" said Steve, who then suggested that they break for something to eat. In the afternoon they completed another three drops together and then Sam completed three solo.

For dinner Sam joined Steve in the officers' mess. He was introduced to the other officers in the squadron. They seemed a much friendlier bunch than the guys at the army camp, maybe because they were an operational unit rather than a training camp.

The next day they started early, taking off in a transport plane at 0,900 hours. Sam felt comfortable with this, as Steve had explained you jump, the shute opens and when you hit the ground, you roll. They had decided that Sam would know this part and they did not need to practice landing from a twelve foot tower as they did with new trainees. The plane circled around the perimeter of the camp and as it did so Sam jumped; it went perfectly. As he and Steve landed a Land Rover came to pick them up to return them to the plane that was just landing. This was repeated three times. Once he was sure that Sam was comfortable Steve moved on to the next phase.

"We are now going to jump with a chute where you will need to pull the chord" he said to Sam. "You will wear an altimeter, its like a watch on your wrist. You watch it as you descend and given the individual chute characteristics and what you want to achieve, you pull the chord when you are at the correct altitude. This is particularly handy when you are jumping at night and don't want to be seen. An automatic shute will open at five hundred feet, you can go as low as two hundred with a manual and sometimes even lower, although that is very specialist and I wouldn't think you would need to be lower than that. I'll be jumping with you to make sure you don't miss the cue. We will be linked by radio mike".

They went back up in the plane and Steve explained to Sam the procedure for pulling the chord and emergency chute backup in case the main chute didn't open. He fitted Sam's radio and they tested that both Sam's and his worked. When it was time to jump Sam felt completely confident. It was arranged that for this first jump he would pull the chord at two fifty feet. He did so right on cue and the shute opened. On the second and third jumps Sam pulled at two hundred and made perfect landings. Both men were pleased with their day's work. Steve slapped Sam on the back as they walked back to the main buildings complex. "You are the perfect student, well done. You'll have no problem out in the field, whatever operation it is that you chaps get up to."

They had an early dinner as Sam had been told that a car was due to collect him at 19.30 hours to take him back to camp. The car was on time, as he expected it would be. He said his goodbyes and was driven away. He was sad to leave. He had only been there for two days and one night but he had enjoyed the atmosphere of the RAF establishment more than the army one. It had seemed more relaxed, they were more of a team.

The next few days Sam found a bit boring. He was introduced to the communications expert, Colin Williams, 'call me Coll', who spent hours going into the greatest details of the radio transmitting equipment that he had brought with him and showing Sam the miniature transmitters that could be used now, explaining the limitations of distance of small transmitters, the way that satellite technology had revolutionized communications and how unsafe a normal telephone was and the how you could use a laptop in conjunction with a satellite. This was mostly beyond Sam although he did think that some of the equipment that he was shown was a bit 'James Bond, radio trackers in the false heels of shoes and fountain pens and watches that doubled as radio transmitters. He decided to nod politely in what he hoped were the right places and when he was given some field equipment, to concentrate on finding out how just that piece worked when it was necessary. The days did not drag too slowly and Sam discovered that his new friend 'Coll' had a car and arranged to take him to Thetford Station when the training had finished. He bunked a lift and returned to London for the weekend.

# CHAPTER 46

The first thing that Sam did when he arrived at his flat was to switch his computer on. It was nice to be home. Only just over a week to go of this training programme. He now only had left a sadist who wanted to hurt him, as all NCO's do to officers; legally if you are teaching them unarmed combat, and then some stuck up major with a degree in the totally useless, telling him how to survive on nettle soup.

As soon as his computer was booted up he e-mailed Irina. He told her he was at home again for the weekend and that he missed her more than ever and loved her loads. Within minutes she responded. She told him that she was still in the office, the other girls had gone home but she had been in meetings with Yuri and the field team members so was working late to catch up. She said that she would phone him in about an hour.

Sam showered and cooked himself one of the instant meals that he had bought the previous weekend. Irina phoned him about one and a half hours later. Sam thought that she sounded tired. He told her about his week, jumping out of planes with the RAF, she laughed when he tried to tell her about what he had learnt from his new friend Coll.

She told him about her week, about Yuri being away investigating a terrorist attack on a police station, about how worried he was about the women being involved in terrorism, but also how he had returned in a very good mood and was joking and laughing with his men but would not tell her why. She told Sam that she had not yet heard anything from her mother but had spoken to Yuri about when she could leave. He had had a meeting with Mr Putin when he returned and he had been authorised to appoint another two people for the office. "But Yuri is very annoyed with his superiors Shammy. He wants to have a meeting with the Americans and the English to discuss terrorism. He says it is a global problem. He wants all the countries to share information. Here in Russia our media is very controlled and most of the terrorist activities are not reported. The politicians do not want the population to know what is going on in case they are made frightened. They do not want to tell the American what they think is still a secret and the problems that we have had. Yuri says they are stupid, the Americans know anyway, they have satellites".

Irina told him that Yuri would be away a lot during March and the office would be busy and that he wanted her to appoint the new people and train them. "Yuri would like me to work all of March and travel to England on the 8ᵗʰ or 9ᵗʰ of April". "He says that if I stay that long he will pay for my ticket as a farewell present".

Sam said that he would have a word with the Brigadier and try and arrange to be off that week. They chatted for another half an hour and then said their goodbyes, agreeing that Sam would phone her on Sunday.

Sam had an early night. The next day was routine, gym, shopping, a pub lunch in the Docklands, some washing of clothes and in the evening he decided to go to the cinema. There was a film called Ghost, showing at the local multiplex and Sam had read good reports about it. He enjoyed the film, a story about a ghost writer producing the autobiography of a former prime minister, but he didn't like the noise of people talking, the noise that the large buckets of popcorn made, the smell of the hot dogs and even a mobile phone going off on two occasions. It had been many years since he had visited a cinema; he thought it would be many years before he went again.

Sunday Sam went for a jog and brought back some Sunday papers to read. Despite his working class background he liked the Sunday Times when he had time to read it. He did some ironing and sat on his balcony overlooking the Thames and had a sandwich at lunchtime. At least it was dry and the snow had finally gone although he needed a jumper on while outside. In the afternoon he telephoned Irina and they chatted. Sam had been thinking about her parents and offered to write to them inviting them to the wedding but she thought that it was too soon for that. Sam told her about his visit to the cinema, Irina told him that she had stayed at home all weekend and cleaned her flat and done all her washing and ironing, the weekends were the only chance she got to do these things. After about forty minutes they parted and Sam phoned for a taxi to Liverpool Street Station. He had decided to return on Sunday evening rather than leave very early the next day.

# CHAPTER 47

Sam was on duty at nine o'clock on the Monday morning. He met with the Sergeant Major who was to teach him unarmed and knife fighting techniques. He was typical of what Sam expected, about forty years old, all muscles showing as he wore a pair of jogging trousers and vest, shaved head and hard as nails. Sam was pleasantly surprised how much he enjoyed his morning. The instructor showed Sam the places on the body to aim for to best disable an adversary. It's a popular belief that when fighting a man, you would aim for his groin. However Sam was told that the groin was well protected and difficult to target. He demonstrated by lashing a foot out at Sam's groin. His reflex was to move away and turn slightly, the blow caught him on the side of the thigh. "See, you avoided it just as a reflex and you were not aware that I was going to do it. It's a small target area and difficult to get a clean blow at" he explained. He told Sam to attack the kidneys, not as painful as the groin but still painful. Also a blow just under the nose, above the top lip is also very painful. He also pointed out various pressure points to aim at and how to debilitate any foe.

In the afternoon they started with knives. This was an area that Sam had had experience with but he had not had training for many years. The Sargent Major started with what he called rule one, "never let go of your knife, never throw it at the adversary. If you do it will give the other person the advantage and he may use your own knife against you. You would be surprised how many people will try and injure somebody by throwing their weapon at them. Rule two, if you are in a knife fight always assume that the other person is trying to kill you, not threaten you, not injure you, kill you. Kill them first. Don't hold back with the knife, go to end the fight in the quickest way you can, the quicker it ends the less likely you are to be injured". They spent the afternoon with Sam being instructed on various moves both defensive and attacking. Despite Sam having been told most of this before he still found his day very enjoyable and instructive.

Sam had dinner on his own as, as an NCO, his instructor was not entitled to eat in the Officer's Mess.

The next day started with a revision of the techniques of unarmed combat that Sam had been shown the day before. The instructor advised Sam on a few of them but in the main he was pleased with his efforts. They then went back to the knives and again Sam showed he was a good pupil although the Sergeant did amend some of his actions and told him that he didn't think that Sam showed enough aggression. At the end of the day Sam felt fairly confident about what he had learnt and the Sergeant Major confirmed that he would be making a very positive report about Sam's ability.

Sam was breakfasting on his own as usual the following morning when a Corporal walked into the mess followed by a Major and approached Sam's table. "Good morning Major Tucker, this is Major Whitecroft, your guest advisor."

"Thank you Corporal" said Sam returning the Corporal's salute. Sam looked at the Major indicating the chair opposite to his. He was momentarily surprised. Firstly the Major was a woman. Although Sam was aware there were many women in the army for some reason he had expected a man. She was tall, not as tall as Sam, about five feet ten. She had shoulder length almost black hair, was slim but not thin, and tried to use her army fatigues to hide what appeared to be a good figure. She sat down opposite Sam and ordered an Earl Grey tea and a bottle of mineral water from the waiter who had appeared at their table. Three minutes after they met each other Sam had formed a significant dislike for this woman. She was everything that he hated in a British Army officer. He knew that she had a good degree, the Brigadier had said that, so she was obviously from a privileged background, parents had money, went into the army because she couldn't get a proper job, all of which was reinforced by the posh, plum-in-the-mouth accent she had. She talked down to Sam as though he was somehow inferior and she came across as being very aggressive. She finished her tea, picked up her water and said "Shall we go then? We don't want to waste time do we?" She obviously thought that she was in charge.

"Just a few more seconds to finish my coffee if you don't mind" said Sam, refusing to be intimidated by this assertive woman.

The day was to be spent in one of the meeting rooms on the base. She started with an introduction which managed to annoy Sam. "Today we are going to deal with the basics of what to look for in flora and forna that you can eat while in the field and the benefits of its nutritional value".

"Like nettle soup" said Sam.

She ignored him and carried on. "I will not go at a fast speed and will treat you as an averagely intelligent adult but if I am going too fast or you need clarification on any specific please raise your hand and I will stop and retrace".

Sam was beginning to fume inside. He was a forty year old man with over twenty years experience in the army, most of which was in the field which he had survived just fine, and he was being told to put up his hand if he had a question. He already decided that there was no way he was going to do that.

She droned on uninterrupted for the next hour. She spoke about mushrooms and toadstools, what to look for to differentiate each, if you cook them in water how they react differently and the difference in smell of the water, and finally, just so that Sam understood, don't eat toadstools. Sam surprised himself by understanding a good part of what she saying. At the end of the section she said "that concludes this section on fungi. You haven't asked any questions. Do I assume that you are an expert?"

"I feel like one now thanks to your very interesting tutorial" said Sam rather sarcastically.

"There will be a test tomorrow afternoon you know and the result will be transmitted to Brigadier Reece-Watkins. Anyway, lets have a fifteen minute comfort break. Back here in fifteen minutes sharp". With that she turned and left the room. Sam walked over to the officer's mess and had a coffee. He returned twenty minutes later. Major Whitecroft watched him walk in and sit down leisurely, she glared at him but said nothing.

"Now we will talk about nettle soup as you call it. Nettles are in fact a rich source of nourishment and should not be dismissed as a food source. If you cook them there is no danger of them stinging as you eat them". She then carried on to talk about berries, how to select them, look to see if they were the type that was eaten by birds and other animals because if they were they were unlikely to be poisonous to humans. Sam began to switch off. He decided that if he failed the test it was unlikely that he would be kicked out of the group.

The major concluded with what she described as natures medicine chest, leaves such as doc leaves, leaves that contain soothing oils for insect bites and sun burn, even a type of wild cannabis that can dull pain. Sam was becoming increasingly bored.

At last it was time to break for the day. "That's it for the day. Tomorrow we shall devote to natural poisons. We start at 0.900. Can you make it on time Major, will that be convenient?" she said sarcastically.

"I'll set my alarm for a specially early start so as not to delay you" said Sam as he got up from his seat and made for the door.

Two hours later Sam entered the mess. He looked around but Major Whitecroft was not there. That pleased him as it meant he did not have to make the decision about whether to sit with her or not. He was just finishing his soup when, ten minutes after Sam had arrived, Major Whitecroft walked in. She saw Sam and walked to a table at the other end of the dinning room and sat down for dinner.

The next morning Sam was in the meeting room fifteen minutes before the nine o'clock start. Major Whitecroft arrived five minutes early and seemed surprised that Sam was already there.

"Good morning Major" said Sam, pleasantly.

"Good morning to you too Major" she replied. Without a pause she carried on. "Today we are going to discuss natural poisons, Did you know for example that ordinary caster beans can be used to produce niacin which is deadly poisonous and will kill somebody very effectively. Caster beans are found in many countries throughout the world . . . . . . ." Sam turned off. If he was going to kill somebody he would use a gun or a knife or he would use his hands to strangle the victim. He was not going to ground down some bean that he had to scrabble about to find.

She called a break at ten thirty and this time Sam did only take fifteen minutes. She carried on as before after the break, "even kidney beans, if not cooked properly, are poisonous . . . . . .". She went on until it was lunchtime. Sam had had many years of practice of appearing to listen to officers drone on without listening. It had been a useful experience for the morning.

"After lunch is the test. It will last about an hour and deal with the points that I have covered over the past day and a half. As I said the results will be passed to Brigadier Reece-Watkins. Fourteen hundred prompt please" she said as she turned and exited the room.

"At least this time she said please" Sam said to himself, "stuck up bitch".

He went to the mess for lunch and was pleased again that she wasn't there.

The exam was a disaster. Sam could only attempt to answer about a quarter of the questions. He finished in twenty minutes. She took his paper, looked at it, and said "it appears that I have been completely wasting my time for the past two days. It's obvious from this paltry effort that you haven't listened to almost anything I have said".

"I am sure that in a stress situation it will all come back to me" retorted Sam. "If my bullets don't manage to kill the adversary and then I fail to finish him off with my knife, and I am unable to deal with him with my hands, I am sure that I will remember to scrub around some waste ground in the bush and find some poisonous beans and force feed him to death." Sam left the room feeling good with himself that he had had the last word. It was on his way to his room that he remembered that he would be spending the next three days alone with her on some Scottish mountain.

# CHAPTER 48

Sam followed his normal procedure. He went to the mess just after seven o'clock, had a drink at the bar where his fellow officers were polite but distant and then he would sit on his own and have his dinner. The only difference this evening was they wanted to know about the female Major, what was she like, a bit of a looker one of them said. Sam told them that she was a dragon, breathed fire, hated men and was probably a dyke. "You just want to keep her for yourself sir" said one of the young Lieutenants jokingly.

"Not likely son" said Sam, "she's poison. If you fancy your chances go ahead, I wish you best of luck". With that he walked to an empty table, the same one he sat at every evening. His tutor arrived about twenty minutes later and sat down as before, on an empty table, as far away from Sam as she could get.

Sam ate his meal deep in thought. He decided that he needed to tackle this problem if they were going to endure each other for the next three days. At least he wanted to know what her problem with him was. When he had finished eating instead of going to his room he went to the bar. She would have to walk past him to leave the mess. Twenty minutes later she was walking towards him, she passed by him and headed for the door. Sam followed. When they were outside Sam said "A word Major if you don't mind". She stopped, turned and looked at him.

"You obviously have a problem with me. I don't know what it is or why you should have one, especially as its been apparent since we first met, before I had any opportunity to do anything from which you could have made a judgment. We leave tomorrow to be dropped in Scotland. Its been bloody cold up there this winter, lots of heavy snow. At least to make the trip bearable we need to have a working arrangement better than we have now, so what's your problem?"

Her face went tense. She looked at him hard, he got the impression that she would like to have hit him. "You have got a bloody cheek, why do you assume that it is my problem. Who was it that played silly buggers yesterday and came back late, who is it that has sat in my classroom for the past two days and hardly listened to anything that I have said, who is it that doesn't seem to give a damn about what I report to his commanding officer because he is probably the blue eyed boy and it won't make any difference anyway because I'm here only to fill up a timetable". She was very angry.

Sam spoke to her in as calm a voice as he could muster. "You had this attitude before I was late back, before I took the test, in fact you had it right from the start, when you were first introduced to me in the mess you had an attitude. And you are wrong about not listening, the first morning, the first lecture, I took that in, but you still tried to lord it over me and you were still remote. As for the report to the Brigadier, of course I am concerned about what he thinks, I don't know where you got the blue eyed boy bit from, but I'll tell you this lady, I have been on more maneuvers in more theatres than you have had clean knickers. I have either been on my own or as part of a team that I trust and can rely upon. This may be a training exercise tomorrow and for the next few days but trust me, Scotland in the winter can be hostile. I am not prepared to put myself or any one of my party at risk I am prepared to tell the Brigadier that and I am quite prepared to take the consequences for my actions.

Now she was really annoyed, she raised her voice to him, almost shouting. "You bastard. You're all the same you public school namby pamby Oxbridge lot with rich parents. You must know that I am being considered for an appointment to your department and running to the c/o will put pay to that. Consequences for you? There aren't any. Consequences for me, they are immense, my chance to get out of the classroom at last. I hope that shit falls all over you." She was almost hyperventilating with rage when she finished.

Sam responded calmly, "I had no idea that you were being considered for the department, you are the fifth tutor that I have had on this course, I thought that like the others you had just been on secondment for a few days. As for being namby pamby Oxbridge, that's rich coming from you. Talk about kettle and black. Who is it that has the fabulous degree, who is it that went to a good university, who is it that talks like Princess Anne? It isn't me. I left school at fifteen and worked in a garage until I was old enough to join up at sixteen. No public school, just a comprehensive in a grotty part of East London, no university, and as for rich parents, there were no rich parents in the block of council flats where I lived in London E16. Do you know how I came to join the army?" I had a probation officer who suggested I join the army cadet core. That was my university".

She was standing still looking at Sam. There was a few seconds silence. She was calming down and breathing normally again."OK maybe I got you a bit wrong, but the principle still applies. However I do agree that you are right about the next three days so lets call a truce and work together to get through it safely". She looked again at Sam. "Goodnight Major, I will see you tomorrow morning". With that she turned and left Sam standing there, in the open, in the cold. Sam shrugged his shoulders and headed towards his room. At least he had got it off his chest. He went to bed and soon fell asleep. Before he did though, he thought about the next three days. He was not looking forward to it. He had once spent a week in the mountains of Southern Afghanistan in the winter. It was not a picnic. He doubted that his erstwhile colleague had any idea what she was in for. Sam had been watching the weather forecast on television for the past week and one thing he was sure about, it was going to be cold.

# CHAPTER 49

Sam was breakfasting in the mess the following morning when she walked in. She headed towards his table. "Mind if I join you" she said.

"Please, be my guest" he replied, indicating to the chair opposite.

"Thank you. I think I will have a full English breakfast today. I am not sure when we will eat a decent meal again".

"My thinking too. That's what I have ordered" and as he said it the waiter arrived and place the plate in front of Sam".

"Ma'am?" the Private who was on waiter duty this morning enquired of her.

"I'll have exactly the same please Private" she said.

"Do you mind if I start" said Sam

"No please, don't let it go cold".

Sam was pleased and relieved that they were at least being polite to each other. "Do you mind if I ask you a personal question Major?" She asked.

"Go ahead" said Sam.

"You said yesterday that your probation officer had suggested you join the army cadet core. Why did you have a probation officer, what had you done?"

"I nearly killed someone, probably would have if my mates hadn't dragged me away".

"Why, what had he done to deserve that?"

"I caught him having sex with my girlfriend, so I gave him a kicking".

Major Whitehead's breakfast arrived quickly, before Sam had finished his and they continued to eat in silence. Sam waited for his colleague to finish before getting up to leave the table. "I'll meet you out front when you are ready. The car should be there any time now if its not there already" said Sam as casually as he could.

"Thank you Major, I will see you there shortly".

The car was waiting and it took them to the same RAF camp that Sam had been the week before for his parachute training. As they arrived and passed through security they were met by the Group Captain that had tutored Sam. He greeted them as they got out of the car. "Sam, can't keep away from us? Morning Major", he saluted Major Whitehead and she returned his salute. He turned back to Sam. "We'll have to make you honoree RAF if you keep coming back here Sam".

Sam smiled. "All I want to do at the moment is get the next few days over with".

"I don't know what your plans are beyond Lossimouth but Scotland at the moment is a bit touch and go. Even yesterday I was a bit concerned whether we would get flight clearance, but you know what we flyers are like, we like a risk. How about a brew before we set off, by the way I'm your taxi driver so it shouldn't be too bumpy on the way up North".

They took off and headed North. They were travelling in a Cessna, plenty big enough for the two of them, they were the only passengers. As soon as they were in the air Sam closed his eyes and leaned back and dozed. Unfortunately the plane had been fitted out for carrying military personnel so the seats did not recline .They had been airborne for about ten minutes when she spoke. "I guess maybe I owe you an apology for jumping to conclusions".

"That's fine, forget it".

"You don't sound as though you come from a rough part of East London".

Sam opened his eyes and looked at her. "I came up through the ranks. When I was a private it was OK to sound like Michael Caine on a bad day, even as a corporal you can get away with it. But when you reach sergeant you have to be a bit posher than the recruits, if you don't you're not accepted. So I changed the way I spoke, I tried not to have an accent. There were times when I was in charge of small groups; detachments on special duties. Even as an NCO in such situations you assume an officer's role, so as time goes by you speak more like them. You spend more time talking to them too so things rub off. I don't talk like you though. Sorry, I didn't mean it like that".

"You mean like Princess Anne" she said in a broad northern accent.

"Bloody hell, that sounds more like Hilda Ogden".

When she spoke again it was in the voice that Sam recognized. "That's how I used to talk, I'm from Burnley in Lancashire. Like you I lived in a council house. My dad was a bus driver and my mum worked in a mill until it closed down. I have two brothers and two sisters, I am the youngest, the one who gets the hand me downs. I was good at lessons and when it came to the final year in junior school they put me in for the exam for the grammar; me and two of the boys. I passed and was offered a place. My dad said no, it was too snobbish, he was mostly worried about what his mates would think. Nobody in our family had ever been to a grammar school. But mum persuaded him so I went. I felt a bit out of it coming from the council estate so I worked hard and helped the other girls with their homework, it was my way of compensating; trying to be popular. Anyway the work paid off. We were the last year to sit GCE's, before GCSE's came in. I got ten. I stayed on for A levels and got four, the most in the school. I was good at science so the teachers said that I should take science subjects; that was the future. By now I wanted to go to university. One of my sisters worked at Woolworths, the other was already married with two kids and another on the way, my eldest brother was a van driver and my youngest, a trainee carpet fitter, and one day I arrived home and said I want to go to university. They thought I was from another planet. My dad told me I should get a proper job and find a fella and settle down. My sisters and brothers just took the mickey. Only my mum supported me and that made me more determined to go. I was offered a place at the University of Bath to do an applied biology degree, that's a four, not a three year degree course. My mum somehow found the money for us to go and visit and I decided that was where I wanted to go, so I did. I had no money from my family, they couldn't afford it, so I worked my way through to my degree, four years. The books alone cost hundreds of pounds. I worked in pubs, I worked at the checkout of Bejams, the frozen food shop, I waitressed at restaurants and yes, sometimes I even lay back an opened my legs while some half drunk, rugby playing hooray henry pumped up and down on me in return for a decent meal. So I qualified with this great degree to find that the jobs I was offered were working in laboratories for peanuts. One day feeling a bit down I passed an army recruitment office and the thought of being an officer was very attractive So I joined up. Even that was wrong; my father said that it was a man's job. Anyway my mind was made up so here I am. And what do I do? Because I am so qualified and so specialist I am part of the army special education core and I go around trying to teach people like you, no offence, but officers mainly, all that I learnt in four years, in four days".

Sam said nothing for a number of seconds, then "Life's not fair, there are the haves and the have nots. There are those who have rich parents and those that don't. But its no good bearing a grudge and letting it eat at you, which I think you are doing. You just have to get on and do the best you can and if you are unhappy about where you are going then do something else. You may not like what you do in the army but you can get out and get another job with your qualifications. Me, all my education has been in the army, all my experience means that the one thing that I am good at is killing people, not a lot of call for that in civvie street".

"I joined the army for action not lecturing to officers".

"Leave then, resign."

"Its not as easy as that". She was quiet for a while. "I guess I owe you an apology, I assumed that you were a normal officer, well anyway, sorry if I prejudged you. Your still an ignorant, arrogant prick, you didn't pay any attention at all to the last part of my lectures, a day wasted as far as I am concerned".

Sam just smiled at her. A voice came from the cockpit. "Belt up you two, we're landing in about fifteen minutes". The plane landed and Sam noticed that it was snowing hard as they pulled up on the runway. The plane coasted to a halt near to what passed as a terminal building on an RAF airfield. The co-pilot came through the plane and opened the door. Steps were put in place and Sam and Major Whitehead walked down them and went quickly inside the building. The Group Captain followed shortly afterwards. "We are pushing off back South straight away, the weather is closing in here and I don't want to get stuck. Good luck Sam, nice to see you again. Maybe our paths will cross again sometime. Major Whitehead, good luck" he said turning towards her and saluting. She returned his salute. He turned and walked briskly out of the building towards his plane.

A Flight Lieutenant had appeared next to them, he saluted. "If you would follow me please we have your winter survival kits ready. We would like to get you off as soon as possible. As you heard the Group Captain state, the weather forecast is not good". They followed him into what was obviously a meeting room. It had two sets of gear laid out on two tables. "This is yours sir and this is yours ma'am. In each pack there are two sets of thermal underwear, an artic sleeping bag which can either be used singly or joined together as may be necessary, there is a pair of waterproof boots, hat, gloves, undershirts, top shirts, trousers, jackets and four pairs of thermal socks each. There is a back pack into which there is already packed a length of rope and in the pockets of each is a details map of the drop area and surrounding country, a compass, crampon metal soles for your boots in case you need extra grip, a sharp hunting knife, a billy can, torch, box of matches, a pair of snow glasses, two emergency flares and some emergency rations, dried food which can be mixed with snow to make a meal. I stress sirs that they are only to be used as a last resort. I was instructed to tell you that. Also to be used as a last resort is the satellite phone. There is one in each pack. If you would like to get changed now, I will see you outside in the reception area in ten minutes.

Sam started to strip off. "Are we supposed to get changed in here?" Major Whitehead said.

"There's nowhere else. Turn around and dress behind my back, I promise I won't look. You wanted bloody equality."

They dressed without further incident and went to the reception and met with the Lieutenant.

They left the airfield in a helicopter. Their landing zone was about forty miles from the aerodrome. It was marked on their maps and they had been told that they would be expected back in three days. The trip to the drop zone was expected to take about an hour, longer than usual because of the weather conditions. It was snowing and windy and cold and Sam could feel the chopper being thrown about in the wind. The two Majors were seated in the rear seats behind the pilot and co-pilot. It was very noisy despite them both having headphones on.

Sam took his off and leant across and removed Major Whitehead's. "Listen, now that we have both established that neither of us is a public school ponce, how about we use first names. I have a feeling that the next three days are going to be a bit tough and whatever else we may think, we are going to need to work as a team. I'm Sam," he said as he held his hand out to her.

She took it and said "my name's Elizabeth, and before you say anything, I hate Betty, it's what my parents used to call me".

"How about Liz?"

"Liz is fine."

An hour later they were at the drop zone. A voice came through the headphones. "We can't land, its too dangerous with this snow, we can't see what's under the snow so we can't put down. I'll get to about six to four feet from the ground and you will have to jump. I would suggest that you keep your packs on your backs as they may break your jump".

The co-pilot showed them how to open the door and as the helicopter hovered Sam and Liz jumped from just less than six feet. They both fell into deep snow as the helicopter turned and peeled away.

# CHAPTER 50

Yuri was back in Omsk quicker than he had anticipated. He had arranged for a small detachment to be posted on the border under the command of a Captain Staveney. Yuri had met and worked with the officer previously and considered him very capable and trustworthy and somebody with initiative, a rare quality among much of the army officer corp. Captain Staveney had been held back during Soviet times due to the fact that his great grandfather, Colonel Staveney, had tried to assist the Czar and Czarina to escape, after which he had escaped to England and lived in London until his death in 1968.

This time the mayor and police chief were unaware of Yuri's visit. Captain Staveney had contacted Yuri with information that large caliber guns and explosives were being collected in a small town just south of the border. The Captain had selected some men to be part of his group that were from the south of Russia so they could pass as locals if necessary when across the border. They had gone on an expedition, visiting some of the local towns, disguised as travelling merchants and found that the residents, while polite to them, encouraged them to move on. They had eventually found a youth who had had too much to drink, throwing up behind a bar and he had informed them that he had been travelling for over two days with a consignment of machine guns and grenades.

"Did they kill the man?" asked Yuri.

"No Colonel, they did not. They thought that if they eliminated him it would raise the alarm"

Yuri was pleased with the reply and told the Captain so. He was pleased that the captain seemed to have selected men with initiative too. Yuri explained that he wanted to know more if possible and asked the captain to arrange another excursion. He told him that he would stay with him in the makeshift camp. He felt that security was vital and did not want his presence known. He felt that spies may be working

198

in the town and may well have infiltrated the offices of the mayor and police department.

The troops were assembled in a meeting tent and the Captain introduced Yuri. He then briefed his men on their objectives. The captain explained that this was an observe and report mission. They were to get as much information as they could without raising any suspicions. Yuri congratulated the men who had reported about the weapon cache and left the informant alive and unaware of any problem. He told them that it was not planned to go in and capture the weapons and the people who had trafficked them, they wanted to try and trace the source and the organisation behind it. A group was selected and left the tent to prepare for the mission across the border.

Yuri returned to his accommodation tent and powered up his new laptop computer. He e-mailed Irina in Moscow to search the files and get names of any regular army, airforce or naval personnel who were from an Uzbekistan or Kazakhstan ethnic background. He had decided that he needed to get somebody to infiltrate this terrorist unit. He hoped that Irina would be able to reply later that day but he thought it would probably be the next day. He considered going into Omsk for the night. The thought of bedding the mayor's wife had crossed his mind a few times, not because he found her sexually attractive, in fact he didn't, but because she and her husband were the type of people that Yuri disliked. He considered them parasites who would creep to any authority. He would bed her just because he knew that the mayor would give her up to an army Colonel from Moscow and that she would acquiesce. Yuri knew he had a mean streak and he knew that he would use her and she would know that she had been used but would say nothing and smile. It had happened many times before, over many years, but Yuri still enjoyed the feeling of power that he had.

He reminded himself that he was on a mission and that secrecy was more important than some fleeting pleasure, anyway he knew she would still be there next time he visited. As he decided that he would stay in the camp, the Captain Staviney came in and invited Yuri to lunch in the mess tent.

Irina received Yuri's e-mail and immediately input the request into the computor system. The secretaries were still imputing information from all of the sources that were contributing data, so Irina was concerned that details of all personnel were not yet available to them.

However within two hours she had come up with five names of what may be suitable candidates.

Yuri spent the afternoon talking to the Captain who he both liked and respected. He told him of his plans to put some men under cover across the border and that the Captain should give some thought to how he would collect and transmit information. They discussed the problems in more detail and Yuri told Captain Stavindy about his distrust of the local authorities. He informed the Captain that he would be returning to Moscow the following day as all seemed to be in good hands here on the border.

Irina e-mailed the details from her search to Yuri and he looked at the files of the potentials that evening. He thought that two looked very good prospects and e-mailed Irina instructing her to arrange for the two selected to report at the Lubianka offices in three days time. Irina knew that this meant an instruction must be sent to their commanding officers in the name of Vladimir Putin. Nobody refuses that sort of instruction. It was late in the evening but before Irina left to go home to her flat she sent a mail to Sam telling him that she loved him and hoped that he was safe and well, although she knew he was on a trip and would not get it until he returned.

# CHAPTER 51

Sam and Liz found it very difficult to walk through the very thick snow. Sam calculated that they had three hours of daylight at the most before they would need to stop for the night. They both agreed that it would be extremely dangerous to attempt to travel after dark. Apart from the deep snow there was also a fairly strong wind and it made it very cold. After less than two hours Sam was beginning to feel tired even though he had been declared as very fit. Liz was putting a brave face on it but he knew that she must be feeling it too and she was beginning to slow down considerably. They were walking when Sam saw an outcrop of rock jutting out of the surface. "I think we should camp here for the night" he said. "If we get up close to that rock face we will be sheltered from the wind, it is blowing the other way. Also there is some moss type growths in the crevices which we may be able to use to start a fire if we can find some dry wood." Liz just nodded. They made their way to the outcrop and took off their backpacks. Sam had been correct, this was sheltered from the wind. Sitting with your back to the rock wall you couldn't feel it at all. Also good news was that the moss on the wall was fairly dry. About one hundred yards further on was a small outcrop of trees. Sam walked to them and scrabbled around under the snow. He came up with a number of twigs and branches of different thickness and carried them back to their makeshift camp.

Liz was still sitting where he had left her, she had not moved. "Those won't burn, they're much too wet".

"Well thank you assisting us with that information, Major survival expert" Sam said cynically. "Perhaps as you are the instructor here and the expert, you could find us some dry wood and while you are at it can you come up with some berries and mushrooms for dinner, otherwise we may starve". Sam sat down with his back to the rock wall and looked at her.

She looked back at him and after a few seconds of silence said "Sorry. This is just not what I expected. I'm freezing cold and want a hot drink, food I haven't thought about yet. How are we, sorry, you going to deal with the wood. Surely it's too wet to burn".

"We dry it. We dry the small stuff which will then hopefully light and then we add the larger stuff which will hopefully dry out before the small stuff burns away and then we put the even bigger stuff on and hopefully that dries and so on and so on. Here, here are some small twigs. Take something from your pack, some socks or a shirt, and dry them as best you can" he said passing her the twigs. She looked at him as though she were going to say something and then took them from him and looked in her backpack for something to dry them on. Sam went and got several handfuls of the moss. He made a small clearing next to the wall, removing all of the snow and digging a small hole about three inches deep. He put the moss into the hole and tried to set light to it. It smoldered. He then took some of the twigs that Liz had dried and placed them on top of the moss. There was a lot of smoke but no flames. Eventually the moss had burnt and the fire went out without igniting the twigs.

"Well that was a great success" she said sarcastically. "What do you do for plan B?"

"Plan B is more of plan A. The twigs will have dried out a bit with the heat from the moss while it smouldered, so we try again but this time with the drier twigs. You wouldn't like my plan B anyway".

"Why wouldn't I?"

"Because if you keep moaning and being sarcastic while you sit on your bum and do nothing and offer no constructive suggestions, plan B is pick up my pack and leave you. So think on and engage your brain before you open your mouth next time."

On the seventh attempt, and after almost an hour of trying the twigs caught light, there was a flame. Half an hour later they had a fire as some of the larger pieces of wood had been put on the fire and caught. Upon Sam's instruction Liz then filled both of the billy cans with snow. Sam put one on the fire and the snow melted. What had been full of snow was now only about a quarter full of water so he put the snow from the second container in the water, and then a third and a fourth that Liz had collected. The sight of the fire seemed to have cheered her up and she was now active again. Soon the water was hot, not boiling but hot enough to drink and warm them. Sam poured some hot water into both of their mugs.

"Cheers" he said, " can't beat a good cup of tea. Pity this isn't a good cup of tea but its hot and wet as my old mum used to say". They both drank the hot water and to them at that moment it was better than a good cup of tea.

They sat in silence sipping their drinks until Liz said "Look Sam, I'm sorry if I was out of order this afternoon. I was very depressed. I've lectured loads of people for years about survival but I have only been on a few courses in the field, and nothing like this. It did cross my mind that we may not survive and I still don't know how we are going to eat. Everything is covered with snow. There is no way that we are going to be able to identify edible plants and even if we could see them there are going to no berries this time of year".

"Don't be so bloody daft, we're not going to die. Christ we have the very latest satellite phones, get on the blower and call a helicab if it gets that bad".

"I can't do that" she said, "that would be to fail and I would have no credibility talking to anybody again about survival".

"Oh right, better to die than fail. Well not me" said Sam. "When I think that we cannot make it you can bet your life that I will be on there phoning a friend. But that time isn't yet. We have a fire, we have water and we have shelter, well of sorts. My suggestion is we bed down for the night now and start as soon as its light tomorrow".

Liz agreed. Sam piled up the fire with more of the wood that he had collected. It hissed and the flame dimmed but Sam knew that it would stay alight for a while now as it would flare up again as the thicker wood dried out.

They both then climbed into their sleeping bags and prepared to go to sleep. Even with the quality of sleeping bags that they had been provided with Sam felt a bit chilly. He lay on his back looking upwards but could see no stars or moon due to the cloud cover. He listened for sounds of birds or animals, potential food sources, but heard nothing above the crackling of the fire. He lay like this, still but listening, for about half an hour.

"Sam, are you asleep?" she whispered.

"No".

"I'm cold".

"So am I, try not to think about it".

"It's a well known fact that you can keep warm using another person's body heat. We should get into the sleeping back together. These are designed to zip together for just that purpose".

"OK" said Sam. "As long as you promise never to tell anybody. I don't want to be known as the man who slept with Major Whitehead."

"Don't worry, its not something that I am going to boast about. This is about keeping warm and keeping off hypothermia."

They both got out of their bags, not a problem as they were both fully clothed, and zipped the two bags together and climbed back into the double bag. They lay facing each other and Liz put her arms around Sam and pulled him close to her. "You'll feel warmer in a minute" she said. Sam lay there. He was amazed to feel that he was getting an erection, he was getting harder. He didn't even fancy this woman and was embarrassed to think that he was reacting in this way. Liz moved her arm which was around him and put her hand over his erection. "What the hell's this" she said, not in the harsh way that he expected but with a smile in her voice.

"Nothing to do with me, he's got a mind of his own".

Suddenly she moved her hand and slipped it inside his trousers, straight on to his now hard member. "I really don't need that" he said. She took her hand out, took his hand and put it down the front of her trousers. He could feel she was moist. She unzipped the front of her trousers and then she unzipped Sam's. She pulled him free of his trousers and suddenly she was on top of him clamping her lips over his, tongue deep into his mouth. She pulled her trousers and pants over his hips and she thrust herself on top of him, driving up and down, consumed with animal passion. She was moaning as she moved faster and faster until she arched backwards screaming out loudly as she climaxed. At the same time Sam came into her despite himself. She collapsed on top of him and they lay there for several minutes.

Sam slept soundly for three hours. He woke as he had planned, his body clock had not let him down. It was dark and cold but it was not snowing. He crept out of bed and moved to the fire. There were still some glowing embers onto which Sam put the last of the wood. He had calculated that the fire would begin to expire at about this time. He took his torch and returned to the small copse where he had gathered the wood earlier. Again he raked around and found a quantity of dead, fallen twigs and small branches. He collected the wood and put it into a small pile. He then carried some back to the fire which had revived. He placed the thicker pieces that he had just collected on the fire and loaded it high with the thinner, kindling type twigs on the top. He returned to his pile and carried more wood over to the fire. As the larger pieces began to dry and catch light, Sam removed them from the fire and putting out any flames put them aside. He then repeated this with the additional wood. He returned to his pile and then back to the fire, repeating his activity each time. The final time he did it he left the wood on the fire and soon he had a fire going and put a billy can full of snow on the fire to heat water. He looked up and noticed that Liz was sitting in the sleeping bag watching him.

"What are you doing, putting wood on the fire and then taking it off?"

"We don't know if we are going to find suitable wood as we journey so we will take some with us. Because this wood has actually started to catch light we know that it is dry. That means we won't have to go through the process of drying out when we next need a fire, it will be ready to light immediately."

Liz just nodded.

They set off as soon as it was light having breakfasted on warm water. They split the wood stock between them and tied it to the top of their backpacks. Sam had told her that for three days only water was vital, that although they may feel hungry, a healthy human could go for three days without food without a serious problem. They both knew though that that was alright normally but not so in the hostile conditions that they were experiencing. The wind was back but the snow held off. Around midday they found a road and although it was thick with snow it did make the going easier. They had walked for an hour, rested for ten minutes, walked for an hour rested for ten minutes, drinking some melted snow at each stop. Sam estimated that in the four hours of travel that morning they had only covered about eight miles. Once on the road their pace almost doubled. They spoke very little, and when they did it was brief and factual. There was no real conversation and neither of them mentioned what had happened the night before.

They were still on the road and walking downhill and Sam was pleased they were picking up some time. "We need to find somewhere to make camp, we'll lose light in about and hour and a half" he said. They carried on walking and suddenly Sam stopped. He pointed ahead, "What do you think that is?"

Liz stopped and looked. "It can't be, but it looks like a bus shelter". The structure was about half a mile away so they quickened their pace towards the building. It turned out to be a small open fronted barn, a rear and two side walls with an oversized roof made of corrugated iron, the type that would normally be used to store hay to feed the sheep that would be out on the hillside.

"We camp here" said Sam slipping his backpack off. There was a small amount of hay still in the barn which Sam thought may help light the fire. Liz too slipped her pack off and stood up and massaged her shoulders.

"We need some food, well certainly I do," she said looking at Sam. "What do you think we should do?"

Sam was a bit annoyed at this. So far he had found the shelter, both last night and this, he had provided the fire, he had sorted the wood provision for today, there were no trees in sight where they were now, it was his routine that had been adopted for travel and he had been the one using the compass and map that had got them this far. He was also still angry about what had happened the night before. It was not what he had intended at all. He had to grudgingly admit that he had enjoyed it, she did have a very nice, well trimmed body, but for god's sake, he didn't even like her. His anger surfaced. "You're the bloody expert, you find the food. You've done bugger all else so far but follow me". He sat down on a small pile of hay with his back to her and leaned on his backpack. Liz said nothing but she got up and left the barn, presumably to find some berries. Sam waited. She was gone about half an hour. "Sam, I've just seen a few sheep in the distance. That may mean that where they are grazing there is possibly something we could use as food, even if it is some leaves which we could use in a soup. It's only a few hundred yards but it away from the road so it would be safer if we both went in case one of us fell over".

Sam agreed, it was sensible to stay together. They walked towards the sheep, there were only three of them. Sitting huddled together. "The farmer must have come and taken the sheep in missed these three. Up here on the hills there would be many of them, these three may not survive with this weather out here". As they approached, the sheep became wary and as they got closer they all got up and started to move away.

"Look, one of them is hurt, poor thing is limping" said Liz.

"So it is, poor thing" said Sam sarcastically, as he hastened his pace and moved towards the injured sheep. As it moved away Sam started to run, the lamb stumbled, moving fast was difficult for Sam but the sheep's injury made it even slower. Sam caught up with it, he grabbed it around the neck, pulled up its head, took out his hunting knife and slit its throat. It was a clean cut and within a minute the sheep was dead. Sam picked it up and carried it back to where Liz was standing, the blood from its throat leaving a crimson trail on the white virgin snow. She was completely still with a look of horror on her face. "Dinner" said Sam as he walked past her towards their camp.

He placed the dead sheep on the ground, dug a small hole, took some of the dried wood from his backpack and lit a fire. He then slid his knife along the back of the sheep cutting the flesh down to the spine, He cut the meat away from the rib cage and then cut it into chunks. Still Liz said nothing, she had sat down opposite him and was looking at him working. Sam then placed about a dozen steaks on the ground.

"What about the fur, what are you going to do about that?" was the first thing that Liz said.

"It will burn off when it goes on the fire" he replied. Ten minutes later the fire was burning well and Sam placed four of the steaks onto it. They cooked quickly and smelt delicious. They tasted delicious too.

"I'm going to let the fire go out" Sam explained. We have used about half of our wood stock and we can't add to it here, there's nothing to gather, so we need to be careful with what we have. I'll wrap up the remaining lamb cuts and they should last us until me make camp".

Liz nodded. "Thanks Sam, I couldn't have done that, slit its throat and then still ate it I mean. I understand that it was necessary and probably an injured animal would have died anyway but all the same, I've never actually seen anything killed before so I'm sorry if you think I froze".

"That's OK, its getting dark, we may as well get into our sleeping bags and get an early night, I would like to get at least close to the camp by tomorrow evening if not actually get there". He stood up and gathered the pieces of meat, he wrapped them in his spare shirt and packed them in some snow just outside of the shelter. The carcass he then dragged away from the shelter, it would probably feed a few dozen birds and save them from starving.

By the time he returned to the shelter Liz had already zipped the two sleeping bags together and was already inside them. Sam slipped off his boots and jacket and slid down inside. She came on to him immediately, putting both arms around him and kissing him hard on the lips. Her hand then slipped down to his groin and despite himself he could feel that he was getting hard again. She quickly undid his trousers and gripped his penis. Sam suddenly realised that she had already taken off her trousers and thermal underwear, she was naked from the waist down. Suddenly she was on top him, she sat astride him, went down and forced him inside her. She was riding him furiously and then almost immediately she came, arching her back and shouting. As soon as she had finished she climbed off. Sam had not come, he was now aroused but had not reached a climax. Liz turned over, turning her back to him. "Night" she said smugly.

Sam lay in the dark. Until the last couple of years Sam's sexual gratification had been achieved with prostitutes, you paid your money, you had sex, you zipped up your trousers and you left. You used the woman and in return you gave her money. Sam realised that he had been used in the same way but without the money. There was no emotion, she had wanted sex and had taken it, his satisfaction was irrelevant to her. Sam was very confused about what was going on. He didn't fancy his woman, in fact he actually disliked her, but still she could get him aroused very easily it would seem.

As before the next morning she said nothing. Sam lit a small fire and heated some water which they drank before leaving. They made much better time this day as the ground was flatter and it wasn't until mid afternoon that they had to leave the road and go across country to find another road that would lead to the destination. They stopped at a small wooded area just before four o'clock and decided they would camp there for the night. Sam prepared to light the fire and this time Liz went off digging under the snow for wood for the fire. She came back with and armful. "How's this?" she said.

"That's fine but we need about four times as much as that to keep in all night. We shouldn't need to take any with us tomorrow because I think that we should arrive at camp at about midday". She went off to get more wood while Sam lit the fire using the dry wood that they had carried. He was very hungry so he was sure that Liz was too so he put almost all of the lamb steaks onto the fire as soon as it was hot enough. They both ate in silence, Sam had been right, it was obvious that Liz was hungry too.

They finished their dinner with some hot water in a billy can and then Sam put some of the wet wood that Liz had collected onto the fire. "Bedtime I think" he said walking towards his pack and picking up his sleeping bag. He zipped it up, took off his shoes and slipped inside. He didn't give Liz the opportunity of zipping them together. Liz did the same. They lay in the darkness. "Don't you want me to ravage you tonight Sam?" she said.

"Not really thanks. Are you that assertive to all of your lovers, or should I say conquests?"

"Conquests? Bit hypercritical aren't you? Men take women, men use women. Many men think that the greatest ecstasy a woman can have is to feel a man come inside her, well that's bollocks. Most men I've been with have just wanted a fuck. I happened to be the convenient female, but it could have been anybody and it would have made no difference. Bit like you really, I felt like it, you were there, you were convenient."

Sam said nothing, he just looked at her with annoyance showing on his face.

"Do you realise how difficult it is for a female officer to get laid in this man's army? It's an offence to have a physical relationship with other ranks, the senior officer's don't want to know for the same reason. You are a major, the same rank as me. Therefore we are two consenting adults of the same rank, so it's OK". Hardly consenting Sam thought, but said nothing.

Morning arrived, they had the rest of the lamb and warm water and set off. Just after ten o'clock they found the road that led to the RAF camp and they arrived there just after 3 O'clock that afternoon, just as it started to snow again.

They were shown to quarters and showered and changed into clean fresh clothes. They had a wait of about three hours until the plane arrived from Cambridge. It turned around in twenty minutes and they were on their way back south again. The pilot was unknown to Sam so they both sat in the rear and Sam was soon asleep. He was woken by a bump as the aircraft landed. A car took them back to the army camp in Norfolk. They had a late dinner in the officer's mess, together but with little conversation. They went to bed with instructions to report to the camp commander at 09.00 the next day.

The colonel was brief, Sam was to report to the Brigadier in London at 10.00 hours on Monday and Major Whitehead to her c/o at the same time and the same day.

# CHAPTER 52

Yuri interviewed the two soldiers that Irina had arranged to attend. Both were ethnically Uzbekistan, both their parents had been born there. Yuri felt that they would be able to integrate into any community across the border. He arranged for them to be co-opted and travel to Omsk the following day.

Despite Yuri being busy and Irina too, Irina had e-mailed him about her leaving date. She had agreed to stay on for March and induct the new people but they were in now and she needed to sort out her travel arrangements and she also needed to tell Sam as he was hoping to get some leave at the time she would arrive in England.

After the interviews Yuri spoke to her. "I am asking that you give me another few weeks Irina. If you will, you could travel on 12th April and as a thank you I will pay your air fare, I will arrange for a government car to take you to the airport and a priority pass through security. I think that you should travel on Aeroflot because British Airways are always on strike now and you may get stuck in the airport for days waiting for a flight. They now have a business class and that is good quality, not like Soviet days. They don't fly those horrible Ilysins planes any more, they fly Airbus planes to Europe and they are serviced by Airbus."

Irina kissed him on the cheek. "Thank you Yuri, I will tell Sam, I will work until 12th April. She immediately e-mailed Sam saying that she would telephone him on the Sunday, knowing that he would be back from his training then.

The following day Yuri went with his two new recruits back to the border and met with Captain Staviney. Once again Yuri's visit was not known to the local authorities.

The two recruits were briefed and within hours they had crossed the border and began their mission to gather information about terrorist activities and arms supply on the borders of Russia. After they left, Yuri was shown the progress being made on the buildings that were being erected to replace the tents that were home to the group at the moment. Yuri placed his kit in the tent that he had been allocated on the previous visit and then he and the Captain had dinner in the mess tent. Yuri had asked the two men to report any progress as soon as possible and to confirm that they had been able to make any contact. Yuri knew that this would take at least three days, probably more, and decided that the following day he would return to Moscow. He briefed the Captain on the procedure that he wanted followed and as the weather was improving, he told him that he hoped he would be able to travel by helicopter rather than train from now on which would result in him being able to react more quickly.

# CHAPTER 53

Sam arrived home just after lunchtime. He stripped, showered, and put on clean civvy clothes. He then went shopping, only to the local shops, he was too weary to get on the train to Beckton and go to Asda. Amongst the large pile of post that awaited him was a letter from his bank manager asking Sam to contact him to discuss investing his money. He advised Sam that he had millions of pounds on deposit earning less than one per cent in interest. Sam made a mental note to contact him as soon as possible.

He read four e-mails that Irina had sent. In one she told Sam that she had heard from her mother. She said that it was a rather guarded letter and in it her mother had said she had not mentioned Irina's letter or the wedding to Irina's father. Another said that she would phone him on Sunday because she had some news.

On Saturday he went to the gym in the apartment complex, mailed Irina that he looked forward to hearing from her, told her about his excursion in the snow covered Scottish Highlands, omitting the details about sex with his Major colleague, and that he was now office based until the Brigadier gave him an assignment.

As he often did when he was on his own, he went to his favourite Italian restaurant in Canning Town. He was up early on Sunday morning, he watched Sky News until nine o'clock and then turned over to BBC and watched Andrew Marr. He knew that he was killing time and he couldn't believe how much he was looking forward to speaking with Irina.

She telephoned him at midday. She told him first that she would travel to London on 12th April. She told him that Yuri had suggested that she flew with Aeroflot because British Airways were always striking and Sam told her that this was true so it was a good idea. They discussed the letter from her mother. After talking about it they decided that Sam would talk to the Brigadier about having a holiday in June or July and when he was told when, they would arrange to get married. When they knew the date, Sam would write to her parents and tell them about the wedding and offer to pay their fare over to London. They agreed that this was all they could do. They talked about how busy she had been at work, how much Yuri was away and the trouble with the terrorists. She gave Sam some of the details of the terrorist attacks that there had been in Russia that they had kept secret from the west. She said that even she was surprised at how many there had been. "Yuri is even now on the border working on a mission to stop guns coming into Russia" she told Sam. Sam didn't really care what she said, he was just so happy to hear her voice and be able to talk to her again. They talked for over an hour and agreed that Sam would telephone her on Wednesday evening and tell her about his new office job.

Sam reported at 10.00 hours as he had been instructed to. He saluted and stood to attention when shown into the Brigadiers office. He was dressed in one of his new uniforms and his shoes were polished to a gloss that his old sergeant major would have been proud of. "Good morning Major, at ease". Sam stood at ease in front of the Brigadier's desk. "Today you will get settled in. I will introduce you to one of our civilian staff who will show you where your work station will be and run you through the computer and the database. It goes without saying that any information on the database is not to be taken out of this building and whatever the content it is covered by the official secrets act". Sam followed his senior officer out of his office and into a large open plan office space. Sam was introduced to a middle age woman, Mrs Clark, who was one of the civilian clerical workers. She was just over five feet tall, plump, greying hair, minimal makeup but had a lovely warm smile. She wore a tweed skirt, matching jumper and cardigan and flat, what his mother would have called, sensible shoes. Sam's initial judgment was that she was probably a great mumsy mum.

The Brigadier continued to address Sam. "The normal dresscode here is civilian, suits, with a stripped or plain shirt and a tie. Unless there is an occasion, in which case you will be informed, it would be a good idea if you could adopt that from tomorrow. You will report to my office at 09.30 hours tomorrow when I will review the reports of your training exercises. In the meantime Mrs Clark will show you the computer system, how to access data and our internal procedures.

I would like you to study what we have on Nigeria". With that he saluted Sam and turned and walked away.

"Well Major" said Mrs Clark, shall we start with a cup of tea while the computer boots up? They are a bit old so take a few minutes to load all of the stuff from the server. They have to deal with a load of firewalls first".

Sam nodded, "Good idea" he said as she flicked the switch on his terminal.

On his way to the small kitchen Sam was introduced to the two other operatives that were in the office that day, both Majors, and to another four civilian staff who all seemed to do jobs like Mrs Clark, a bit of clerical and secretarial support. Mrs Clark told Sam that she was his link in the office, whether he was here or out on assignment, so anything he needed or didn't understand, he was to ask her.

He returned to his desk with his cup of tea and accessed the departments file on Nigeria. He became absorbed in what he was reading. He knew that Nigeria was basically a Muslim country had not realised that there were Muslim extremists in the north of it. There is a group called Boko Haram who model themselves on the Taliban. In 2009 the group were alleged to have killed over seven hundred people. He read that it's members had attacked police stations and fought with security forces. Their leader, Mohamed Yusef was arrested and gunned down by police. It was alleged that he was shot while trying to escape but British Intelligence information suggested that he had been murdered, as he may have implicated some important political figures who are supporting the group. The movement is centered around Malduguri, a town in the North of the country, which is currently surrounded by tanks and armoured vehicles of the national army, in an attempt to stop supplies of arms and explosives coming in from Chad and Niger. A spokesman for the group, Musa Tanko, told Arab media recently that the group are affiliated to al-Qaeda in the Islamic Maghreb, which is operating in Algeria and has links with other fundamentalist groups throughout the Middle East. He went on to say that Islam does not recognise national borders and has the right to pursue Islamic justice throughout the world. Intelligence from both UK and US sources have linked Umar Farouk Abdulmutalab, who tried to blow up an American airliner with explosives hidden in his underpants, as a member of this group.

Mrs Clark brought Sam a sandwich for his lunch and he spent the afternoon as he had spent the morning, looking into various reports and information filed about the terrorist threat in Nigeria, not only from Muslim groups but also from groups of armed criminals, whose source of income was ransom payments from Western companies, especially oil companies, whose employees are kidnapped and returned for substantial amounts of money.

The next morning Sam was sitting opposite the Brigadier as he looked at Sam's file that was open on his desk. "I have the reports of all of your instructors here from your training programme. Health, excellent. Fitness, very good, with a rider that at your age you need to keep on top of it. Therefore I have arranged for you to spend two hours, two afternoons a week while you are based in the office, at the gym of the Household Cavalry which is not far from here. Marksmanship excellent, unarmed combat and knife combat, very good. Freefall, parachuting and abseiling, all very good. Communications, good, all very acceptable except for the report from Major Whitehead. She has reported that your performance and attitude were far below the level that she would consider to be satisfactory. When trying to de-brief you, you told her that her tutorial was irrelevant because if you were going to kill somebody you would do it with a gun or a knife". The Brigadier stopped talking and looked at Sam.

"Yes Sir, I did say something like that". Sam was astonished. They had spent almost four days marooned together, he had fed her, fended for her and generally kept her going and kept her alive, God she had even fucked him. She never once read the map or used the compass, she didn't help with the fire or the preparation of the wood. It was Sam who provided the food and this was the thanks he got. What an ungrateful cow she was to put in a report like that after all he had done for her. However Sam kept his opinion to himself.

The Brigadier continued, "You need to remember Major that nothing I do or arrange to be done by others is irrelevant. Everything I do has a purpose and that is something that you need to accept without question. You say that you would kill with a knife or gun if you needed to dispose of somebody. Sometimes people need to be dealt with who, for various reasons, cannot be shot or knifed.

Let me give you and example. Around the middle of last year an African politician died. He died in great pain and slowly and his tribal witch doctors claimed that he died as a result of a curse that they had placed upon him. However a French doctor working for a local aid agency, carried out a post mortem and he found that the man had died from septicemia, blood poisoning. He found traces of a poison in some of his body tissues. The CIA had some of the tissues analysed in more depth and found that not only was there poison in the tissues but also a residue of human waste. There are a number of African tribes that dip spears in human fasces but looking at the decay and absorption time they concluded that the poison would probably have been administered while the man was in Ireland. In fact Major you may have met him. You were in Ireland at the same time and so was your chum Major Dolchenko, or should I say Colonel as he now is. So you see major somebody wanted our African friend dead and make it look like it was a local issue, no guns and no knives."

Sam looked at the Brigadier. He knew instinctively that the Brigadier knew that Sam had been involved. Sam was thinking where the hell did he get his information. "Yes sir, point taken", was all Sam could think to say.

"In future please don't make it necessary for me to explain myself again Major". There was a silence for a few seconds. The Brigadier looked at Sam. "Despite the report that Major Whitehead compiled about you, she goes on and reports how you performed on your field trip. Apparently you performed in an exemplary way, providing for heating, shelter and food. She did admit at her debriefing that she would like to include details of the trip in future lectures, an excellent example of using the resources that are available. So well done there Major".

"Thank you sir", at least the cow had given him credit for that part of their time together.

"Now Major, have you read the files we have on Nigeria?"

"Yes Sir I spent all yesterday reading all that we have".

"Good. You will be going there soon, I'm not quite sure when yet. It's not a killing job, its observe and report. We need to know how serious the terrorist threat is, how widespread the support is, what weapons they have and a supply line if possible. I do need somebody however who can handle themselves. The last chap who we put in there couldn't, not one of mine, he was MI6".

"What happened to him" asked Sam.

"He was found hanging from a tree, from a branch that hung out over a river that had crocodiles in it, they had managed to bite both his legs off well above the knee before he became too high for them to reach. We are not sure at which point he died but certainly after the crocs had had a bit of a feed. You will spend three days, starting tomorrow, learning about African birds with an expert at Regents Park Zoo. When you go to Nigeria your cover will be as a consultant doing work for the RSPB". With that Sam was dismissed.

Back in the office Sam asked Mrs Clark about the procedure for booking holidays. She gave him a form to fill in, he was to give it back to her and she would get the Brigadier to approve it or not, as the case may be. Sam filled it in for April 12th.

The next day he reported to the London Zoo bird expert. Whatever the subject he was determined to pay attention and look interested: Actually he did find it was interesting, he didn't need to pretend. Because of the climate the plumage of birds in that part of Africa didn't deteriorate with age as it did in Europe. You needed to catch the birds and examine their eyes to determine age. Sam was told how to trap birds humanly and what to look for. He was taught how to ring them for future identification and how to release them unharmed. He spent almost two days looking at slides of the birds that he would be likely to see and at the end of the week he could name them all within a second or two of them appearing on the screen. His instructor was obviously impressed and told Sam so. He also told Sam that if he had another couple of weeks he could teach Sam about their various mating rituals and habits and the type, colour and size of egg that they laid. He could tell him about their migration habits, did Sam know for example that many African birds migrated north, to cooler climates in the summer, to mate and lay their eggs. Only when the young were strong enough to fly did they return to Africa. Sam told him that he would read up on the subject when he had a bit of time.

# CHAPTER 54

Yuri arrived back in Moscow. He asked Irena to set up a data base with details of all seconded operatives, the two that he had appointed the previous week and the special troop that he stationed on the border in the South. If he had such a record he could select from experience when he needed outside recruits in future.

He also reviewed intelligence that had been received and put into the data bank which was expanding at a huge rate. It was Irena that had researched the computer system and he had to admit that this Rackable storage was excellent, its response time when information was requested was very impressive.

Yuri was restless. There was so much going on in his world and yet he was waiting on all fronts, he needed some action. He had not spent much time recently with his latest mistress, in fact he was tired of her already. She had been his mistress for just over two months and already he was about to tell her to leave, but tonight he would take her out for a meal and work off his frustrations on her in bed afterwards. It was almost the end of March so the weather was improving so going out to a restaurant was not a problem. Irena entered his office and asked for him to write his comments on the files that she had compiled on the troops stationed at the border. He only had comments about the Captain so far but the more he met him the more he was impressed.

He telephoned his mistress to tell her to be ready at 7.00pm prompt, he would collect her, and to make herself ready.

He read various reports and files for the rest of the day and left the office at five o'clock precisely. Irena left just thirty minutes later. She was at home when Sam telephoned her as arranged. He told her that he had had the day's holiday approved for 12th April so would be at Heathrow to meet her and take her home, their home in his flat, until she chose a house and they moved some time in the summer. He told her that there would be a general election in Britain soon and he wanted to wait until after it to buy as houses may be cheaper then. He told her that he had visited his bank manager and he was investing a large amount of his money so that they would have a good income when he left the army. He told her that he had been told what his first assignment was to be but he couldn't tell her when or what it was. She understood that having worked for Yuri. She told him that Yuri seemed unhappy and was very worried about some of the information that was coming in to the office about terrorism activity and threats in the countries that bordered Russia. She too felt that she couldn't give Sam the details. Sam told her that he had ordered two made to measure suits for work and five shirts from the same tailor, he had also order two new pairs of shoes, all for work. He explained to her that he did not need to wear an army uniform when he was in the office in London.

Irina gave Sam the name and address of her parents and said that she would be happy if he wrote to them. Maybe hearing from an English officer would impress her parents. She told Sam that she had looked online and that there were three flights from Moscow to London every day so she would have a word with Yuri as to which flight she should take. She told him that when it was booked she would e-mail Sam. Irina became exited when she talked about it; it was, after all, only a couple of weeks away. Sam too was beginning to get exited about it. He realised how important it was to him to have Irina with him in London and Irina could tell this just by listening to him. They spent a few more minutes talking about the weather, talking about buying furniture for their home when they bought the house and then said their goodbyes.

Yuri's current mistress, Magda was ready when he called for her promptly at 7 o'clock. Yuri could see that she had obviously made a big effort for him. He hadn't given her that much notice but she had had her hair washed and make up done and wore a mid blue low cut dress that showed off her big bust to it maximum effect. Yuri had to admit that she looked good tonight, and very sexy. They had dinner in a central Moscow restaurant that Yuri particularly liked, where he had an account and where he was well known so the service he received was as a priority special guest. He started with three glasses of vodka and then he had a rare steak which was cooked exactly as he liked it and Magda had the same, a steak, but she had a small glass of wine.

They hadn't spent an evening together for more than two weeks and although Yuri had told Magda that it was due to him being so busy, she did suspect that he was tiring of her. She knew that with men like Yuri the relationship was only for a limited time. She had met many powerful men in her job as a hostess at an exclusive Moscow bar, but she liked being Yuri's mistress. The apartment that Yuri had put her in was a nice one. He was fairly generous with the expense account and all she had to do was be there for him when he called and provide whatever he wanted.

Tonight Yuri was morose. It was nothing to do with Magda, he was frustrated and annoyed about the progress he was making with the project that he was involved in. He had so much information stored at his offices at the Federal Security Service, at the Lubyanka building, too much probably, but he still couldn't get definite information that would enable his teams to make an effective killer assault. The only firm information he had at the moment was about six teams, in six very different locations, not linked as far as he could tell. All small fish. He wanted the big men, the organisers, the men running the groups and supplying the arms. Despite Magda looking so good, and despite the food being so good, Yuri was drinking more vodka and gradually becoming more depressed and frustrated. Suddenly he had had enough. He stood up ready to leave. Magda was still drinking wine but she too stood up immediately ready to leave. Two waiters quickly brought their coats and they left, getting into Yuri's official car which had waited for them outside.

They returned to Magda's apartment. She knew that he was tense and unhappy so immediately they closed the door she started to seduce him in an attempt to take his mind off of whatever was troubling him. The apartment had one living room and one bedroom as well as a kitchen and bathroom. The rooms were large and the flat was comfortably furnished, it was warm despite the cold weather outside, with good quality furniture and a large, king size double bed. Magda stood in the middle of the lounge floor, took off her coat and slipped the dress over her shoulders. It slipped to the floor and she stepped out of it.

"You like Yuri?" she said. "I get them to please you". She was wearing sexy, but tastefully expensive underwear made by Agent Provocateur. It was pink satin edged with black lace, the bra, brief panties and a suspender belt holding up black stockings. The picture was completed by the black, highly polished shoes, with five inch stiletto heels. "Let me soothe your troubles away" she said as she came towards him. She took off his coat and his jacket and started to unbutton his shirt as she moved close to kiss him. He was suddenly very aroused. He picked her up and carried her to the bedroom. He threw her on the bed and started to kiss her roughly, she kissed him back while feeling for his trouser button and zip at the same time. He stopped kissing her and moved to unfasten the stockings from the suspenders. She had opened his trousers and was now going down on him with her mouth. He pulled away and stood up at the end of the bed, pulling both of her stockings down and off of her legs, he then roughly turned her onto her front and lay on top of her. He grabbed her right wrist and tied a stocking to it and then tied it to the bedpost. He then repeated this with the left wrist. She soon found herself bound by the hands lying on her front. Magda had been with many men when she had been a club hostess, but she had always drawn the line at bondage. This time though she knew that not only would it be useless to protest but that it would also be end of her relationship with Yuri. He was her master, he owned her and in return for her acquiescence she had the apartment, and the clothes and the comfortable lifestyle. She had made her decision to go along with whatever he wanted months ago when Yuri first propositioned her. Tonight she didn't really have a choice. She felt him rather than saw him remove his trousers. She moved her hips slightly upwards so that it would be easier for him to enter her but he pushed her rear down as he climbed on top. All of a sudden he thrust into her. She was in agony, he had entered her anus, he was buggering her. She wanted to scream out but knew that she couldn't. She couldn't help but make a small noise when he hurt her the most. Yuri thrust and thrusted again, he knew that he was hurting her, he could hear the whimpers as he pushed and pushed. Finally he came into her and all the frustrations he felt with the situation released into her body. He climbed off of her. He knew that he had not been fair to her but he felt no real remorse and no sympathy. She was a tart, his tart, and she would do what he wanted in return for her position. He quickly dressed and said "see you soon my love" as he left the apartment and left her still tied to the bed and sobbing quietly into a pillow.

As he sat in the back of his car being driven home, Yuri reflected on this evening. Maybe it would be nice to have a wife, somebody to come home to and share the problems of the day with. Sam Tucker seemed to have settled for that and he was doing so with one of the few women that Yuri had actually felt affection for and respected. But he knew that he could never be monogamous and woman like Irina would demand that. He couldn't see the point of that when there were so many women available. Also sex was a good weapon, it was not only something that could be used against the women but it could be used against her husband, boyfriend, father or indeed any male relative. His thoughts went back to the mayor's wife. He would bugger her as well as soon as the opportunity presented itself. He got out of the car at his apartment with a smile on his face at the thought of it. He really didn't like her or her husband. Yuri decided that he would never have a real relationship. This was his lot in life and as he walked into his new, very luxurious apartment in the centre of Moscow, not far from Park Kultury, he reflected that it wasn't such a bad life after all. If only he could nail some of these bastard terrorists. Monday was the twenty ninth of March. Irina would be leaving in two weeks. The weekend she would leave work was also Easter in Russia, at least it was for the Russian Orthodox Church. That gave him two weeks to get all of the pieces together so that he was ready to move when the holiday weekend was over. He would bully and cajole all involved for more action in the next two weeks and make sure that things moved forward. His interlude with Magda this evening seemed to have given him fresh impetus.

# CHAPTER 55

Sam was back in the office Monday morning. He was accessing information about birds of Nigeria when Mrs Clark told him that the Brigadier wanted to see him.

"Sit down please Major" said the Brigadier as Sam walked into his office. "I understand that the woman that you are intending to bring to England works in the FSB office which is now located in the old KGB offices in Lubyanka."

"Yes sir that is correct". Sam was suddenly very worried. He had never hidden where Irina worked and what she did. Was there now suddenly a problem in her coming and living in Britain?

"There is probably no cause for alarm but I have just received intelligence that a large bomb was detonated on a train at the Lubyanka Station. You know what the Russians are like, we cannot get any information at the moment but I did think that you would like to try and make contact with you fiancée to check that everything is alright".

Sam's mind was swimming, "Thank you sir, I will try and contact her now".

"I am just about to go out for a meeting so you can use my office if you like."

Sam held the phone. He realised that Irina did not have a mobile phone and he didn't know her office phone number. He telephoned Yuri instead as he had his mobile phone number. He got straight through to Yuri who sounded very tense. He told Sam that Irina was fine and gave him a number where she could be contacted. Sam phoned immediately.

"Oh Shammy it's awful, there are many people dead from the train and another bomb has gone off near where Yuri lives, where there are lots of government offices". She went on to tell Sam that she had gone to the office early as she had lots of work to do before she left to live in England. She had arrived at almost 7 o'clock so was working when the bomb went of just before 8.00am. He assured himself that she was indeed alright although a bit shaken, so they agreed to talk that evening and both went back to work.

The Brigadier returned at lunchtime and Sam was asked to go to see him once again. "Did you make contact with Moscow?" he asked.

"Yes thank you sir, she's fine. She was already in the office when the bomb went off".

"There were two I hear. Usually the Russians give very sanitised reports of activity within the country or deny that anything happened at all, but in this case there are lots of pictures taken with mobile phone cameras and posted on the internet. Thay show victims in railway carriages. Both bombs were apparently were detonated in stations. That is peculiar. If they wanted to create more mayhem it would have been better to detonate in tunnels, more difficult to get to for rescue teams, more difficult for survivors to exit, more difficult to remove debris and it would close the underground system for several days at least. This way the Ruskies will have it up and running by tomorrow morning I would suspect."

"Yes sir, I agree. Are we involved at all here sir, are we investigating or co-operating at all?"

"No. We will always co-operate if asked, but our Russian friends never do. Their problems and ours are different. Most of their dissidents, the potential terrorists come from former Soviet states. The Russians were fairly brutal in the way they put down any resistance in the Caucuses especially. They had an almost zero tolerance of religious practice. They just about tolerated the Russian Orthodox church but that was fairly benign. Islam was not and their solution was to suppress it and kill those who did not acquiesce. If women and children got in the way, well that was just hard luck. What they never understood is that the culture of blood revenge is very strong in the culture of some of these people, those in the Northern Caucasus especially. It is seen as a duty of surviving members to avenge the killing of relatives. They killed men and their sons but often left the women alive. Our intelligence suggests that many of these women feel that they have little to live for with no husband or family and are ideal fodder to be blackmailed or indoctrinated to being part of assault teams, even suicide bombers, to avenge their family. Because they traditionally wear loose fitting, full length black dresses, it is not difficult for them to disguise the fact that they have explosives or small guns under their robes".

"Maybe sir, the reason that the bombs were detonated in stations was that they were detonated by a third party. It could be that the third party was outside the station so would not be harmed. I do remember from my course that the chap from communications said that a mobile phone can easily be used to detonate a bomb and that this had been done a few years ago during the troubles in Northern Ireland".

"Good point Major, that's true. Maybe that is what happened. Anyway, to more relevant issues. You are taking a day's holiday on 12th April I understand".

"Yes sir if possible"

"Its fine. I would suggest that you also have the Tuesday off to make sure that you lady is properly settled. On Wednesday back here for a briefing and on Friday 16th you are booked on a flight to Lagos. You are Sam Tucker, Ornithologist, working for the RSPB. You have read our files about the dissidents?"

"Yes sir".

"Good, read them again and again. See if you can find pictures in the press of the main characters, Tanko, the police chief Azare, even the Mullah Omar. If any of them appear you will need to know who they are. As I have said before this is only an intelligence gathering mission with the secondary purpose of getting you to establish a presence. I would anticipate that you would be there less than three weeks on this trip but depending upon the results, you will probably have to return for longer in the future. I must say the report from the chappie at the zoo was very good, he said that you showed a great interest and thought that you had a natural enthusiasm and talent for the subject. Read up on all of the material that you can find about the birds as well. Your knowledge and your ability to appear genuine may save your life. Get Mrs Clark to help you source information, that's what she's there for. Everything understood?"

"Yes sir". Sam stood and saluted and left the room. He went back to his computer and found out more information about the birds he was likely to see in Nigeria. He found a section describing their eggs that had been produced by the instructor from Regents Park.

He telephoned him to tell him that he was studying his paper and the ornithologist seemed both pleased and flattered.

Towards the end of the day, Sam wrote a letter to Irina's parents. He introduced himself, told them that he had met their daughter over a year ago (God, was it only a year he thought to himself?). He told them that she was coming to England in two weeks time and that she was going to live with him and that they intended to get married in the summer. He went on to say that he understood that there had been some problem in the past between them but he hoped that they could put it all behind them. He hoped they would wish them good luck and that they would come to England and visit at the time of the wedding. Sam said that he had independent means and would be pleased to pay for their flight tickets at the time should they wish to come. He hand wrote the letter and one of the secretaries who spoke Russian, translated it and typed it up for him, He placed both the translation and the written original in an envelope and posted it on his way home.

# CHAPTER 56

Yuri had enjoyed his weekend. He had followed his recreation with Magda with a dinner on Saturday evening with two old KGB colleagues. They had concluded the night with some young, active hostesses from the bar they finished in. Sunday, he spent reviewing the latest information he had received from the various units that he had working on his behalf. He even went for a walk in the crisp Spring sunshine that was now the weather in Moscow. He had enjoyed his weekend also, because it was the first weekend that he had not really worked for months, certainly since the New Year.

On Monday he was up early, he was refreshed and felt better than he had felt for weeks. He powered up his laptop and sent an e-mail to one of the new administration assistants in the office telling her to book a flight for Irina on 12th April to London, business class. As he started to check his e-mails he realised that she would be going in exactly two weeks. He felt genuinely happy for her. He suddenly saw an e-mail from Captain Staveney. He had heard from one of the undercover soldiers that had moved over the border. The information suggested that arms and explosives were being moved to the Northern Caucuses. The information they had was that the explosives were going to be used in some sort of terrorist attack which would take place soon, they did not yet know where. They believed that there was a new group being set up which was made up of family members of people who had been killed by the Russians, some of whom were women.

He was in his car travelling to the office when he heard a dull noise in the distance. Yuri was experienced enough to know it was an explosion, the only question was where. Shortly afterwards there was another, the second one seemed to come from somewhere behind him and slightly further away. As he got close to his office he saw people running along the pavement, away from the station. His car got caught up with crowds running along in the road. Yuri got out and walked the last two hundred yards to his office. He arrived shortly after eight o'clock.

Irina was in the office looking out of the window. "What's happening?" he asked.

"I don't know Yuri. I heard a noise, it sounded like an explosion and then the building shuddered and then it was all very quiet. Then I heard lots of screams and saw people running from the station some had blood on their clothes".

Yuri picked up his phone, he punched in a number and barked some orders to the person on the other end. Less than an hour later Yuri was with the leader of the police task force investigating, standing on the station platform at Lubiyanka. The police had taken some of the passenger's mobile phones and sent the pictures that they had taken to a central computer base at the Central Moscow police headquarters. They had over one hundred of them. Yuri had only seen the e-mail that morning about women terrorists being involved in an attack. The police had established that there at least three women involved in the two bombings.

Later that day, having investigated the evidence that they had gathered, the police issued a statement saying that the terrorists had concealed the explosive in belts together with metal fragments and nails. They were designed to cause maximum damage. Because the news was already public knowledge the authorities sought maximum media coverage instead of their usual method of hushing it up.

Yuri was still in his office at six o'clock watching the television. The television evening news reported that the two explosions were timed forty minutes apart, Yuri could not yet work out why that was. It was now public knowledge that the two bombers at Park Kultury were women. They were officially described as being of Eastern appearance, with black hair and wearing black clothes. The report included some CCTV footage the police had retrieved, taken from the stations and the trains. This had enabled the authorities to identify the bombers. They went on to report that the FSB were now heading the operation and asked for the public's help in locating a man with a short beard, wearing a blue jacket with white insets, a dark baseball cap and white trainers. According to accounts, one of the groups boarded the train at Yugo-Zapadnaya station and the news broadcaster asked for anybody who was on the train at that station who had not yet given police a statement to come forward. The report continued saying that Chechen terrorists had used women before in July 2003 and a previous bombing on the Metro in 2004, that had killed forty one people and injured over two hundred and fifty.

Suddenly Yuri took notice of the news item. President Medvedev was criticising the security forces for failing to do more to protect the country and its people. Mr Putin, who was on a trip to Siberia, just said that 'the terrorists will be hunted and destroyed'. Yuri was furious, Medvedev blaming the security forces, blaming Yuri's section, blaming Yuri as he saw it. "Bloody cheeck of the man. We have only been in operation for a few months. We had to wait ages for equipment. He will not follow the more open policy with the West to exchange information as I have suggested and its my fault. Shit on him". Yuri threw the vodka glass in his hand at the television screen in anger. He phoned Captain Staveney and told him that he would be back in Omsk tomorrow and that he wanted to make contact with his men over the border. He told him to tell the local police chief that he would be coming down and to book him into the hotel for at least two nights. He said to tell him that he wanted a meeting late afternoon the next day, the Tuesday. He grabbed his jacket and coat and stormed from the office without even saying goodnight to Irina who was still there working.

The following day Yuri left early for Omsk. He took a helicopter and was met by Captain Staviney shortly before eleven. The two men who were under cover in Kazakhstan had made contact early with the base. They reported that not only had more arms been delivered but there were also another four widows traveling with the arms who were to be used in the next attack. The store they had located was in a small village, half way between the border and a town called Pavlodar. The Captain had a large scale map spread out on a table and the village located.

Yuri spoke. "Contact the men, tell them to get themselves an alibi for tonight and tomorrow morning. Maybe they should get drunk and be with a group who can alibi them. Have your men ready at 05.00 in the morning, we will go in and get them. If that idiot Medvedev wants action, we will give it to him".

After some discussions about strategy for the next day, Yuri arranged for one of the Corporals to drive him back into the town.

He told him to collect him at the hotel entrance at 04.00 the next morning. He then walked into the police headquarters unannounced. They had been warned that he was in town; security was tight. He was asked to identify himself three times before he was shown into the office of the Chief of Police. The Mayor was already there waiting. Yuri received an update about the change in policing methods throughout the district including an upgrading of the communications equipment. There was also a training programme to improve the performance of the police especially in marksmanship. Yuri tried hard to keep his emotions under control, the Police Chief was talking as though all of these initiatives were his, but in fact Yuri had suggested all of the changes to the Police Chief during his previous stay. Yuri needed to remind himself that the most important thing was that the changes had been put in place.

When the business was concluded it was the Mayor who spoke, "We know that you were up early this morning and have had a full day so we assume that you would rather spend the evening on your own and have an early night".

"No, not at all. I enjoy the company of both you your good ladies and it will be my pleasure if you would all be my guests tonight". They could not refuse a colonel from Moscow and arranged to meet at the hotel at seven thirty. Yuri left and walked to the hotel. He was smiling, he was making mental notes of plans for the Mayors wife later that night.

They met as arranged in the hotel bar. There was the Police Chief and his wife, the Mayor and his wife, and the niece Tanya, who had been at their first dinner. The conversation was rather forced. Obviously, given Yuri's performance during his last visit they were apprehensive about his plans for the evening, and more importantly afterwards. They asked him how long he was going to be here and how often he thought he may visit. He said that his was just a routine check on the squad at the border and he didn't expect to be around for more that a couple of days. He realised that the presence of Tanya was as a decoy from the other women. Half way through dinner Yuri accepted that the ploy had worked. He had wanted to totally humiliate the Mayors' wife and use her in a degrading way but the more he thought about it now he was looking at her, he decided that he found her repulsive. She was very overweight with huge hips, she had a bad haircut and in a style that was twenty years out of date, she wore far too much makeup and was smothered in a perfume that reminded Yuri of a urinal building in an army barrack block. Tanya on the other hand was young, attractive and as Yuri already knew, was an expert in bed.

After the meal he was the first to leave the restaurant, returning to his hotel with Tanya on his arm. They got to his hotel room, he went to the bathroom to wash his hands and when he returned Tanya was already naked, in bed waiting for him. She was just what he needed, good, uncomplicated sex with an attractive woman who knew how to please a man.

He was up early the next morning, at the steps of the hotel when the driver arrived at four thirty sharp.

Dressed in camouflage fatigues the group was ready when Yuri arrived at the base. They set out immediately and arrived at the outskirts of the target village just over two hours later. They had no recognisance information so spent about an hour studying the layout and likely arms storage places. It was a very small village, only eight houses, too small for a school and any sort of church or mosque. This would make their task a bit easier. At one end of the town was a house larger than the other with a barn behind it. Yuri and Captain Staveney agreed that this was the most likely target. Yuri assigned two soldiers each to watch the other houses and the main group moved forward to the target. It was reminiscent of the attack he had been involved in a few months ago at New Year. The target was the correct one. They rushed the house, some from the front and some from the back. The occupants were still asleep. Two of the men managed to fire some shots before being shot themselves, they killed two of the Russians in the process. A third man had tried to fire his gun but it had jammed. He was quickly disarmed and one of the Privates stabbed a knife in his chest rather than shoot him. He looked around at the Captain and said "They have killed my best friend, he will die more slowly that way".

In another bedroom they found four women. All looked to be in their early twenties. The problem was that so far they had found only a few guns. Yuri knew that if the information about the house had been correct, and the information about four women, then the arms had to be somewhere. They secured the men and the women in their rooms and left a guard with them. They searched the house and found nothing. They searched the barn and there, hidden underneath hay, were the arms, automatic rifles, hand grenades, explosives, pistols and detonators. Yuri's men piled the guns and grenades in a field on the edge of the village. They put the grenades on the pile and took the explosive material and laid it around the cache, attaching the detonators. They roused all of the villagers and made them stand and look as they brought the men out of the house, and the bodies of those that they had killed, and placed them next to the pile. They then detonated the explosives, blowing both the men and bodies into vapour. The Captain then addressed the villagers. "We will not tolerate enemies of Mother Russia plotting against us. Anybody supporting subversives will be executed. You are being spared this time to warn others who may wish to plot and scheme against us. You will tell them to desist. They cannot win". With that he sent them back to their homes telling them to stay inside until the operation had finished and they had left the village.

"What about the women Colonel?" asked the Captain.

"Let your men do what they want with them and when they have had their fun, kill them" was the reply.

The women were stripped naked and lay motionless as they were repeatedly gang raped. When the men were unable to perform any more the soldiers emptied machine guns magazines into the womens bodies. When they had finished the scene was like a slaughterhouse. The bloodied shapes bore no resemblance to human bodies, they were just a mass of bloodied meat.

They returned to their base over the border, job done.

Yuri returned to Omsk where he had dinner in his hotel room, just him and Tanya, and then they spent the night together before he headed back to Moscow. Now he had something positive to report to his political masters. Another attack dealt with before it happened. He enjoyed Tanya, both her company and her body. He thought that maybe he would invite her to stay in Moscow with him.

# CHAPTER 57

It was Friday afternoon in London. Sam was with the Brigadier being debriefed about his knowledge of birds. When they had finished the Brigadier sat back. "Bloody fools the Russians".

"Who sir?" Sam didn't know how else to respond.

"GCHQ reported that earlier this week a group from the Russian army crossed into Kazakhstan and wiped out a group, presumably terrorist suspects, and blew up the explosives and ammunition they had captured with the men tied to it. Locals allege that they also raped and murdered some women. The Russians deny it happened but it was all seen on a US surveillance satellite. The Russians have no idea how accurate and clear the pictures are from these satellites. The problem is that they just don't get it. They go into the old Soviet countries and deal with dissidents as they always have done. What they don't understand is that the psyche of these fundamentalists is revenge. This group will be revenged. If they murdered six people there will be twelve ready to take their place. History tells us that they should negotiate".

"But sir, we claim not to negotiate with terrorists."

"We may claim not to, but that is politicians talking. But of course we talk, we have to otherwise people would just go on being killed, civilians with no involvement in conflict. You were in Ireland. Look at what has happened, hundreds killed, soldiers, terrorists, civilians, and now the terrorists we fought are in government and the killing has stopped. Look back fifty years at Kenya. The Mao Mao terrorists fought the British army for independence. Their leader Kenyatta was a terrorist with a price on his head. A couple of years later he is welcomed to London by Her Majesty the Queen and Prime Minister as leaders of our nation. A turnabout maybe, but the killing stopped."

"Should we not assist them in some way sir, after all terrorism is an international problem. One of the things I read in our Nigeria files is about a Muslim leader saying that Islam does not accept national boundaries."

"They don't want our help. In the few conversations that I have had with them they think their terrorist problems are domestic and that those we and America have are not related to their situation. Also, we have to be careful what we say about what we know. As I said, they don't realise how accurate the US satellite cameras are. That may be an advantage one day. The US share their information with us, at least most of it, and also with other European countries and the Israelis. Its an advantage that some powers don't know how much detail we have available. Do you know that we could print photos of those soldiers faces in Kazakhstan that would be almost as good as if we had taken them with a small digital camera from six feet away? That's how good the detail is. Anyway, time to head home for the weekend. By the way Major, the Quartermaster will be here on Wednesday to kit you out for your trip".

"Thank you sir", Sam stood and saluted and then left the room.

For Sam the weekend dragged. Apart from going to the gym on both Saturday and Sunday he had little to do. It was raining so he didn't fancy going out anywhere. Apart from the hour on Saturday evening and the hour on Sunday when he phoned Irina, the days moved slowly.

Irina told him that she had received her flight tickets and that Yuri had organised for her to travel business class, but not only had he booked her one seat but two, seats 1A and 1B. As there were only four seats abreast in business class it meant that she had nobody sitting next to her. "I am flying on flight number SU 241 and it arrives in London at twelve ten".

"I will be there to meet you of course" Sam responded.

She told him that Yuri was also lending her his official car to travel to the airport so there would be no delay if there was traffic, Yuri car had police sirens and concealed lights fitted, but as an official car it could park in the restricted area in front of the terminal. Sam was pleased that she sounded so happy and bubbly and her mood was infectious. He kept reminding himself that it was a little more than a week before she would be here in London with him.

Sam told her that he had written to her parents and he had had his letter translated into Russian. Irina said she had not heard from them further and that she hoped that they would respond to Sam. When she talked about her parents it was the only time that Sam thought she sounded a bit sad.

They finished the phone call on the Sunday professing their love for each other as they always did and saying that in just over a week they would be together forever.

Sam came off the phone feeling both elated and down. He really loved Irina and couldn't wait for her to come and be with him but at that moment a week seemed an age. Added to that he would only have a few days with her before he went on assignment. That was a very short time, but he knew that was the army and he was much more fortunate than his former colleagues fighting in Iraq and Afghanistan.

# CHAPTER 58

Monday morning, less than an hour after Yuri had arrived at his office there was a message instructing him to go and see Mr Putin immediately. Not much frightened Yuri but being summoned to see Mr Putin at short notice was one of them. He knew that the fallout from the bombs on the subway network would arrive on his desk eventually, especially after the speech by President Medvedev. On the way to the Politbureau offices Yuri decided that he would be vigorous in his defence. He would tell the Prime Minister about the lack of information, lack of resources and lack of liaison that had been going on for years. Even now some agencies only gave up their information reluctantly and slowly.

He was shown into Mr Putin's office and stood to attention at the Prime Ministers' desk.

"At ease Colonel" said Putin. "Congratulations on a job well done. I have just read the report of your successful mission last week, the elimination of a terrorist cell and destruction of their arms dump. Excellent work".

"Thank you Prime Minister" said Yuri, waiting for the 'but'.

It didn't come. "We need to give some good news to the people. I have issued a press release saying that we have destroyed the cell that launched the attacks on the subway and dealt with all of their weapons. I am having a weapons destruction staged this morning. We will say that they were captured and are being destroyed. The population believe pictures more than words. I would like you at the ceremony as the officer in charge of the action. Eleven O'clock at the Sekorski barracks please Colonel. I will see you there". Yuri stood to attention, saluted and left.

Later that morning he stood next to a Captain as the television cameras destroyed about fifty old and broken guns and blew up a small amount of semtex explosive.

It was Irina's last week so she started it going over all of the tasks that Yuri's office had to undertake and making sure that everybody knew their responsibilities.

Sam felt that he was just wasting his time. Mrs Clark had told him that she had arranged for a gym timetable at the Guards' gym as the Brigadier had instructed her to do but as yet no programme, date or time had come through Sam was just sitting in the office playing with his computer. He decided to phone the ornithologist from the zoo. He seemed pleased to hear from Sam. They arranged that Sam would go there the next day and use it as revision. Sam told him that he had been looking up on the web, information about eggs and other information and he seemed delighted to hear about Sam's interest. They would talk about the additional things that Sam had learnt too. Sam told Mrs Clerk to put it in the diary, he thought that she seemed pleased that he had something to occupy his time.

After Yuri's meeting with Mr Putin he decided that a good lunch was called for. He phoned his mistress and told her to be ready in an hour. She was surprised but pleased to hear from him in the middle of the day. She assumed that the phone call also meant that she was still in favour. She was still in some pain from Yuri's sexual actions when he last was with her but she knew better than to mention that. She had known enough men, none of them as influential and powerful as Yuri, who, if their women complained, would just cut them out of their lives in an instant. Yuri had hurt her, quite badly, but she was prepared to put up with a bit of pain once in a while for the nice flat and clothes and food, and the prestige of being with such a man. The alternative was to go back as a hostess in a club and she was beginning to get a bit too old for that. Many young attractive women were coming in from the countryside and the men seemed to prefer them.

They ate lunch in a small but expensive restaurant not far from Red Square, a favourite in days past with members of the politburo. During lunch Yuri decided this was his last meal with his lady, it was time for a change. She bored him. He realised that she had nothing to talk about, she was a sex object, not company. Irina had been company, they had sat and talked. Tanya was company, at least she seemed to be from little time he had spent with her. He thought again about bringing Tanya to Moscow from Omsk. He thought that she would fit well into the big city. She was smart, good company, was nice looking, had a good body and he enjoyed her in bed. He would see to it soon, in fact he would see to it tomorrow.

Sam visited the zoo on Tuesday. He was surprised how much he enjoyed himself. He lunched in a cafeteria overlooking the elephant house and the day flew by. If it hadn't been for his appointment with the quartermaster on the Wednesday he would have arranged to return the next day.

Yuri flew to Omsk on the Tuesday. He had instructed one of the secretaries to phone the Mayor, instruct him to book the hotel for one night and arrange for his niece to have dinner with him. He went and visited the small garrison on the border and was pleased to see that the accommodation construction was going well. The troops would be in timber buildings very soon and out of the tents.

He had dinner with Tanya and told her that he would like her to come to Moscow with him. She understood exactly what he meant and accepted without much thought. Yuri knew that most of the women he had set up with over the years knew the score, they were his mistress with a fairly short lease on the apartment, but they all thought they would change him and would be the first to win him over and make the arrangement permanent. He knew that Tanya was no different in that respect but he also thought that apart from Irina, Tanya was the first one that may actually achieve it.

On Wednesday the Quartermaster visited Sam. Sam smiled to himself when he was introduced to him. His name was Jeffrey. He was rather lacking in personality and had a tendency to talk as though he was lecturing someone. He reminded Sam a bit of the Q in the James Bond films, before John Cleese took the role. He couldn't wait to see the gadgets he would get. He was to be disappointed. He was issued with a watch. It didn't strangle anybody, have an integral saw to cut rope, or blow people up. It was a normal watch except that it was linked to a satellite so it was always correct to local time wherever in the world he was, to an accuracy of one hundredth of a second. He was issued with a Blackberry, a phone that was also able to send and receive e-mails. This one was converted to receive signals from a satellite phone rather than an antennae. He also had a conventional cell phone. The phone had a local Nigerian sim card in it. He was also issued with a two guns, a Glock 17, the same model that he had practiced with a few weeks ago. He also had three rounds of spare ammunition. With the one in the gun, that gave him sixty-eight shots; should be enough for any eventuality. The other was a very small Smith and Wesson handgun, a 340 model. It was the sort that ladies in the United States may carry in their handbags for protection. They were known sometimes as a Saturday night special. He looked at this 'toy' quizzically.

Jeffery saw his look. "It may not be a crowd stopper but its advantage is that it is light. With a full stack of shells, it only weighs twelve ounces. Small, just over six inches long as you can see, only five shots at a time and you would need to be close up for it to be accuarate but we feel it a useful weapon in a clandestine situation. You could strap it inside your underwear or tuck it in your sock and it's likely missed if you are being tapped down. Its five bullets could save your life".

Sam nodded, "Point taken".

He was also issued with a knife, a long bladed, thin shafted knife, almost a stiletto. "Again good for concealment" Jeffery explained. "Think about your experiences tapping people down or being tapped yourself. Rarely do people check the centre of the front of the upper body, unless they are checking for a wire tap. This blade taped in the middle of your chest bone would likely be undetected. A thicker knife could be more easily seen or felt". As soon as he had checked the issue they were all boxed up.

"What are you going to do with them?" Sam asked as they were being packed into an anonymous brown paper sack.

"You don't think that you are just going wander through security with this lot do you?" said Jeffery. "Don't be daft man. They will go over to our high commission in Lagos in a diplomatic bag and when you are met at the airport by one of our embassy staff, they will give you the bag". Sam felt a bit foolish. He hadn't thought about setting alarms off at Heathrow and certainly not getting into Lagos.

"Finally there's the computer". Jeremy pulled a small Dell Notepad from his briefcase. "This is the latest Dell small computer. Its only got a 1 gig but that is plenty big enough for what you need. You have an e-mail address, samt@rspbuk.gov. Any mail sent to that address is also routed here into the office. Your contact address here is polly@rspbuk.gov. That address is issued to Mrs Clark and a copy goes to the Brigadier. You should check in by e-mail every day when you are on a field assignment such as this. That way we know if you are alright. The computer is also loaded with information about birds. There are some memo's and mails from the RSPB and there is a diary. You should make an entry in the diary every day about your bird watching so that together with the information already loaded, if anybody checks it, you will look legitimate".

Friday arrived and Sam had collected all the information he could on Nigeria, the birds that he was likely to see, the background of the oil industry in Nigeria and the problems of kidnapping in the region. He also received an envelope containing his travel documents, including flight tickets, economy class from London to Lagos. His passport was in the name of Sam Tucker showing his occupation as ornithologist. He had return tickets for three weeks after his arrival. There were five pages of instructions and information including that he was to be met at the airport by a member of the embassy who would supply him with his 'package' and would give him details of the accommodation that was booked for him.

Yuri was in his office early on Friday, even before Irina who arrived shortly after eight. Everything was normal until, at eleven o'clock Mr Putin arrived. Obviously Yuri was expecting him but nobody else knew he was coming and all were amazed. He went into Yuri's office and emerged about fifteen minutes later. Yuri called them around and Mr Putin addressed them all.

"I would like to say how important all of us in government think that your work here is. If anybody needed reminding how much we are under threat from terrorists they only have to think about what happened less than two weeks ago at the station underneath this very building. I would like to thank you all for your efforts. This is a new unit and we have to appreciate what Colonel Dolchenko has achieved in the time he has had to set it up. But my main reason for being here today is to also thank his assistant Miss Kirilova. Irina, who has also been here since the beginning and who has organised this very impressive computer system which I am told is the best in Russia. We are sorry that she is leaving today and even more sorry that she is leaving us for an English army officer".

Irina was stunned and speechless. Mr Putin, probably he most popular man in all of Russia, the Prime Minister, here in her office talking about her. As Mr Putin was talking, a man walked almost unnoticed into the office.

Mr Putin continued, "As a thank you Irina I would like to make this small presentation to you. It is a copy of my book, my autobiography, which I have signed and I would like to wish you every happiness in England". He moved towards her and held out his right hand to shake hers and give her the book with the left. The man who had entered the room stepped forward. He was Mr Putin's personal photographer. He took a picture of Mr Putin shaking hands and presenting the book and another of Mr Putin standing between Irina and Yuri. Mr Putin then shook hands with everybody in the room and left with photographer following him. Irina was still in a daze as were most of the other staff members.

"I would like to make a small presentation now" said Yuri. He pulled a small packet from his pocket. He gave it to Irina who could still not speak. She opened the box and looked inside. "It's an Apple i Phone" said Yuri. "It's the latest model. It is registered in England, at Sam's address, so you will able to use it anywhere in the world but in England the calls will be cheaper. I think it will be useful as it means that you can invite me to the wedding on it, you can send me pictures of your first baby, and it also means that I know how to get in touch when I need your help or advice".

Irina burst into tears, she grabbed Yuri, held him close and kissed his cheek.

"Careful, careful, I don't want to make my new girlfriend jealous" he said with a laugh. "Anyway its lunch now, an early lunch, lunch for Irina, I'm paying". Five minutes later they left the office and went to a new fish restaurant in the tourist area of the city near to the cathedral.

After a long lunch Irina returned to the office to find that her desk had been decorated with flowers. There was very little work done that day.

Irina left to go home and pack for the last time. Yuri left to go to Omsk. He was going to stay there the night and on the Saturday he was returning to Moscow with Tanya. He had refurnished his old apartment in Krasmaya Presnya and he was loaning it to her. It was more luxurious than any he had put his mistresses in before but he had a special feeling about Tanya. Maybe this was the time for him to settle down. What a pity that Tanya wouldn't get to be friends with Irina.

# CHAPTER 59

Irina telephoned Sam that evening on her new Apple i Phone. She was so exited and Sam found it infectious. She told him that about the day in the office and the present that Yuri had brought her. They laughed together when she told him about Yuri saying he wanted a picture of the baby. They talked for about an hour and when at last they hung up Sam was feeling so exited that he had to sit down to catch his breath.

On Saturday Sam cleaned the apartment more diligently than he had ever done before. He was in the middle of washing the kitchen floor when his phone rang. It was Irina. "Shammy, Shammy, I have a letter from my Father. Your letter worked, he is pleased about me getting married and says it is wonderful that I am going to live in England. He is talking to me again and it is because of you, your letter to him". She was so excited.

"How about writing back to him and telling him that you are coming to England on Monday and maybe he and his wife, your mother, could come over and visit soon, before the wedding. We can find a nice hotel near the apartment and take them out and show them where we are looking to find a house for the two of us. I will pay for the tickets, that's no problem".

Irina told him that she would write back straight away and give them the address of the apartment in London so that they would know where to write to.

Sam felt great as he went out and purchased new towels and air fresheners. He wanted the apartment to be perfect when Irina arrived. He was so pleased that her parents had contacted her and seemed to have got over their problem of her leaving to go to Moscow with Yuri.

On Sunday after going to the gym he went and had brunch at a bar in Saint Catherine's Dock. He was so exited about tomorrow. He was sitting having a drink and realised that he felt like a adolescent, not a mature man, an officer in the British Army, somebody who had tortured and killed men without giving it a second thought. He sat and laughed to himself. He thought about what Irina had told him Yuri had said. Kids would be nice, and soon. He didn't want to be an old father. He felt sure that Irina would like lots of children.

The afternoon dragged and Sam went to bed early in the hope that Monday morning would come quicker.

# CHAPTER 60

Yuri woke early on Monday. He had returned with Tanya to the apartment in Krasmaya Presnya. He lay in bed thinking how long it seemed since this apartment had been used as his place of work. It was only a few months before but it seemed like years ago. Tanya was asleep next to him. He had enjoyed being with her in every way. The day before, on the Sunday, they had walked around some of Moscow. She had never been to the city before but knew lots about it and many of its sights like St Basil's Cathedral, the art galleries and the museum. Yuri not only enjoyed being with her but he felt relaxed.

He crept out of bed so as not to disturb her and went into the bathroom for a shower. When he came out she was standing in the kitchen holding out a freshly brewed cup of coffee for him. He took it from her and kissed her as a thank you. He had ordered his car early today so that it would not be delayed to pick Irina up for the airport after it had delivered him to his office.

He sat back in the car for the short journey to the office and considered his life. He felt as enthusiastic about the future as he could ever remember. He had a feeling that Tanya was right for him. He didn't expect to be faithful to her but he did think that he would only have sex elsewhere for the sadistic pleasure it sometimes gave him or to punish somebody. Sex in such cases was not about physical pleasure, it was about power. He believed that for pure sexual pleasure Tanya would provide all he ever wanted. He also found her good company and enjoyed being with her. She was attractive and wouldn't let him down in company. She was street wise and clever and most of all, he really liked her. He thought of Irina and her going to England to marry Sam. He was happy for her, happy for both of them. He had liked Sam, imagine that, him liking an Englishman. He grinned to himself. Mr Putin was pleased with him and maybe, just maybe, he had stopped any terrorist attacks on Russia for a while. Yuri exited his car feeling very pleased with the world. All he had to do today was get one of the secretaries to write to his mistress, his now ex mistress, and tell her to leave the flat. Yes, life was good and he thought; beginning to get better. He had a very good feeling about that. He arrived at the office and looked around at the new furniture and computers. Irina had done well but she would not have got this equipment if it hadn't been for the personal involvement of Mr Putin, further evidence of his position in the new Russia. Life was good and getting better, even the sun was shining.

It was just after nine o'clock on Monday, on a bright sunny morning in Moscow, when Yuri's limousine and driver collected Irina, together with two large suitcases from her apartment and drove her to Domodedova Airport. She had only packed some of her clothes and a few personal items. Yuri had told her that he would arrange for everything else to be packed up and shipped to her when she and Sam had moved into a bigger house and she would have room to store everything. They arrived at the airport terminal. Irina wasn't prepared for what happened next. The car entered the airport by a side gate marked "Authorised Persons Only". It pulled up outside a door at the side of the terminal building. As soon as it came to a halt, a man came from the building and opened the car door. "If you will follow me please Miss Kirilova, I will escort you to the VIP lounge".

Irina got out of the car and moved towards the rear to get her luggage from the boot.

"Your luggage will be looked after ma'am, we will make sure that it gets to the plane". She was escorted into the building and to a large, well furnished, comfortable, warm room with a buffet breakfast bar, tea and coffee and an assortment of alcoholic drinks. It had comfortable chairs and copies of all of the most popular European newspapers. "Please make yourself comfortable here. I will be back to escort you to the plane in plenty of time".

He was good to his word, he returned at ten thirty and showed Irina to the waiting aircraft. She was the first to board. She was shown to her seats in the front row and while other passengers boarded she was given complimentary champagne and little snack biscuits. The cabin crew made a big fuss of her and she made a mental note to phone Yuri and thank him. Obviously all this treatment was because of him. While she waited for the other passengers to complete boarding she telephoned Sam and told him about her morning so far. He was again struck by her excitement and felt very happy for her. He knew that she would never forget these last few days. She told him that she was on the plane and that other people were now getting on so she hoped she would be taking off on time and it was only a few hours before she would be in London. Sam told her that he was leaving the apartment immediately so although he would be there very early, he would wait for her at Heathrow.

As they were taxiing the pilot came on the speaker system. He announced himself as Sergi Ramkorkov, he told them they would be flying at twelve thousand metres. They would be flying across Russia, crossing the outskirts of St. Petersburg, then across Poland, Germany, France, going over Paris and then across the English Channel to London. He reported that the weather conditions were good for the trip and that he anticipated that they would be landing on time.

It was a smooth take off and as there was little wind they ascended smoothly and quickly to their cruising altitude. They had been airborne for about half an hour, Irina and the other business class passengers were being served drinks. Because of the way she had boarded the flight and the fact that she was sitting at the front of the cabin, Irina had not noticed any of the passengers that had boarded in the normal way. Had she done so she would probably have been suspicious of three of them, three women, dressed in long black dresses, with black scarves covering their heads. It was not the women themselves that she would have been suspicious of but the fact that they did not sit together on the plane. One sat towards the front, one in the middle and the third almost at the back. All three had aisle seats. What nobody knew is that they were part of a terrorist group. A fourth member of the group, a Chechnyan, had obtained a position as a baggage handler three months before. Early on the Sunday morning, the day before, he had helped to smuggle three cases packed with high explosive, into the secure area in the airport. While the plane was unoccupied he had placed all three cases in the hold without being detected.

The first any of the passengers knew that something out of the ordinary was happening was when the woman at the front of the aircraft stood up, moved into the aisle and shouted in Arabic, praising Allah. The other two rose immediately and also started to shout, praisng Allah, denouncing Russian oppression, declaring they were avenging brothers and sisters that had been murdered. All three produced mobile phones and held them high. They all pressed the redial buttons on the phones. These connected with three phones, one in each case. As the connection was made it detonated the explosives. All aboard the plane died instantly. The aircraft disintegrated. It did so as it was flying across the outskirts of St Petersburg.

The first to notice a problem was Russian air traffic control. The plane was being monitored by the St Petersburg controller and it suddenly disappeared from his screen. At the same time he was checking that his connections were in order, debris started to fall on the outlying suburbs. Twenty minutes later Yuri's telephone rang. He was told that an aircraft that had been flying over St. Petersburg had disappeared from radar screens and that debris was falling on civilians on the ground in St Petersburg. As it was a suspected terrorist attack, Yuri had been informed as the head of the main anti terrorist unit. He knew from the details that he had been given that it was the London flight that Irina had taken. He put his phone down and sat for a moment. He felt an overwhelming sadness, unlike anything he had felt before. This feeling was soon overcome by rage. He ordered his car to be brought to the front entrance immediately and instructed one of his assistants to organise a helicopter from an army base on the outskirts of Moscow to take him to St Petersburg. As Yuri was travelling to the base he thought over the situation. It was complex for him. It was personal, he had been very fond of Irina, he knew that she would not have survived. It was professional, he hadn't predicted this, he had no intelligence reports of an imminent threatened attack. He also knew that as it was over Russian airspace the authorities would hush it up. Even if they admitted the explosion they would not admit that the aircraft had been sabotaged. It was not how they handled things. That meant that Yuri could not ask for foreign assistance with intelligence information.

Sam arrived at Heathrow less than two hours after he had spoken to Irina from the plane. As soon as he arrived he looked at the arrivals board. He was surprised to see that the flight was showing as cancelled. He double checked, there it was, flight SU 241 from Moscow—cancelled. Sam couldn't understand it. Irina had phoned him from on the plane. If it was cancelled she would have disembarked and phoned him. He tried to phone Irina. The phone was turned off. He went to the information desk but they had no information. They referred him to the Aeroflot desk. They too told him that they had been advised that the flight had been cancelled due to technical problems. Sam tried to phone Irina again; still the phone was off.

Sam went to the Costa Coffee shop, ordered a cappuccino and tried to telephone Irina yet again. He still could not get through. He didn't know who else to phone. He had a bad feeling about a situation where he couldn't get a response from anybody. His sixth sense had kicked in and he trusted his sixth sense. In different circumstances it had kept him alive. Now it was just telling him that there was a problem with Irina.

Yuri's car pulled alongside the helicopter that was waiting for him. He flew quickly to St Petersburg and landed in a wide road that had been closed to allow him access. There was debris in the area he landed in. He was met by a major from the local army unit. Yuri instructed him to secure the area and search for the black box, the in-flight voice recorder. He got into a jeep with the major and toured the immediate area viewing the damage. There was a considerable amount of it in one area of the city particularly, where the main area of the fuselage had fallen. He had been touring the area for about an hour when his mobile phone rang. The caller ID showed it was Sam. He suddenly realised again that there was a personal aspect to this. He looked again at his phone and let it ring, he couldn't face talking to Sam at the moment. He thought that Sam would not yet know what had happened, probably just that the flight had been delayed. He knew that Sam would be devastated when he heard about the crash and Yuri could not bare to be the one that told him. He also did not want to lie to Sam and say that he didn't know anything. A man like Sam deserved more than that. He continued to look at the phone until it stopped ringing.

Sam had decided to phone Yuri. He thought that he may know what had happened or where Irina was. Yuri didn't answer his phone. Sam didn't know who else to phone, he tried Irina again.

About the time that Sam was ordering his coffee an e-mail arrived on the screen of the security computer in the Brigadiers' office. It was from GCHQ who had been advised by US security that a plane had exploded over Russian airspace. The explosion had been detected by a US surveillance satellite. Their computer system had calculated the time and trajectory of the flight and had analised that it was headed for London. They suspected that it was a mid-air explosion probably a terrorist attack, and so had advised British security. The Brigadier realised the potential implications and summoned two of his men immediately. He also knew that no information would be forthcoming from the Russians, certainly not today. He needed to get to Sam, he would be unlikely to know what was going on. He would be waiting at Heathrow. He would still need to be on the mission to Nigeria in only a few days time.

Sam had finished his coffee, tried again to contact Yuri and Irina. He returned to the Aeroflot desk in case they had any more information and they said that they didn't. He was walking back to the coffee shop which was located within sight of the arrivals door. Just as he approached the counter a message came over the tannoy, "Would Mr Sam Tucker, awaiting a passenger from Moscow, please go to the airport information desk immediately".

Sam turned and hurried to the other end of the terminal towards the information desk. As he approached it he saw two men waiting there. They wore pin striped suits, white shirts and regimental ties. They were the same two men that had removed Sam from the police station many months ago. They were the Brigadier's men.

As he approached them Sam thought to himself "I'm on holiday; what the hell do they bloody well want?"

# THE END

# About The Author

Richard Pennell was born and brought up in East London but he has lived in Berkshire for the past thirty years. He has traveled extensively throughout Europe mainly as a result of working for various European producers in the plastics industry. Richard has a keen interest in history and has achieved an Open University degree in the subject.

Richard's hobby's apart from writing are traveling and golf. He is an active member of his local golf club.

Snow In Gorky Park is Richard's second book to be published, a sequel to it is in the process of being produced and Richard also has plans for a historical novel.

*If you have enjoyed this book and want to read more about Sam, read on and enjoy a taster of the next book featuring him,*

# ON THE EDGE OF THE WORLD.

## Chapter 1

Sam Tucker looked out of the window as the British Airways Boeing came into land at Lagos airport. Sam was numb. He hardly noticed the heat, the dust, the noise and the hustle and bustle as he departed from the plane, went through passport control and collected his bags from the luggage carousel.

More importantly, he didn't notice the two men whose eyes followed him as he headed away from the baggage area and walked towards the exit, or the fact that they turned and followed him as he approached the doors.

Sam almost missed the young man standing by the doors, wearing a suit and what looked like an old school tie.

"Mr Tucker?" he asked as Sam approached.

Sam jolted back from his almost automaton state.

"Yes, that's me".

"Good morning Sir, my name is Kevin Bailey and I've been sent to collect you and take you to the High Commission. If you will come this way sir, I have a car waiting".

Sam meekly followed the man to a black Ford Granada and as Kevin took his cases and put them in the boot of the car, Sam opened the door and got into the back seat.

Neither of them noticed the two men from the airport wave at a parked car, which drew up alongside them and as they got in, left the curb and followed the Ford.

Kevin drove to the Commissions' offices, through the gate that was flanked by two armed members of the Irish Guards, stopping outside of the front doors. He got out of the car and as he did so another soldier came out of the building and opened the door for Sam. Kevin gave the car keys to the soldier and asked Sam to follow him into the building.

As they walked into the reception area another man approached them.

"Good Afternoon Mr Tucker. My name is Norris, Steven Norris, I am assistant attaché here and I am responsible for you short time with us and it is I who have arranged your accommodation in the bush to enable you to study the birdlife. We will take you there tomorrow and you can move in any time you would like. Your trunk from the RSPB has arrived and we have arranged to have it delivered to your accommodation whenever you wish. It must be fascinating to study the wide variety of birds that we have here in Africa."

"Yes, thank you" was all Sam could think of saying.

"We dine at 7.00pm and would be delighted if you would join us but if there is anything that we can do in the meantime please let us know ."

"All I would like at the moment is a rest and the opportunity to freshen up."

"Of course, of course" said Stephen Norris, "follow me please."

# Chapter 2

Sam had been shown to a large, comfortable room, with a double bed, an en-suite bathroom and air conditioning.

He collapsed on the bed near to exhaustion. It was Thursday afternoon and Sam had not slept since he had got up on Monday morning. He lay back and his mind reviewed the week so far.

On Monday Sam had been waiting to meet his fiancé at Heathrow Airport. She was coming to London from Moscow to live with Sam and to get married shortly. Her plane had never arrived, it had been blown out of the sky by terrorists. Sam had made contact with her and his, ex boss, an ex KGB officer who was heading up a special anti terrorist unit in Moscow. His name was Yuri Dolchenko and he was personally heading the investigation team in St Petersburg and Moscow. Sam had a lot of respect for Yuri and although he would ideally like to have been working with him in Moscow, he trusted Yuri to do his best.

Going to Russia was out of the question for another reason. Sam was a Major in the British army, part of a small group of specially selected operatives who go under cover, and clandestinely observe and report back on a given brief. Sam's mission was to investigate terrorist activity in Northern Nigeria and his cover was as a specialist from the RSPB, studying birds in the country. The mission had been planned for months and despite his loss and his state of mind, the Brigadier who was in charge insisted that he go ahead as planned.

Sam decided to take a shower at least, although he felt that he should get some sleep before he started his mission. In his present state of mind he would not be able to do the job properly and in a country like this, in a situation like this, that could be dangerous.

Lightning Source UK Ltd.
Milton Keynes UK
UKOW04f0201140214

226455UK00002B/108/P